Heart in Hand

Other books by the author

A Time to Love, book one in the Quilts of Lancaster County series
A Time to Heal, book two in the Quilts of Lancaster County series
A Time for Peace, book three in the Quilts of Lancaster County series

Her Restless Heart, book one in the Stitches in Time series
The Heart's Journey, book two in the Stitches in Time series

HEART IN HAND

Stitches in Time Series

Barbara Cameron

Abingdon fiction
a novel approach to faith

Nashville, Tennessee

Heart in Hand

Copyright © 2013 Barbara Cameron

ISBN: 978-1-4267-1434-4

Published by Abingdon Press, P.O. Box 801, Nashville, TN 37202

www.abingdonpress.com

The persons and events portrayed in this work of fiction are the
creations of the author, and any resemblance to persons
living or dead is purely coincidental.

Library of Congress Cataloging-in-Publication Data

Cameron, Barbara, 1949-
  Heart in hand / Barbara Cameron.
    pages cm. — (Stitches in Time Series)
  ISBN 978-1-4267-1434-4 (Book - Paperback / Trade Paperback) 1. Amish women—
Fiction. 2. Amish--Social life and customs—Fiction. 3. Amish decorative arts—Fiction.
4. Grandparent and child—Fiction. 5. Widows—Fiction. 6. Widowers—Fiction. I. Title.
  PS3603.A4473H43 2013
  813'.6—dc23

2012041285

Printed in the United States of America

1 2 3 4 5 6 7 8 9 10 / 18 17 16 15 14 13

For Eva

Acknowledgments

A cousin asked *that* question recently: Where do you get your ideas?

It always makes me groan. I'm usually a pretty polite person, but I always want to say something like, "The idea tree in the backyard," or "I bought this book of them years ago."

The truth is there are so many places that writers get ideas. And sometimes we don't even know where they come from. Some come as niggling little things, and other times, the whole book is just there. Of course, the ones that come full-blown are great! Sometimes it's even an idea that just won't let go.

Once, when my doctor and I were talking about our families, she asked how my then teenagers were doing. Well, they were great kids, but all kids seem to go through challenges at one time or another . . .

"You're a writer," she said. "Bet you could learn what to do if you wrote about it."

What an idea. And that is not only how so many projects begin for me—it's how I end up learning something for myself. One of my favorite times in my life was when I got to stay home for a while with my two children and be a homemaker. I cooked everything from scratch, sewed most of their clothing, and reveled in a role that felt so right. When I was able to sneak time during their naps to write, I felt like the world was perfect.

As I've worked on my Amish books, I've learned a lot about forgiveness and inner peace and big themes like that—and I've learned about fun activities like quilting and weaving and so on. I found myself yearning for those days sewing and doing so many domestic crafts, so that I visited a quilt shop. I wanted to write about three Amish cousins who are as close as sisters . . . and there, in the quilt shop, the idea of a series about them sewing and quilting and weaving and falling in love with three Amish men began to form. And so I created this series.

Thank you to Magrieta of Magrieta's Quilt Shop in St. Augustine for being so gracious to me and answering so many questions and letting me wander the shop. I enjoyed the times I visited so much.

Thank you, too, to Wendy Ashton, who runs PA-Dutch-Travel and helped me with some research.

Thank you, as always to Judy Rehm, such a good friend and inspiration to learn more about God and His endless ideas for our lives.

A thank-you should go to my mother, May, and her twin, June, for teaching me how to sew—seemingly a lost art these days. The memories of working on such simple but necessary things like clothing and creative additions like embroidery warmed my heart so many times as I stitched. I used those memories as I wrote the three books of Stitches in Time.

My mom was one of nine children, so there are many cousins. Memories of growing up with some of them gave me material for the relationships of the cousins in the books. So thank you to them.

Thanks, as always, for the encouragement of my editor, Ramona Richards, and all the staff at Abingdon Press who take these ideas of mine and help me turn them into books with such beautiful covers that get sent out there into readerland. I am so grateful for the many readers who write me and tell me they've given you a few hours to read of a peaceful place where people still care about each other.

Blessings to you.

1

*I*t felt like dawn would never come.

When Anna first realized that it was going to be one of those nights . . . one of those awful nights that felt like it would never end . . . she reached for the book she'd been reading and read for a while with the help of the battery lamp on the bedside table.

Reading didn't help. Knitting didn't, either, and knitting always relaxed her. Reaching for her robe, Anna pushed her feet into her slippers and padded downstairs to the kitchen. There was no need for a light for she knew her way from all the dozens—no, hundreds—of nights she'd gone downstairs in the dark.

Even before the first time she stepped inside this house she knew it like the back of her hand. She and Samuel had drawn the plans, spent hours talking about how he and his brothers were going to build it. As soon as the house was finished, he'd started crafting furniture for it. The final piece he'd made was a cradle for the baby he hoped they'd have soon.

His sudden illness stopped him in his tracks. Leukemia, said the doctor. One day it seemed he was an agile monkey climbing up the frame of a barn he and other men were raising and just a few days later he could barely get out of bed and she'd joked he'd turned into an old man.

She'd insisted that he see a doctor, and reluctantly, he'd done so.

Six months later he was gone, and she'd shut the door to the room with the tiny crib. She buried her dreams the day she buried Samuel.

She filled the teakettle and set it on the stove to heat. *How many cups of tea have I drunk in the middle of the night?* she wondered as she reached for a cup and the box of chamomile tea bags.

Before Samuel had died, she'd heard about the seven stages of grief. She'd been naïve. You didn't go through them one by one in order. Sometimes you walked—faltered—through them in no certain order. Sometimes they ganged up on you when you least expected them.

And sometimes—it felt like too many times—no one seemed to understand.

She couldn't blame them. The only way she got through the first month, the first year, was to put on a brave face and pretend she was getting through it. There was no way she could get through it otherwise—she'd shatter into a thousand pieces that no one would be able to put back together again.

Humpty Dumpty, she thought wryly. Then she frowned, wishing that she hadn't thought of the childhood story. A closed door didn't keep out the memory of the tiny crib that lay behind it.

The teakettle's whistle broke into her musing, its sound so sharp and shrill that she put her hands over her ears to block it while she got up to take it off the flame. She poured the hot water over the tea bag and took the mug back to the kitchen table and sat there, dipping the bag in and out of the water.

Finally, she pulled the bag out and set it on the saucer. Sighing, she massaged her scalp and wondered if she should take an aspirin to stop the pain. Then she flicked her hair behind her shoulders and hunched over the cup. In a minute, she'd get up and get the aspirin. Her mind might be awake, but her body felt tired and full of lead.

As she trudged back up the stairs a few minutes later, she heard something—it sounded like a laugh, a high, excited one that went rushing past her and up the stairs. She watched, tired, leaning against the wall as she saw herself, lifting the hem of her nightgown so she wouldn't trip, Samuel reaching for her as she flew up the stairs to their room.

She blinked, not sure if she was dreaming or seeing a ghost of the two of them, so young and in love, so unaware that anything bad could touch them.

When she reached her room, no one was there. Climbing back into bed, she pulled the quilt around her shoulders and lay on her side facing the uncurtained window. The wedding quilt that her cousins Naomi and Mary Katherine and her grandmother had sewn for her and Samuel lay wrapped in muslin and tucked in a box in the closet of the same room as the cradle. She hadn't been able to bear lying under it after Samuel died.

She'd thought she wouldn't be able to bear living without him in this house they had built, but her grandmother had brought her here after the funeral to pack and she'd found she couldn't leave it. Somehow it felt like she'd be abandoning everything they'd worked so hard for.

Her grandmother had understood. She'd done the same thing—continued to live in the house she'd shared with her husband who'd also died too young. She'd continued to stay there for nearly two decades, and only in the last couple of years had Mary Katherine and then Naomi come to stay with her.

Hours passed. Anna remembered reading that it was always darkest before dawn. She could vouch for that.

Finally, the sky began lightening. She got up and made the bed before she went to shower. The reflection in the mirror made her wince. She looked tired, with faint lavender shadows under her eyes.

Funny, everyone said that she and her two cousins who worked with her at Stitches in Time—Mary Katherine and Naomi—all looked so much alike with their oval faces and brown eyes and brown hair. But she felt she just looked like a dull version of them lately. She looked older and more subdued.

With a sigh she center-parted her hair and began arranging it in a bun, then she placed a starched *kapp* on her head. She chose her favorite dark blue dress and hoped the color would make her look less pale.

Her first cup of coffee helped her get moving. The knock on the door startled her as she sat eating her breakfast.

She opened her door to find Nick standing there.

"Sorry, I had to come a little early," he apologized as she invited him inside.

"It's okay. I'm ready."

He touched her shoulder. "You look tired."

"I sure hope you don't ever say that to Naomi," she responded testily. "No woman wants to hear that kind of thing."

"I'll remember that."

She regarded this man who was engaged to marry Naomi. He had dark hair, angular features, and sharp green eyes. Not as handsome as Samuel had been.

Nick was quiet and serious and had a heart just as big as Samuel's. She could trust him with someone as dear as Naomi . . .

"Want some coffee before we go?"

He shook his head. "I have a thermos in the car."

She took a plastic box filled with sandwiches from the refrigerator and tucked it into a tote bag. A bag of cookies was next.

Catching Nick's interest, she pulled another plastic bag from a nearby cupboard and filled it with half a dozen and handed it to him.

"Oatmeal raisin," he said with a satisfied sigh. "Will you marry me?"

"Sorry, the Amish don't believe in plural marriage."

Gathering up her sweater and her purse, she walked to the door with him and locked it behind her.

After they climbed into the van, Nick set the cookies on the seat between them.

"You know you're going to eat them now."

"They're oatmeal," he reasoned. "Just because it's not hot and in a bowl . . ."

"So very logical," she agreed, trying not to smile.

"That's me, logical."

She opened the bag so he could slide his hand inside, pull one out, and take a bite.

"Please give Naomi the recipe."

"Are you sure you want to tell your intended that you like my oatmeal raisin cookies better than hers?"

He considered that. "Maybe not. She wasn't happy when I complimented Leah's rolls."

"Exactly."

"Maybe you'll sneak me some of these now and then?"

"Maybe," she agreed with a grin.

Nick glanced at his watch and turned the radio on. "I want to check out the weather forecast. We're certainly having a cool November, aren't we?"

Anna nodded as the jingle that announced the news broadcast filled the interior of the van.

"The forecast is partly sunny and cool in Paradise, Pennsylvania. Chance of afternoon showers," the announcer said cheerfully.

"Tell me how it can be partly sunny. It's either sunny or it's not."

Nick chuckled. "I agree."

They listened to the quick news report and then the weather before Nick turned the station off.

A yawn overtook her. She covered her mouth and shook her head. "Sorry."

"S'okay. Rough night?"

"Yeah."

"Why don't you close your eyes and try to get a little shuteye?"

"Don't want to be rude," she said, stifling another yawn.

"I don't mind. I might fall asleep in front of you someday."

She blinked at him. "Don't do that when you're driving!"

He laughed as he reached for another cookie. "I saw Abe Harshberger asleep as he was driving the other day."

"Abe was driving his buggy," she pointed out. "I heard the horse got him home okay." She studied him. "How are the lessons going?"

"The last time I remember being around a horse my mother was putting me up on it for a kiddie ride," he said with a grin. "I was five. I didn't really like it very much and never wanted to be around a horse again. Now here I am buying a business where I'll have to work with horses for hours every day. Feed them, water them, care for them. Hitch them to a buggy, persuade them to walk along a route for me."

He glanced at her. "Deal with manure." He made a face, then patted his steering wheel with one hand. "Big change from this horseless carriage."

"It sure is."

"Thank goodness I made training me a condition of the sale," he said.

"How's the other instruction going?"

Nick reached for a third cookie. "Just as hard. I thought I knew what was involved, but there are so many more rules than I thought . . ."

He began telling her about the lessons he was taking to become Amish. It hadn't been all that long ago that she'd taken them as every Amish did before joining the church. She found her attention drifting off even as she frowned and wondered why she'd never noticed how Nick spoke in a monotone. Snuggling her cheek against the upholstery of the back of the seat, she heard him chuckle.

"Am I boring you?" he asked. "I never bore Naomi."

"She has to put up with you." Anna felt her eyelids growing heavy, and she jerked awake once, then twice.

"You're chicken-pecking," he told her. "Relax and shut your eyes. Don't worry. Your cousins will wake you up."

❧

"Let her sleep," Nick was whispering. "I don't have to be anywhere for another half hour."

"I'm awake," Anna said, yawning and straightening in her seat. "There's no need to babysit me while I nap."

She saw that they were parked in front of the shop. Turning, she saw Naomi and her grandmother sitting in the backseat, staring at her, concerned.

"Rough night?" her grandmother asked, her eyes kind and a little sad.

"Had trouble sleeping." She unsnapped her seat belt. "I'm fine."

Anna stepped out and looked at the shop while her grandmother unlocked the door. The name of the shop, Stitches in Time, was emblazoned on a sign with needles and thread and little quilt squares dancing around the letters. She'd just changed the window display the night before so she stopped to examine it before going inside.

Everything about the display was designed to say "fall." Anna had knitted warm woolen mufflers, caps and gloves in earth tones of brown, gold, and green. Cupcake hats for babies featured little pumpkins, owls, and forest animals.

Naomi's log cabin quilt had been tucked around Leah's handmade Amish dolls. A little fireplace complete with a glowing "flame" made a cozy scene.

Mary Katherine had spent hours weaving placemats and napkins for tables set for holiday feasts. She'd made sturdy woven tote bags to carry home all the fall fruits and vegetables from the farmer's market and roadside stands.

Jamie's contribution was a wall hanging with a scene of the Amish countryside at harvest time. She'd used a traditional image but worked in pieces of bittersweet, pussy willow, and twigs.

And there were kits for customers to get started on their Christmas gifts.

She started to go inside and then realized that Naomi still hadn't gotten out of Nick's van. There was nothing she liked better than teasing—not just the two of them but particularly them. Marching back to the van, she knocked on the window.

"Hey, you two, no PDAs!" she called.

Naomi rolled down the window. "You are so obnoxious! All we're doing is exchanging a good-bye kiss!"

"You're steaming up the windows," Anna said with a grin. "Get inside before you get arrested."

Nick leaned over and gave Naomi one last kiss. "Have a great day."

"You've been cheating on me!" she exclaimed, licking her lips. "Whose oatmeal cookies have you been eating?"

"I don't know what you're talking about," he told her as he brushed crumbs from his tie.

"You!" Naomi said, pointing a finger at Anna. "You've been tempting him with your oatmeal cookies."

"Guilty," Anna agreed, grinning. "Maybe if you help me with a design idea I'll share the recipe."

Naomi climbed out of the van. "Maybe I should rethink this wedding if my *mann* can be so easily tempted."

Nick got out and rounded the hood. "You know you don't want to do that," he told her, his eyes alight with mischief.

He swept Naomi up into a kiss that had some tourists laughing and clapping as they stood observing on the sidewalk.

She beat her hands on his chest. "Stop that! You know you can't behave like that!"

"I'm not Amish yet," he told her, unrepentant.

Backing away, Naomi tried to look stern. "And at that rate, you're not likely to be." She glanced around her. "What if the bishop had seen you?"

He winked at her before strolling back to his side of the vehicle and getting in.

"Men!" Naomi huffed, and she walked inside the shop.

"*Ya*, men," said Anna, suddenly feeling like a balloon that was deflating. She sighed and went inside.

The interior of the shop, crammed with colorful fabrics, yarns, and supplies, raised her spirits. What would she have done if her grandmother hadn't asked her and her two cousins to join her in opening it? She wondered about this as she walked to the back room to store the sandwiches in the refrigerator.

She'd needed the creative work, the company, the daily routine so much after Samuel died. What did people who were grieving do when they didn't have the support of their loving family and community, the people they worked with in a job that fulfilled them?

Chiding herself for the way she'd vacillated between self-pity and sadness during the sleepless night, she stopped, closed her eyes, and thanked Him for reminding her that she should be grateful for all she had and not focus on what she didn't.

Determined to live with a grateful heart—even if today it meant moment by moment—she walked back into the shop to ask her grandmother what she should do first.

2

"If business is as good this afternoon as it was this morning, this may go down as one of our best days," Leah announced as she turned the sign to "Out to Lunch" and locked the door. "I don't know about you two, but I can't wait to get off my feet for a few minutes."

"Me, too," said Naomi.

They walked to the back room where Anna insisted that her grandmother allow herself to be waited upon.

"You look as tired as I feel," her grandmother said.

"That's the second time I've been told I look tired," Anna said, frowning as she got out the sandwiches. "You're just making me feel worse."

"Sorry, *kind*, you're right." Leah sighed. "Wonder when Mary Katherine's going to get here? We really could have used her help."

"Where is she?" Anna asked as she passed around plates and sat down.

"I don't know. She just asked for the morning off."

"Don't go asking if she's pregnant when she comes in," Naomi warned.

"Don't look at me," Anna told her, making a face at her cousin. "I'm not the only one who's been asking her."

They heard the shop door being unlocked, and Mary Katherine called in that it was her. A few moments later, she walked in with Jacob.

"We just got the most amazing news," Mary Katherine announced.

Anna, Naomi, and Leah exchanged hopeful looks.

"The farm next to ours came up for sale," Jacob announced. "We put in an offer, and it was accepted!"

Anna, Naomi, and Leah exchanged disappointed looks.

"I thought you'd be excited for us," Mary Katherine said, frowning.

"We were hoping for different news," Leah told her gently.

"Different news?" Jacob sounded puzzled.

"I think she means they were hoping we were going to say I was going to have a baby," Mary Katherine said.

"Oh."

"We're happy for your news," Leah gave Anna and Naomi a look.

"Yes, of course," Naomi said, jumping up to give Mary Katherine and Jacob an enthusiastic hug.

Suddenly everyone was talking at once. It was like looking into a mirror to see her cousins, Anna thought. Mary Katherine and Naomi looked more like sisters and were just as close as if they were siblings. Mary Katherine was taller and her hair a bit more auburn but other than that they might have been triplets.

But things were changing. Her cousins would be doing more with the men in their lives—had already been doing so—and soon much of Mary Katherine's time would be taken up with a baby when she had one.

Anna felt a mixture of joy and melancholy. "I'm so happy for you both," she said, rising to give Mary Katherine and Jacob a hug.

"Jacob, can you stay and eat with us?"

He looked to Mary Katherine. "I was going to take Mary Katherine out to celebrate—"

"I'd rather stay here," she said quickly. "Can we?"

Jacob didn't even need to say anything. Anna didn't think she'd ever seen any man so hopelessly in love with his wife.

Her heart actually hurt at that moment. Samuel had looked at her like that. Anna looked away, and as she did, she saw that her grandmother was watching her. She smiled to show that everything was okay because she was determined not to behave in any way that would take away a moment of her cousin's and her husband's happiness.

Mary Katherine walked out to say good-bye to Jacob, and Leah went to open up the shop.

"I can clean up," Anna told Naomi as they cleared the table.

"I know."

Anna glanced up at her as Naomi continued to help.

"I know that you can do whatever you have to," Naomi said quietly. She touched Anna's shoulder. "But I want to make sure you're okay."

"I'm fine," Anna said. "People have been getting married and having babies all around me since Samuel died."

"I know."

Naomi held out her hands for the dishes Anna held, and for a moment there was a tug-of-war over them until Anna was forced to look at her.

"I'm proud of you for how you behaved just now. You thought of Mary Katherine and Jacob and not of yourself."

She set the dishes in the sink and then surprised Anna by hugging her.

Anna hugged her back, and then she turned to the dishes. "Why don't you go see if anyone's come in before we think about doing these?"

"Good idea. Be right back."

She ran water into the sink and squirted in dish soap. When she heard footsteps behind her, she reached for a dish towel and held it out. "I'll wash, you dry."

A hand took the towel, and then Anna felt herself hugged from behind.

"I'm okay, really," she said. "Come on, we don't want Mary Katherine walking in and thinking I'm not."

"Mary Katherine's afraid that you're not and you're protecting her feelings."

Anna closed her eyes. It was Mary Katherine.

She turned, and her cousin kept her in her embrace. "I'm happy for you. I truly am."

"I know. Because you're a good person, Anna. But I've seen your face when you hear this kind of news, and it can't help but make you think of Samuel."

Anna hugged Mary Katherine, and then she stepped back. "It makes me think of the happiness I had with him, and I'm glad to see someone else having it."

"Mary Katherine? Fannie Mae's here to pick up her order."

She hurried into the shop, and Leah walked over to the sink and took the towel Anna clutched in her hand.

"How are you doing?" she asked Anna as she turned back to the dishes.

"Will it do any good to say I'm fine?"

Her grandmother met her eyes. "*Schur*," she said. "You can say it, but I know it's not easy."

Anna stared down at the bubbles popping in the sink. "So many people came up to me after Samuel died and said they knew how I was feeling. But they didn't. They hadn't had a husband die. But you had. You knew."

Leah slipped an arm around Anna. "But that didn't mean I knew exactly how you felt. I didn't lose my *mann* so soon after we married."

"No." Anna washed a plate, rinsed it, and handed it to her grandmother.

She felt the loss of comfort when her grandmother had to remove her arm to have both hands to dry the dish, but it helped her not to sink into self-pity at the moment.

"It helped when Waneta and I talked since her husband died young," Anna said after a moment. "But then it wasn't long before she remarried and moved away."

"Another loss," Leah said, setting the plate down and holding out her hand for another.

Anna nodded. "But it was so nice to see her happy again. I got a letter from her from Indiana last week. She had a little girl. They're both happy and healthy."

"I hope for that for you, too, if it's God's will. There's no reason to believe that God hasn't set aside another *mann* just as wonderful as Samuel for you."

"I know," Anna said, summoning up a smile for her grandmother.

But deep in her heart, she didn't believe that.

⌘

"Well, well, look who's here," Naomi said, peering out the shop window.

"Who?"

"Gideon Beiler."

"What's he doing coming to our shop?"

"He's got his daughter with him."

"Oh, she's so sweet." Anna frowned. "But too quiet."

"I'm going to go help Grandmother in the back room," Naomi said, and she turned away.

"Wait! I need to finish this hat for—"

But Naomi had already hurried toward the back of the store.

Sighing, Anna got up and tucked her knitting in the basket beside her chair. She walked to the front counter and watched as Gideon strode toward the store, his daughter's hand tucked safely in his. She looked a lot like her father with his sandy brown hair and brown eyes, but her face was more delicate and heart-shaped. Anna remembered Gideon's wife and could see her in the way she looked up at him, lifting one brow as she listened to him.

Anna had always thought that Gideon was cute when they were in *schul*, and he'd grown into a handsome man, tall and strong and hardworking.

But like her and Samuel, Gideon and Mary had only had eyes for each other.

And like Anna, Gideon had been widowed early. Mary had died not long after Samuel.

Anna opened the door. "Welcome! What brings you to the store today?"

Gideon reddened. "I brought Sarah Rose to get some sewing stuff."

"*Daedi*! Stuff?"

He spread his hands, looking clearly out of his element. "You know, whatever it is you need."

She stared up at him. "I don't need any of it. Save your money."

Gideon looked at Anna. "I want her growing up knowing how to do girl things."

"Girl things?"

He grew even redder. "You know. Sew. Knit. That kind of thing."

Anna noted that Sarah Rose's bottom lip was jutting out. "What sort of thing do you like to do?"

She shrugged. "I don't care."

Looking at Gideon, Anna tapped her lips with her forefinger. "Who's going to teach her?"

"I—don't know. I guess I thought we'd learn together."

Anna pressed her lips together and tried not to laugh. After all, it was so terribly sweet that he was obviously trying to be both *dat* and *mamm* to her.

"Well, are you interested in knitting, quilting, what?" she asked him.

Gideon knelt down so that he could meet his daughter's gaze eye to eye. "Let's decide on something together."

"But I like it when we play catch."

"We can still do that. But I made a promise to your mother that I'd see that you would grow up a young lady, not a little wild thing."

He'd certainly tried, thought Anna. She'd seen the zigzag part in Sarah Rose's pigtails as he learned how to do them in the early days after Mary's death. There had been an occasional burn mark on a dress and that sort of thing, but gradually he'd learned. Anna supposed it wasn't easy to know how to do such things. After all, he'd grown up male.

And a handsome one at that, she couldn't help thinking now. Her cousins would probably be surprised that she was attracted to Gideon. But after all, she wasn't dead.

Shaking off such irreverent thoughts, Anna gestured at the rocking chairs in the center of the store.

"Let's think about this a minute," she said as they took their seats. "Maybe we can figure out something you like."

"My sisters have taken her to a quilting or two, but they said she's not interested."

"I never liked quilting as much as my cousin Naomi when I was growing up," Anna said. "I didn't have the patience for all those little stitches. Mary Katherine loved weaving from the time she sat down at a loom. I like working with yarn—just the feel of it, the colors, all the shapes and designs I can make. I think my favorite is making hats for babies. Like those over there. We call them cupcake hats because they look like little cupcakes."

Sarah Rose smiled one of her rare smiles. "They're silly."

Anna saw Gideon shoot her a quick glance to see if his daughter had offended.

"I know." Anna grinned at her. "That's probably why I like them so much. We need something silly sometimes, don't we?"

"There are lots of easy and fun projects to knit if you'd like to try one." She looked at Gideon. "Men knit, too. Probably more often than quilt."

He gave her a dubious glance but got up and held out his hand to Sarah Rose. "I'm willing to try."

Anna led them to where the children's crafts were grouped, and the three of them enjoyed a discussion of what might be a fun project. Father and daughter decided on the simplest knitted muffler, hers in shades of pink, her father's in blue.

The bell over the door jangled as it opened.

"Gideon! So you took my advice!" a woman said loudly.

Anna recognized the voice. Gideon's oldest sister had a voice that was like no other—loud and a bit shrill. She knew it wasn't nice to think such a thing. But truth was truth.

"I thought you were going to get Sarah Rose some quilting supplies."

It wasn't polite to eavesdrop. But then again, Martha made it impossible for what she said not to be heard.

"This is what Sarah Rose wants to do."

"But I don't knit much," his sister said. "I don't know how much help I can be. I was thinking if she went to a quilting circle she could learn to quilt there."

"But she did that and didn't seem very interested," Gideon pointed out. "So we decided to come here and see what she might like to try."

Sarah Rose slid her hand into her father's and gazed up at him. "*Daedi* will teach me how to knit. He's going to make something, too."

"Really?"

"It'll probably be the blind leading the blind," Gideon admitted. "But Anna helped us pick something simple."

He picked up a multicolored skein of yarn and held it to his face. "What do you think of these colors?" he asked his daughter. "Do they flatter my skin tone?"

Anna couldn't help smiling when she heard Sarah Rose giggle. *What a sweet sound*, she thought. She hadn't heard her laugh since Mary died.

When she glanced at Gideon, she saw his grin widen. She must have made some movement because he looked over at her then. No one understood loss like one who'd suffered such a loss, and in that moment, she saw his expression lighten for a moment. She smiled, happy for him. He was so lucky to have someone in such a time of grief, someone who made it worth getting up each day.

She realized she'd stopped and forced herself to keep walking toward the front counter where Gideon's sister stood, watching her. Her heart sank. The other woman was regarding her with a calculating look. *Oh no*, Anna thought. Martha loved to gossip. If she took a simple shared moment as more than it was, if she thought that Anna was interested in her brother, it would take little more for her to speculate—and maybe start a rumor. Marriage, family—both were such touchstones of the Amish life that those who were widowed didn't stay single long.

There were many reasons to be attracted to Gideon. But no man held a candle to Samuel . . .

And since Gideon hadn't remarried, she suspected that no woman had matched Mary in his eyes, either.

"How can I help you today?" she asked Martha.

"I need some thread. These colors," she said, holding out a piece of paper she'd taped pieces of several colors onto.

"*Schur.*" Anna walked over to the thread display and quickly found what was needed. "Anything else? No black or white? They're used so often many people often forget to get them."

"You're right. I'll take a large spool of each. You're a good saleswoman." She turned and nodded toward the display of baby hats. "And an amazing knitter."

"Thank you."

"Maybe you can give Sarah Rose and her father some lessons, *ya*?"

Anna avoided meeting the other woman's eyes by concentrating on adding up the order and taking Martha's money. She counted out change into her hand, then piled the threads and a schedule of upcoming classes into a bag.

With a big smile, she handed the bag to Martha. "All of our customers know we're here to help however we can."

Martha smiled and nodded. "Ya, I know." She glanced back at her brother and wiggled her fingers. "See you on Sunday at *Mamm's.*"

The bell jangled over the door as she left.

Mary Katherine joined Anna at the counter. "So, did she come in to check you out?" she whispered.

Anna shook her head. "Apparently she sent Gideon in to get something for Sarah Rose. I need to get back to them."

She walked over to where Gideon stood considering a pattern in his hand. "You sure I can do this?"

"I remember you were very good with your hands in *schul*," she said, then realized how that sounded. She blushed and unfolded the directions. "It's just a matter of following directions, counting out rows, that sort of thing, see?"

Remembering what she'd told his sister, she smiled at him. "If you or Sarah Rose have any problems, just come see us here."

Gideon glanced up and studied her. "You'll help us with questions?"

Funny, but her throat went dry. "Any—any of us can help you."

"But you're the knitting expert."

She nodded.

"Well, then, we'll come see you if we have any questions."

She started to nod again and then realized she probably looked like one of those silly bobblehead dolls that they sold in a nearby toy store. Turning, she looked for Sarah Rose and found her in an adjoining aisle, staring hard at an object in her hand. It was a thimble, one that bore a carved silver flower design.

"It's pretty, isn't it?" she asked.

Sarah Rose jumped and dropped the thimble. "Sorry," she said as she scrambled for it.

"No problem. I'll go ring up the things you and your *daedi* chose."

Turning, she made her way back to the counter and added up the purchase, then reached for the schedule of classes and with a pen circled the knitting class before handing it to Gideon.

"You might want to attend a class since you're taking up a new hobby," she said.

"Me in a class with a bunch of ladies?"

"You never know, you might meet someone," she teased. The minute the words were out, she wanted to call them back.

"And where do you meet men?" He watched her with an intensity she found unnerving.

Frowning, she shook her head. "I don't." She bit her lip, then took a deep breath. "I'm sorry. That was insensitive of me to suggest you'd want to meet someone. You might not be any more ready than I am. I just thought—"

"You just thought?" he finished for her.

Oh, well, in for a penny, she thought. "I just thought since you have Sarah Rose you might be looking to get married again."

"To give her a *mamm*?"

She lifted her shoulders and then let them fall. "It's what many men do. It's hard to raise a child on your own."

"True. But I figure when God feels it's the right time, He'll send along the woman he has for me."

His words threw her. "You think that God has more than one person set aside for us?"

He nodded slowly. "I can't think He gave us a taste of heaven only to yank it away forever, do you?"

"I—I don't know," she whispered, at a loss for words for perhaps the first time in her life.

"*Daedi*, can we go now?" Sarah Rose said, appearing beside him. "I'm very hungry."

Gideon blinked and dragged his gaze away from Anna. "I promised her we'd eat while we were in town."

"I'm glad you stopped by," Anna told the child. She smiled at her. "If you have any problems, you and your *daedi* come see us here, all right?"

Nodding quickly, Sarah Rose tugged on her father's hand. "Can we go?"

Shrugging, Gideon allowed himself to be led to the door. "Say thank you to Anna, Sarah Rose."

"*Danki!*"

And they were gone.

"Anna?"

"Hmm?"

"Anna!" Mary Katherine said more firmly.

"What?" Anna turned to look at her cousin.

"I didn't know how to tell you this while they were here."

Anna rolled her eyes. "Don't start acting like I'm interested in Gideon."

"I don't have to state the obvious," Mary Katherine said dryly. "But it's not that. Anna, Sarah Rose stole while she was in here."

3

She did what?"

"Sarah Rose stole." Mary Katherine's voice sounded flat and disappointed.

"Are you sure? I didn't see anything."

Mary Katherine sat down on the stool behind the counter. "I couldn't believe my eyes, either. She took one of the silver thimbles."

"Why didn't you say something while they were here?"

"I was so surprised, I didn't know what to do. I think we should ask Grandmother what she wants us to do about it."

"Do about what?"

Anna pressed a hand to her heart. "I didn't hear you coming."

"Do about what?" Leah repeated as she walked around the counter and checked the cash register.

"Sarah Rose stole something while she was here—one of the fancy carved silver thimbles."

Leah stopped and stared at Mary Katherine. "Sweet little Sarah Rose? Gideon's daughter?"

"I saw her holding it, but I thought she put it back," Anna said. "Mary Katherine said she was too shocked to say anything."

"Well, Gideon must be told."

Anna nodded. "I'll go see him after work. He's going to be appalled. What would make her steal something?"

"She lost one of the two most important people in her life two years ago."

"You're saying she stole because her *mamm* died?" Anna asked, not believing what she was hearing.

"Grief affects people in different ways," Leah said quietly.

"I don't believe what I'm hearing." Shaking her head, Anna walked around the counter. "I'm going to go finish unpacking the delivery I started before we got busy today."

It is downright ridiculous the way people blame everything on grief, she thought as she opened a box and pulled out skein after skein of yarn and checked it off on the shipping invoice that had been included. She'd lost Samuel and not turned into a kleptomaniac, hadn't she? And she hadn't heard of anyone she knew who had lost a loved one who'd resorted to larceny. Mood swings, sure. Sleepless nights. Difficulty concentrating. She could personally verify that all those were symptoms of going through grief.

But stealing? Never.

The day had gone by so fast, but the last hour before closing dragged. Anna knew it was because she was dreading talking to Gideon. She went over and over what to say: "I'm concerned about Sarah Rose. I'm sorry to tell you that your child stole from us. Maybe you should get her counseling." No, that was telling him what to do.

"Give us back the thimble and we won't press charges." Ouch.

Or—the door opened and her grandmother stepped inside the storage room.

"Do you want me to go with you when you talk to Gideon?"

Surprised, Anna shook her head. "No, why?"

"I know it's probably going to be awkward."

Anna shrugged. "I imagine it will be. But I've known Gideon for years. And Sarah Rose since she was born. I'm hoping he'll realize I'm there to talk to him as a friend."

Leah sighed. "I hope so, too. Get your things together. We're closing a few minutes early."

Well, that certainly caused mixed emotions, Anna thought. Part of her just wanted the workday over with, and part of her knew she still had to talk to Gideon. Anna winced. So sad. She'd always liked Sarah Rose with her big, solemn eyes and sweet nature. She hated having to tell Gideon that the child had done something wrong.

Gideon was a good father. She could tell from seeing him with his daughter in church. Such obvious love and care couldn't be pretense. And the fact that he'd brought her to the shop to find something to do with her—something he thought her mother would have done with her. Well, that was so sweet.

"What are you going to say?" Naomi wanted to know as Nick, her fiancé and their driver for the past couple of years, drove them to Gideon's home.

"I have no idea."

She turned to Leah. "What would you say?"

"No parent likes to hear that his child has done such a thing," Leah said, turning to stare out the van window with a faraway expression. "I remember when your mother's teacher called me. I was appalled. I—well, that's for another time."

She looked back at Anna. "Be prepared for Gideon to be defensive because he won't think his little girl could steal. It's the boys we expect such behavior from." She pressed her lips together to keep from smiling. "Sorry, Nick."

He laughed. "No offense taken. My mother had a lot of those conversations with teachers and others, I'm afraid. About my brother, not me. I was the good son."

His fingers tightened on the steering wheel, and he glanced at Naomi sitting in the front passenger seat, then away. She reached over and squeezed his arm and he nodded, but no words were exchanged.

Something was obviously wrong. Anna glanced at her grandmother, but she shook her head and touched her forefinger to her lips to indicate now wasn't the time to be asking.

Anna knew her cousins didn't always appreciate her curiosity, but it wasn't as if curiosity could be—should be—contained. She believed it was like trying to hold back a sneeze. Maybe it would do something to you inside.

That was her story and she was sticking to it.

But she was getting That Look from her grandmother so she stifled herself. She hoped her grandmother realized what an effort it was taking.

A few minutes later, Nick drove into Gideon's drive.

"I'll be back in an hour," he told her. "Will that give you enough time?"

She took a deep breath. "I might need just five minutes. It could be that he'll slam the door in my face."

Her grandmother patted her hand. "Gideon won't do that."

"But who knows what Sarah Rose will do?" She got out of the van and straightened her shoulders. "Well, here goes."

She looked at her grandmother, then Naomi. "See you both in the morning."

"We'll pray for you and Sarah Rose," her grandmother said. "And Gideon."

Anna nodded. "Good idea." She glanced at Nick. "See you in an hour."

As she walked toward the house, she couldn't help thinking how glad she was that she had tomorrow off.

The door opened before she could knock.

Sarah Rose stood there, frowning. "What are you doing here?" she demanded, not sounding like the sweet little girl who'd accompanied her father just hours earlier.

"I think you know," Anna said quietly, trying very hard not to sound accusing.

Sarah Rose reached into her pocket and threw the thimble at Anna's feet. "There!" she cried. "Take the stupid thing."

Anna's eyes widened at the girl's rude action, then she glanced down where the thimble glittered in the fading sunlight as it lay on the wooden porch.

"Sarah Rose? Is someone at the door?"

The child went white as she heard her father call. "No, *Daedi*!" She slammed the door.

A moment later, the door opened and Gideon stood there, looking puzzled. "Anna? What's going on?"

Anna bent down to pick up the thimble. "We need to talk."

"*Schur.*" He held the door open wider and gestured for her to enter. "We just finished supper. Have you eaten? Can I offer you something?"

"No, thank you. I'll eat when I get home."

"Some coffee?"

Anna hesitated. A cup of coffee after a long day might be nice, but she wasn't sure how he'd feel about offering it after what she had to say.

"Let me get you some. Come on into the kitchen."

The room was warm and homey, with crisp curtains at the window. Anna knew that Mary had made them because she'd bought the material at the store. Mary had been quite a seamstress, even in a community filled with good ones.

If Anna hadn't already been feeling a little hungry for her evening meal, she would have been now. Unless she was mistaken, they'd had vegetable beef soup and—sniff, sniff—grilled cheese sandwiches.

Gideon chuckled and shrugged as he noticed her looking over at the stove.

"Soup and sandwich night," he said, setting a mug of coffee in front of her. "Sarah Rose isn't much for fancy food, and that's good considering my cooking skills. Cream? Sugar? I'm afraid I don't have any of that sugar substitute stuff some women are so fond of."

"Milk and regular sugar are fine."

He got a small carton of half-and-half from the refrigerator and pushed a small sugar bowl toward her.

She fixed the coffee to her taste and noted that he took his black. When she tried hers, she found it so delicious she probably didn't need the cream and sugar. Who knew a man could make such a good cup of coffee?

"I'm afraid we haven't tried the kit yet so I can't tell you how it is."

Anna smiled. "I didn't figure you'd had time. I—I came to talk to you about something else. Something that happened at the store today. I'm afraid I have to tell you that Sarah Rose stole something."

She wished she'd timed it better—Gideon choked on his coffee. He reached for a napkin and wiped his mouth. "I'm sorry—you said?"

"Sarah Rose stole this." Anna held out the thimble.

Gideon looked confused. "If she stole it, how can you have it?"

Anna sighed. "She just—gave it to me at the door when I arrived."

She didn't want to tell him that his daughter had thrown it at her. It was enough to have to tell him his daughter had shoplifted.

He put his head in his hands, his elbows resting on the table, and then he straightened and looked at her. "I am so sorry she put you through this trouble. I'm going to have her apologize."

He stood, pulled out his wallet, and began pulling bills from it.

"There's no need to pay," she said quickly. "The item's been returned, and it wasn't damaged. But I do think an apology is in order. I think it would be good for Sarah Rose."

"You're sure about the money?"

She nodded.

"Let me call her down."

He went to the stairs and did so, and they heard her slowly descend them. When she entered the kitchen, it was obvious that she'd been crying. Gideon pulled out a chair and indicated she was to sit between him and Anna.

"Sarah Rose, Anna had to come here this evening after a long day working to tell me something. Something disappointing."

"I gave it back to her!" she cried, her lips trembling.

"That doesn't make it right," he said firmly.

Big tears began rolling down her cheeks. Anna's stomach twisted and she felt like crying herself.

"Why did you take it?" he asked her.

She wiped her tears away with her fists. "I just wanted it."

"Why didn't you ask me for it?"

"It was too 'spensive."

"But that's no reason to steal it. I hope you haven't done that anywhere else?"

She shook her head hard.

"You owe Anna an apology."

Sarah Rose turned to Anna. "I'm sorry."

"Go to your room now, Sarah Rose. We're going to talk some more about your punishment before you go to bed."

She slid off her chair and threw herself into his arms. "I'm sorry," she cried as she pressed her face against his chest. "I'm sorry."

He patted her back, frowning as he looked at Anna. "Go get ready for bed."

She ran from the room and Gideon sat there, lost in thought. Then he looked at Anna.

"Can I see that thimble again?"

"Sure." She held it out, and he studied it for a moment and then handed it back to her. "Wait here just a minute."

He left the room and took the stairs two at a time. She listened to his footsteps overhead, then he returned to the room carrying a sewing basket.

Sitting, he opened the basket, his hands looking so big and masculine on the delicate woven basket. He reached inside and withdrew something, holding it out in the palm of his hand.

The thimble was exactly the same as the one Sarah Rose had stolen.

"I thought it looked familiar," he said. "This was Mary's."

"She must have taken it because it reminded her of her mother. Mary probably bought it in our store. She shopped there for her quilting and sewing supplies."

When he nodded, she stayed silent for a minute, thinking hard. "Gideon, why haven't you given the basket to Sarah Rose?"

"She wasn't old enough when her mother died. I thought I'd give it to her when she would appreciate it more."

"Maybe she's old enough now," Anna said. "I think when she was in the store and she saw the thimble like her mother's, it stirred something in her. Maybe you should give it to her."

"My daughter's something of a tomboy," he said. "She hasn't really been interested in sewing and that sort of thing. That's one of the reasons I brought her to the store today—the promise I made to her mother that I wouldn't let her become a wild little thing."

"This isn't about her having the basket so she can sew. It's because she wants something that reminds her of her mother."

Anna touched the basket. "I remember what tiny stitches Mary made when she quilted. How she made a crib quilt before Sarah Rose was born and talked about how much she was looking forward to holding her."

She looked at him. "I'm sorry, I don't mean to make you sad."

"Can't be helped," he said, putting the thimble back inside the basket and closing it. "At the same time, it helps to hear a good memory, don't you think?"

She nodded, but the truth was, she didn't often let someone speak of Samuel. It just hurt too much. Glancing at the kitchen clock, she stood.

"I need to go outside," she said. "Nick will be by in a few minutes for me."

He walked outside with her and invited her to sit in a rocking chair on the porch.

"Do you want more coffee?"

"No, thanks."

"I'm sorry this kept you from your supper."

"It's okay, really."

She didn't have much appetite in the evening anyway. Sometimes all she wanted was a sandwich or a bowl of soup eaten far away from the big kitchen table Samuel had built.

"I don't know which is better," he said finally. "Being left alone or being left with someone whose grief you apparently have failed to help." He sighed and leaned back in his chair.

"I don't think you can blame yourself."

"No? Well, you would if you were me right now."

"Gideon, one incident doesn't make you a failure."

He dropped his head into his hands, then looked up at her. "It isn't the first incident. Her grades have been dropping. I've had two teacher conferences this month."

Anna fumbled for something to say. She hadn't had children, and even though she had siblings, none of them had ever behaved like Sarah Rose.

She felt a rush of relief she tried to hide when Nick pulled into the driveway.

"I'm sorry. I have to go," she said, getting to her feet. "Maybe we can talk sometime."

He got to his feet and nodded. "Thanks."

Anna got into the van, and Nick pulled out of the drive. When she looked back, Gideon waved at her and then thrust his hands into his pockets.

She couldn't forget the image of him staring off into the distance as they drove away.

≈

Gideon tried to concentrate on the directions for the knitting kit he and Sarah Rose had gotten at Anna's store.

He'd decided Saturday was a good day for the activity after the morning chores had been done. Even though it was something fun and he thought Sarah Rose should stay in her room and think about what she'd done, he figured that it was a chance for them to talk father/daughter.

So after lunch they cleaned up the kitchen and got out the kit and spread it out on the kitchen table.

After donning an apron, Sarah Rose read the directions— only stumbling over a few words he helped her sound out—good practice for her reading. Her teacher had said she needed to work on it for twenty minutes a day.

Gideon spread the packets of Kool-Aid out on the table. *Interesting idea to use it as yarn dye*, he thought. The drink mix was a summer favorite Sarah Rose was allowed now and then.

"We each get to pick a color," he told her.

"I want pink so I want strawberry," she said immediately. "Do we get to drink some before we use it?"

"After. Let's make sure we have enough for the dye first."

"Grape for you?"

"I'm not wearing purple." He hesitated, wondering what he'd gotten himself into. "Maybe blue moon berry if we make it dark."

Gideon opened the packet of strawberry and stirred it into the big bowl of water sitting in the sink, and immediately the fruity smell of berries filled the kitchen.

"*Mamm* used to make that kind for me," Sarah Rose told him as she carefully lowered her skein of yarn into the water. "She knew strawberry's my favorite."

In the act of dumping the blue moon berry in his bowl of water, Gideon's head jerked up. He studied her, head bent as she poked at the yarn with a big plastic spoon.

"I know your *mamm* always made you strawberry."

She looked up at him and gave him one of her solemn smiles.

"Sarah Rose, I know you miss your *mamm*. But she's watching over you, and I think she's feeling sad that you're hurting still."

"I don't want to forget her."

"No one expects you to. But we need to remember how God gave her to us for a time."

"But why do other kids get to have their *mamms* a long time and not me?"

He searched for the right words. It didn't seem fair to him sometimes, but it was God's will.

"We don't always know why God does what He does," he said, swirling the drink mix into the water and pushing his yarn into the bowl until it was submerged in the dye. "We have to trust that He knows what He's doing."

Her bottom lip stuck out as she stirred. "I know." She sighed, a huge sigh that said she didn't really like what she heard but had heard it enough to know it was the truth.

"How long are we supposed to let it sit now?"

She set down the spoon and picked up the directions. "Thirty minutes."

"So how long is that?"

She frowned. "Half an hour?"

"That's right. How about we have some Kool-Aid and cookies while we wait?"

"That would be *gut*. I'll get it."

"No!" he said quickly. "The pitcher's full. I wouldn't want it to get spilled."

He withdrew his hands from the bowl and wiped them on a kitchen towel.

Dye came off on the towel but remained on his hands half-way up his forearms. Shrugging, he turned on the faucet, careful not to let the stream of water into the bowl of dye. But no matter how much water he ran over them, how much soap he used, his hands were still stained blue moon berry.

He glanced over and saw that Sarah Rose was studying the directions, her lips moving as she read the words.

"Sweetheart, what does it say about getting the dye off your hands?"

"I didn't get any on my hands, *Daedi*. I used a spoon to stir."

He dried his hands on the towel. "Let me see that."

She handed the paper over and then her eyes lit up and she started laughing. "Oh, silly *Daedi*!" she laughed. "You didn't use the spoon!"

"Why didn't you read this part?" he asked, pointing at the big warning at the top of the page.

"I didn't know how to pronounce that *r* word."

"This one?" he asked, pointing to it.

"*Ya.*"

"It's *rubber*," he told her dryly. "*Rubber gloves.*"

"Oh," she said but with the air of unconcern that told him she really didn't understand. "Are you getting out the Kool-Aid?"

"*Schur.*" Shaking his head, he poured her a glass and brought the cookie jar to the table.

He fixed himself a cup of coffee and sat down with the directions, praying they'd offer him some suggestion on how he was going to get rid of blue hands and forearms.

Otherwise he was going to look pretty silly at church tomorrow.

4

Anna couldn't put her finger on what it was, but something was definitely wrong with Gideon.

Oh, he looked as handsome as ever in his Sunday church clothes, his hair neatly combed, his smile warm and friendly.

Then he reached for the plate of food she offered and her eyes widened and she bobbled the plate. He caught it before it could fall and grinned.

"I'm hoping you can tell me what to do about my little problem," he said, glancing down at his hands. "We were using the Kool-Aid kit, and I didn't put on rubber gloves."

She tried to hold back a giggle, she honestly did, but it slipped out anyway.

"What's so funny?" Sadie, one of the women helping with the small meal after church, wanted to know.

Then she caught sight of Gideon's hands and started to laugh. She covered her mouth. "I'm sorry!"

Sarah Rose appeared at her father's side and frowned. "It's not funny! *Daedi* scrubbed and scrubbed his hands."

"You're right, Sarah Rose, it's not funny," Anna said. "Gideon, I thought that kit came with rubber gloves."

"We found them in the box," Gideon told her, nodding. "After."

John Stoltzfus clapped his hand on Gideon's shoulder. "My son Henry says you're turning into one of those Smurf cartoon characters he saw in a library book. They're blue, you know?"

Sarah Rose went still, then backed away and walked toward the front door.

Anna started to say something to Gideon, but after the initial laugh at his expense, Gideon and the other man had launched into a business discussion.

"I'll be right back," she told Sadie.

She walked out onto the front porch and found Sarah Rose sitting in a rocker she'd pulled into the farthest corner. The child slumped down in the chair, her lip trembling.

"Sarah Rose? Sweetheart, are you all right?"

"Fine." She turned her face away.

"You seem upset."

She turned around. "It's all my fault *Daedi's* hands are blue."

"Oh, I'm sure he doesn't blame you." She was silent for a moment. "I'm kind of surprised he didn't think of the gloves."

"I skipped that part in the d'rections."

Directions. "But still—"

"We started talking about *Mamm*." Her eyes grew bright with unshed tears. "I think—well, he always gets sad about her. He put his hands in the water with the dye 'cause I think he was upset and he forgot."

She hung her head. "That's why I don't talk to him about her. It hurts him too much."

Unsure what to say, Anna glanced back at the door, but Gideon was still inside.

She had to choose her words carefully; she knew from experience how the wrong ones could hurt even more than silence.

"Your *daedi* loves you so much," she said softly. "He'd want to talk to you about anything that's hurting you. He wouldn't care about himself."

Anna sighed. "And sometimes you just have to talk about things no matter how they hurt. Sometimes it can hurt more to hold things in."

She reverted to a childhood habit and chewed on her thumbnail. "Sometimes I do that because I don't want to talk about how I'm hurting about—about Samuel. Sometimes I think it'll hurt someone like my grandmother because it'll make her think of my grandfather dying young."

Sighing, she shook her head. "Sometimes I'm up and down with my moods still. Sometimes . . . well, I'm not so pleasant with the people near me like my cousins and my grandmother."

She remembered how after she'd found out that Sarah Rose had stolen, she'd thought about how she knew people did all sorts of things, behaved all sorts of ways when they grieved, but she'd never heard of anyone stealing.

But the way she was sometimes—was that any different from the way Sarah Rose had been acting out? The only difference was that they weren't at the same maturity level . . .

She almost laughed. Her cousins might have disagreed with her on that.

The door opened, and Gideon came out.

"What are the two of you doing sitting out here?" he asked, his tone neutral.

But Anna saw the expression of concern in his eyes.

"Girl talk," she said lightly.

"Oh. I guess I'm not invited." He pretended to be disappointed and wiped away an imaginary tear.

Anna watched Sarah Rose stare at her father's blue hands.

"*Daedi*, maybe if Anna saw the d'rections she'd know what to do to make the blue go away."

"We read them, remember? I don't think there's anything else we can do. It just has to wear off." He bent down to kiss her head. "Stop worrying. I'm not upset with you. I should have been paying better attention."

He glanced at Anna. "I know some things can stain, so even if I'd never used the dye kit I should have known better. After all, I use gloves sometimes working on the farm."

With a shrug, he shoved his hands into his pockets. "It'll just be a funny story I trot out after I knit my muffler."

"That's true," Anna agreed. "Since so many people saw your hands today, they'll want to see it when it's done."

Gideon straightened and gave her a rueful look. "Thanks for reminding me how many people noticed the blue hands."

Anna grinned. "No problem."

"*Daedi*, I'm hungry."

"You didn't have anything to eat?"

She shook her head. "I wasn't hungry then."

"Let me go see if anything's left." He turned to Anna. "Did you eat?"

"No, but I'm fine until I get home." She'd seen a number of people leave and had a suspicion that any remaining food had been packed up and was going home with them.

When Gideon returned, his blue hands were empty.

"Sorry, Sarah Rose. The food's gone. Let's go home and I'll make you a sandwich."

She stood up. "Can Anna come with us and you can fix her a sandwich while she reads the d'rections?"

Gideon looked at her. "Anna may have plans."

Plans. She almost laughed. She'd been throwing herself into her work at the shop and chores at home in an effort to keep busy, her mind occupied with anything but thoughts of Samuel for so long.

And she didn't need to add more problems on to her already full plate. She had a feeling she could be drawn into the problems of these two people . . . this little girl and her too-appealing widowed father.

But she suspected that had already happened.

Sarah Rose tilted her head as she looked at Anna. "She solded it to us, *Daedi*."

Anna laughed as Gideon reacted with a gasp and a frown. "Now don't get upset with her," she said quickly. "She's right. Okay, I'll come. And I'll take you up on your offer of a sandwich. I confess I'm feeling hungry!"

∾᪽

Anna had already been in his home a number of times visiting Mary and again the other night, but Gideon still had that momentary feeling of anxiety when he opened his front door and stepped aside for her to enter.

He knew he hadn't been able to keep it at the level of cleanliness that Mary had, but he did the best he could. Besides, he had to be two parents now . . . and Anna certainly knew that.

They'd known each other since childhood, of course, but from the time he decided girls were not only okay but pretty special, he'd only had eyes for Mary. It had been the same for Samuel. He and Anna had been inseparable and were one of the first couples their age to marry.

"Coffee?"

"Yes, thanks."

Anna turned to Sarah Rose. "So, where are those directions?"

Sarah Rose ran to get them, and the two of them sat down at the kitchen table.

Gideon rinsed the percolator, filled it with fresh water and coffee, then set it on the gas range. He opened the refrigerator and stuck his head inside. There were plenty of sandwich makings.

"So what'll it be?" he asked, straightening and glancing back at Anna and Sarah Rose.

Their heads were close as they bent over the directions. He paused for a moment and studied them. Sarah Rose had been sulky that day when she was called downstairs to talk about the stealing. Her apology hadn't been as willing—or remorseful—as he'd have liked.

But apparently his daughter wasn't holding a grudge at Anna telling on her. Not that she should. He'd just been afraid she'd be like *kinner* could be when they got into trouble—and he wondered if the conversation they'd been having on the porch today had anything to do with it.

Anna glanced up and caught him looking at them. She lifted her brows in question, and he realized that he had to think of something to explain why he'd been staring.

"We have chicken sandwiches—it's left over from last night—and ham and Swiss and some egg salad . . ." he trailed off. "No, wait, I had the egg salad last night."

"He eats a lot," Sarah Rose said, shaking her head. "Boys eat a lot."

"They do," Anna agreed, grinning at him. "The chicken sounds good. Maybe with a little mayonnaise. But I can make it."

"No, you're a guest. We have some chocolate chip cookies we made, too. Sarah Rose, time to wash your hands and set the table."

It was a new feeling to be waited on, one she felt a little uncomfortable with, but she told herself to sit back and enjoy it.

She went back to reading the directions. "I'm sure you tried scrubbing them really well with soap and water."

"*Ya.* Maybe I should try some bleach."

"Absolutely not!" she cried. "Don't even think of doing such a thing! Don't you know how dangerous that is?"

"Don't yell at *Daedi!*" Sarah Rose said.

"I'm sorry, I just don't want him to use something that can hurt himself to get rid of the dye," Anna said quickly.

"It's all my fault!" Sarah Rose's lip began trembling. She opened her mouth to speak, and then she turned and ran from the room.

Gideon sighed and set the plate of chicken on the table. "I have to go talk to her."

"Wait," she said, stopping him. "You need to tell her the worst that can happen is it might take a few days to wear off."

"So she's overreacting?"

Anna nodded. "But please don't use that term. Girls—women—don't appreciate hearing that kind of language from a man."

He met her level stare. "All right." Turning, he started up the stairs.

People were always saying that children grew up so quickly. His baby had turned into a child, and yes, she was growing up too fast. But Anna was, in effect, telling him that she was a girl, and he was going to have to start watching what he said to her.

No, life was going too quickly.

He'd barely gotten to the top of the stairs when Anna was calling to him, her voice sounding excited.

"Gideon? May I use your phone?"

"*Schur.* It's in the shanty. The key's on a hook by the refrigerator."

Sarah Rose had thrown herself on her bed, but at least she'd stopped crying. He sat down beside her and placed his hand on her back. No telling her she was overreacting, he warned himself.

"I want you to come downstairs now. I'm not upset, and I don't want you to be. But we have a guest in our home, and it's not polite for us to be up here and her down there. And she's sitting there hungry, too, remember?"

"I know," she said with a sniff.

"So why don't you go wash your face and let's feed our guest—and you."

Sarah Rose sat up, wiping her tears away with her fingers. When she went to wipe her nose with the cuff of her dress, he stopped her, shook his head, and gave her a handkerchief he pulled from his pocket.

"Maybe she'd like to see my room after?"

"I bet she would."

She considered that. "Okay." Cheered, she wrapped her arms around him and hugged him, then slid off the bed.

Crisis averted, Gideon went downstairs and found Anna looking inside his refrigerator.

"You don't have to make your own sandwich."

She jumped. "Oh, didn't hear you. Do you have pickles?"

He pulled out a jar and handed them to her. "Dill?"

"Doesn't matter. What about toothpaste?"

He eyed her warily. "We have mayo."

Anna laughed. "Just get the toothpaste, please."

She'd told him that he needed to be careful what he said to Sarah Rose because she wasn't so little, she was becoming a big girl. Mary had never been hard to understand. He knew from what other men said that some were but not her. She had always been so easy to be around. Interesting that her daughter was looking like she might not have that easy personality Mary had.

Sarah Rose joined them. "I'm sorry I ran upstairs, Anna. You must be very *hungerich*."

She nodded. "I am."

Gideon walked back into the kitchen and handed Anna the tube of toothpaste.

"You're going to eat toothpaste?" Sarah Rose asked her.

Anna grinned. "No, your father's going to wear it. Or pickles."

Now it was Gideon's turn to stare.

"Excuse me?"

She walked over to the sink. "After you two went upstairs I suddenly had this idea. I called Jamie. You know Jamie? She's come to church a couple of times."

"The *Englisch* girl with the colored hair?"

"That's right. She works at the shop part-time. Well, I remembered that she sometimes uses Kool-Aid to color her hair. I called her, and she told me what to do if you get it on your skin."

"Pickle juice and toothpaste?" Gideon asked, wondering if he was hearing correctly.

"One or the other. Not both at the same time."

Gideon looked at Sarah Rose and then shrugged. "I'm game."

A few minutes later, he watched as the pickle juice did its magic. "Well, how about that," he said as dye ran down the sink. "Who knew it could be that easy? Nothing to get upset about after all, right?"

"Except Henry said you looked like a Smurf," Sarah Rose said with a giggle.

Gideon gestured for them to sit. "I can handle being called a Smurf," he said grandly.

It wasn't what he'd like to have been called, but now, if teasing him put that smile that he loved back on her face, well, the world could call him a Smurf and he wouldn't care.

Then he looked across the table at Anna and saw that she was smiling at his daughter. She glanced at him, and he saw something he had never seen before.

He saw a woman he wanted to know better.

Reminders of Mary were everywhere in the house, but nowhere more than in Sarah Rose's bedroom.

Perhaps it was because this had been one of Mary's favorite rooms. He knew many people called the kitchen the heart of the home, but for Mary, their long-awaited first—and only— child's room became the place he'd often find her.

He wasn't as good a carpenter as other men he knew, but he'd done his best on the rocking chair he gave her the Christmas before Sarah Rose was born. She'd sit in it and read during the time before she delivered, and then she'd rock their baby many a night when she was colicky or teething.

Near the end, when he'd wake and find Mary's side of the bed empty, he'd tiptoe into Sarah Rose's room and find Mary sitting in the rocker, watching her sleep in her big girl bed.

It was as if she tried to cram in every moment with her child in case she didn't survive the ovarian cancer that the doctor discovered during one of her checkups.

The rocking chair wasn't the only thing that reminded him of Mary. As his gaze swept the room, he saw the old chest of drawers that had been hers and her mother's and her grand-mother's. There'd been a pad on top of it she'd sewn so that she could change Sarah Rose's diapers, but that was long gone now.

A shelf he'd made held some of the cloth dolls and stuffed animals she'd made for their daughter, most of them lovingly tattered by a little girl who used to take them to bed. Now she acted like she was too old for even her favorite doll.

Fortunately, she hadn't yet grown too old for story time before bed.

He sat down on her bed with the book she'd chosen for tonight's bedtime reading and waited for her to finish brushing her teeth. She always kept her bedroom clean and her bed made, but she'd obviously used the time-out yesterday to make it spotless.

Lost in his thoughts, she surprised him when she padded barefoot into the room and climbed onto his lap.

Her hair was soft and clean and smelled like the baby shampoo he still bought. The snowy white nightgown she wore smelled of sunshine. He wrapped his arms around her and hugged her before she slipped between the sheets.

She looked like such an angel, but as he opened the book she made a face. "You still smell like pickle juice."

Gideon picked up a pillow and put it over Sarah Rose's face. "Now you don't have to smell it."

She pummeled him with her fists and wiggled to get free.

He pulled the pillow off. "Did you say something?"

"Smurf!"

Clapping the pillow back over her face, he said loudly, "Can't hear you!"

She pushed at him and got the pillow off her face—it wasn't hard since he barely held it on her. "Smurf, Smurf, Smurf!" she giggled.

He held his hand over her face. "Here, have a nice whiff before you go to sleep."

"Ugh! Now I'll dream about green pickles chasing me."

Without turning, she nipped at his fingers with her teeth.

"Ouch! You're so obnoxious!"

"I know what that means!" She pretended to be offended.

"I bet you do," he said, getting up. "I'll be right back."

"Bring me a glass of water. Please," she added.

He rolled his eyes and then left the room. When he returned, he brought her a glass of water, but he also carried something that made her eyes grow big. Setting the glass on her bedside table, he sat down on the bed.

"When Anna showed me the thimble, I recognized it," he said, opening the little wicker sewing basket. From it he withdrew the thimble and held it out to her. "This was your *mamm's*. I was going to give it to you when you got older. But Anna said I should give it to you now."

He placed it back in the kit, closed the top, and held it out to her.

Sarah Rose took the basket and hugged it to her chest. "*Danki, Daedi*."

"Just take good care of it."

She nodded, then slipped out of bed and set the basket on top of her dresser. When she returned to bed, she didn't get in but instead threw her arms around him. "I love you."

"I know. I love you, too."

"I'm sorry I've been bad. I don't know why I do things sometimes."

"Maybe it's time for you to go talk to somebody who can help you understand."

She pulled back and frowned. "Like who?"

"Like a counselor."

Her bottom lip jutted out, and she frowned. "I'm not crazy."

"People aren't crazy because they see counselors."

"David Stoltzfus says they are."

"David Stoltzfus is something else," Gideon muttered.

"What?"

"Nothing. Come on. Get back in bed and let's read our story and get some sleep. Monday's going to come awfully early."

"Why do people say that? It comes at the same time, doesn't it?"

Gideon rolled his eyes. "*Ya*. Bed, Sarah Rose. Now."

She climbed into bed and he tucked the quilt around her, then he kissed her forehead and rose.

"I like her."

He stopped and turned back to look at her. "Who?"

"Anna. She doesn't pretend to like me to be near you."

Gideon walked back to the side of the bed. "Who does that?"

"All the ladies who aren't married."

5

*N*aomi got into the van, gave Nick a quick kiss, then turned around to stare at Anna. "So what happened?"

"Well, that was romantic," Nick said wryly.

Embarrassed, she turned around, put her hands on his face, and looked him in the eye. "Sorry," she told him, and this time she gave him a proper kiss.

Then she turned around and stared at Anna again. "Tell me what happened."

Anna met Nick's gaze in the rearview mirror, and a little exasperated, Naomi looked at Nick again. "I don't think I should be expected to give you a better kiss than that in front of my grandmother and Anna."

He laughed and shook his head. "Of course not. I'm waiting for you to buckle your seat belt."

She rolled her eyes but complied. "Are you going to make us do that when you drive a buggy?"

Pulling down the visor on the passenger side, she narrowed her eyes at Anna. "Now tell me. I saw you leaving with Gideon after church, and I didn't have a chance to call you last night."

"He gave me a ride home." Then she bit her lip. "Well, we went to his house for lunch. Sarah Rose, too," she added quickly. "He wanted my help with something."

Naomi turned to their grandmother, but before she could ask the question, Leah shook her head.

"I don't know more than you do," Leah said.

"Come on," Naomi said. "You've always been so nosy about our lives."

"Why that's—" she cast a glance at her grandmother— "absolutely true." She grinned.

Then she told the story as quickly as possible but without the mention of the way Gideon had looked at her a couple of times. That was absolutely no one's business. And she wasn't even sure there was anything to it.

All she knew was that it was the first time that she'd even remotely been interested in being around a man, let alone a little attracted to him.

Besides, what had struck her was the way she had felt an unexpected bond with his little girl. She loved children and babysat often for her twin siblings, but it was usually younger children that she related to best.

"Oh, somebody got quiet and thoughtful and in her own little world."

"What?"

"Is it possible that you're interested in Gideon?" Naomi wanted to know.

Anna caught the look she got from Nick in the rearview mirror.

"What?"

He shook his head and grinned. "I just remember how you were like an Inquisitor with Mary Katherine and then Naomi about their dating," he said. "It's nice to see the shoe on the other foot, so to speak. Turnabout's fair play."

"Any other clichés you want to use?" she muttered.

"No, two a day is my limit."

"Thank goodness."

Laughing, he flicked on the turn signal and pulled in front of the shop. "Have a good day, ladies."

Anna and Leah climbed out, letting Nick and Naomi say good-bye. Well, kiss good-bye was more accurate. Anna had teased them a couple of times about it, but she really was so happy that they'd found each other and were getting married that she tried to hold back the teasing.

As she walked to the back room to put her things away, she passed the shelf with the knitting kit Gideon had bought his daughter.

She found herself remembering what she'd said to Sarah Rose after church. She'd really meant what she said about how her moods were still up and down and she wasn't always so pleasant with the people around her.

Anna had hesitated about sharing something so personal with a child, but it had seemed right when Sarah Rose had been so upset. She hadn't experienced losing someone she loved as a child, but it didn't seem to her that it was much different from losing anyone important to you. Sarah Rose had listened but hadn't said much so she didn't know if she'd helped at all. But it didn't really matter. Anna had felt moved to say what she had, and that was all that mattered to her.

The morning moved slowly because it was raining.

So they sat in their chairs in the circle before the crackling fireplace and worked on their respective crafts. Mary Katherine sat weaving a beautiful blanket in earth tones of russet, gold, pine green, and burnt sienna, and Leah sewed and stuffed her little Amish dolls. Anna's needles clacked as she knitted a new cupcake hat for a baby—it was hard to keep them in stock this time of year. Naomi stitched on a quilt and occasionally stopped to scribble something in a notebook she was using to plan her wedding.

Naomi didn't talk much about wedding plans in front of her. Anna had noticed that Mary Katherine hadn't, either.

It didn't take a genius to figure out that they didn't want to upset her, but it was time to stop that. She'd been so self-involved she hadn't noticed Mary Katherine doing this, but now, as time had passed and the grief wasn't quite as raw about Samuel, she realized Naomi seldom talked about wedding plans.

Well, Anna told herself, *I'm not fragile and even if I was, Naomi deserves to have every minute of joy talking about her wedding in front of me.*

"Not much longer now, is it?"

Naomi glanced up, and when she realized that Anna was looking at her, she frowned. "Not much longer for what?"

"Your wedding." She shook her head. "You haven't forgotten it, have you?"

"Of course not!" Naomi bit her lip. "I just—well, I—"

"You don't have to hold back from talking about it because of me."

"I'm not doing that."

"Liar." But she smiled to show she wasn't being mean.

Naomi set her quilt down. "What do you want to know?"

"Anything—everything."

Naomi's cheeks bloomed with pink color as she talked about the upcoming wedding. Anna had already heard about the color of the dresses she, Mary Katherine, and the others would wear because they'd had to pick out the material to begin cutting it and sewing the dresses.

The food would be simple for the wedding meal and the evening supper but all wedding favorites: roast—roasted chicken and filling, vegetables, salads, rolls. Pies and cookies and cakes galore. And, of course, the wedding cake. All of the food would be made by friends and family with loving hands. She couldn't wait to surprise Nick with the flavor of the wedding cake; she'd narrowed it down to three choices.

Anna let her cousin's words wash over her as she knitted, determined to concentrate on them and not let herself drift away into a daydream about how she'd felt planning her own wedding years ago.

"So you think he'll like the flavor of the cake?" Naomi asked a little loudly.

"Yes, of course," Anna said. "Why wouldn't he?"

"Most people don't like to eat mud cake with dandelion frosting."

ﾟ

She stood staring out the window of the shop with a pensive expression on her face.

Although the day was a bit chilly, Gideon used the excuse that Sarah Rose wanted to look at the display window to give himself a few minutes to study Anna.

Gone was the carefree expression she wore so often when he saw her. Once, when he'd had a particularly difficult night thinking about Mary, he'd been a little resentful of her healing from her loss. It didn't seem to him that she could be feeling what he'd been feeling, seeing his late wife everywhere he looked.

Even looking at his daughter had been painful. Sarah Rose was the image of her mother from her daintily pointed chin to that funny little frown she'd get when she concentrated on something.

Today, not knowing that someone looked upon her, he saw the vulnerability, the shadow in her eyes. Maybe his assumption that she'd been recovering from her loss faster than he had was wrong.

When she moved and caught sight of him, he looked away quickly, pretending to study the window display. Somehow he didn't think that she would appreciate him seeing her having a private, thoughtful moment. Anna had always been friendly, but there was a reserve about her since Samuel had died.

He raised his hand and waved, and she waved back, smiling as she glanced down and saw Sarah Rose.

Anna opened the door. "Well, hello."

"Are we in time?"

"In time for what?" she asked.

"The knitting class," Sarah Rose said, looking around her. "There's nobody here."

"We're early," her father told her. "I told you that I needed to ask Anna if we could join it, remember?"

Sarah Rose shifted the handles of the cloth tote bag on her shoulder. "I think we're going to be the only oneses, *Daedi*."

"They'll be here," Anna told her. She looked at Gideon. "Would you like some coffee?"

He nodded and rubbed his hands. "*Ya*, it's a bit chilly today."

"Black, right?" She poured him a mug. "Sarah Rose, would you like some hot chocolate? It's not homemade—it's a packaged mix—but it's good. It even has mini marshmallows."

She looked to her father for permission. Then when he nodded, she said, "Yes, please." They went into the kitchen, and Anna made it for her.

"Gideon! How nice to see you," Leah said as she entered the room. "And Sarah Rose as well."

Anna set the mug before the child, cautioning her to wait until it cooled to drink it.

"We're here for a knitting lesson," Sarah Rose told her, swinging her legs under the table as she stirred her hot chocolate, making the mini marshmallows bob in it.

"I'm probably the only man who's ever taken the class, right?" Gideon asked, his mouth quirking in a grin.

"*Nee*, Daniel Yoder was in here last year," she said, pouring herself a cup of the hot water Anna had just boiled on the stove.

She took a seat at the table and reached for a tea bag. "He came in intending to just take the class for some therapy— he hurt his hands in an accident on his farm, remember? Then he decided he liked knitting mufflers for a charity project, and he came for quite a long time."

"We're just here to learn how to make our project," Gideon told her. "Although the coffee is worth coming for."

Sarah Rose took a sip of her hot chocolate and licked at the white marshmallow mustache that appeared on her upper lip.

"May I see the yarn you dyed?"

Taking a ball of raspberry-colored yarn from the tote bag, Sarah Rose handed it to Anna.

"So this is the color you chose," she said, looking at Gideon.

He gave her a look. "You know I chose the blue that matches my hands so well," he told her. Reaching for the tote, he pulled out the ball of blue yarn and tossed it to her.

She examined the ball. "Turned out nice."

He held out his hands. "And fortunately the dye wasn't permanent."

"I like it," Sarah Rose said suddenly. "Mine's the kind my *mamm* used to make me."

Anna smiled. "My favorite was grape. My *mamm* would make it for me sometimes in the summer."

She looked at Gideon. "What about you?"

His eyes were warm on her. "Grape. Always grape."

Mary Katherine poked her head in the door. "Your class is here."

Gideon stood. "Well, I'm going to go brave the ladies."

"You'll be fine."

There was a loud slurping noise as Sarah Rose drained the last of her hot chocolate.

"My daughter, the delicate young lady," he said wryly as they walked into the shop.

Anna introduced Gideon and Sarah Rose to the members of the knitting class and got them started on the week's lesson, then sat in the chair beside Sarah Rose to help her cast her yarn on her needles.

Sarah Rose chewed on her lip as she struggled with the task, but after she got the first couple of loops safely on the needles, she smiled. "I did it!"

"You did!"

Anna remembered the first time her grandmother had helped her do this. Quilting hadn't interested her as much as it had Naomi, but she loved the feel of the yarn in her hands, the thing she was creating—a muffler had been her first project just like Sarah Rose—emerging from the needles with their comforting clacking noise.

Her father insisted that he loved the muffler when he opened it on Christmas even though it was overlong, contained a number of dropped stitches, and looked slightly crooked. He didn't mind the length, he said, and wrapped it around his neck an extra time or two. Years later, in her teens, she'd tried to exchange it with a better one, but he'd refused, insisting that he loved her first effort.

Poor Samuel had been the unfortunate recipient of some of my early knitting as well, she thought with a smile. He'd gotten many beginner projects that made her wince today: sweaters with one arm too long, a cap that covered his eyes but he swore was his favorite for keeping his head warm. Truth was, it slipped and often covered his eyebrows. That was okay, he said. They got cold in a Pennsylvania winter, too.

She'd teased him that there was room enough under the hat for two. Laughing, he'd pulled her close, tried to drag it over both their heads, but only succeeded in bringing their faces so close that they'd ended up staring at each other, the cold-smoky plumes of their breath intermingling. Then they'd kissed, and nothing had been the same again. They'd been schoolhouse friends one day and inseparable the next.

"This is hard," Sarah Rose said, breaking into her thoughts.

"You're doing really well," Anna told her. "Look at how much you've done so far."

She looked over at Gideon. "I'll help you in just a minute."

"No hurry," he said, watching his daughter's progress.

A few minutes later, satisfied that her new student was doing well, Anna got up and moved to a chair next to Gideon. "Oh, my."

He held up his hands tangled in yarn, laughed, and shook his head. "Not so good."

She leaned forward and began unsnarling the yarn. Just as she had the day she helped him get rid of the dye on his hands, she noticed how his hands looked so strong and capable. Although she was careful not to touch him, one of her hands accidentally brushed his and her fingers tingled. Looking up, she saw that his eyes had suddenly grown intense. Quickly, she finished pulling the yarn away.

"Now, if you'll hand me the ball of yarn I'll rewind it and get you started again."

He picked up the ball from his lap and went to hand it to her, but he dropped it and it rolled under his chair. Anna bent to catch it, but he'd done the same thing and they knocked foreheads together.

"Ouch!" they cried simultaneously and sprang back to rub their foreheads.

Sarah Rose giggled, then slipped from her chair to retrieve the ball and hand it to Anna.

"I'm doing real good," she said in a lofty tone, climbing back into her chair and resuming her knitting.

Anna rubbed at her forehead. "You certainly are." She turned back to Gideon. "You're not usually this—" she paused, searching for the word.

"Klutzy?" he asked, rubbing his own forehead.

She bit her lip, trying to stifle her smile as she rolled the yarn back on the ball. "There, now just go back to what you were doing but slower and with . . . a little more attention."

"I got distracted," he said in a low voice.

She blinked at him, and then understanding dawned as he continued to stare at her. Feeling flustered, she got to her feet. "I need to check on the other students."

Betsy, a stay-at-home mother with two children, had knitted twice as much as Anna expected. "You've made great progress!" Anna told her.

"I've been taking some time to myself lately," Betsy told her, grinning up at her as she knit. "Both my boys are in school all day now, and I finally have a little time to do something I enjoy."

"I remember those days," Thelma said. A whirlwind in her seventies, she was newly retired from working at the phone company. "I was always so busy taking care of the kids and the husband—he was like a fourth kid himself—and the house. I never had the chance to have a hobby. Now, the hubby says I'm busier with all my hobbies than when I worked. I come here to knit, to quilt. There's that Indian cooking class I take at the senior center."

"You're making me tired thinking about all you do," Anna said with a laugh.

"And you, young fella, you came here with your daughter. Are you a single parent?"

Oh no, thought Anna. *Here come the questions, the prying.* She hadn't thought Thelma was that kind of woman. She cast a glance at Gideon, and he shook his head and shrugged, as if indicating that everything was okay.

"Sarah Rose and I like to do things together," he said, taking a moment to study his work. "I didn't want the two of us to always be doing things like toss a baseball."

"It's nice when fathers do things with their kids," Thelma told him, nodding. "And not just toss a baseball."

"*Daedi* says he thinks we kids should all learn how to do all kinds of things."

"He's a smart *daedi*." Thelma smiled.

Anna saw how Thelma's eyes grew sad.

"How does this look, Anna?" Ella wanted to know.

A shy, quiet wisp of a woman, Ella was taking the class more to learn how to relax, she'd told Anna, than to create things from it. She ate lunch at her desk and took the time later in the afternoon once a week to take the class.

Anna was determined that she'd have some fun, not just learn to relax.

Although this was a great solution she'd come up with since classes weren't offered in the evening at Stitches in Time, it had probably made her feel even more stressed. So far, Ella was beginning to relax because she said she couldn't multi-task here in the shop when she was knitting. Anna had to admit that she needed this multitasking explained. How much calmer to do one thing at a time—and do it well.

Sure, there were a few times when people needed to do two things at once. If you had to care for your new baby at the same time as start supper, that was when you quickly put together a casserole or a roast with vegetables or a big pot of soup and it cooked at the same time.

This sense of having to always do two things at once was one of the things that seemed to stress the *Englisch* the most and made them envy the Amish. When they walked into the shop, they reacted with yearning, wanting to learn how to quilt or knit or sew or pick up their UFOs—unfinished fabric objects—like a quilt they'd started and let sit gathering dust.

The class members were welcome to get up and visit the restroom or fix something to drink or snack on a cookie any time that they liked. However, Anna had found that the students liked stopping for a break together a few minutes and chatting before turning back to their projects.

She was pouring herself a cup of tea when Thelma sidled up to her and asked, "So, this Gideon is a widower, eh?"

Surprised, Anna blinked and then nodded.

"So maybe the two of you are interested in each other?"

Such things were usually very private in her community, but Anna knew they weren't outside it. Not that the Amish didn't gossip—they weren't perfect, after all. But she wasn't accustomed to talking about anything so personal.

"Gideon is a friend," she said.

Thelma suddenly clamped her mouth shut and gestured with her head toward Sarah Rose. "Little pitchers," she said and moved away.

Sarah Rose stepped closer. "You're *my* friend."

Anna looked down at her and nodded. "You and your *dat* are both my friends."

"But I'm yours first," Sarah Rose insisted.

Someone moved on the periphery of Anna's vision. Looking up, she saw Gideon watching her, his expression conflicted. She felt the same.

Knowing how vulnerable she was feeling judging by her behavior of late, Anna wanted to be sensitive to her.

"Yes, I'm your friend first," she said quietly.

Sarah Rose smiled. She looked up at her father. "May I have a cookie?"

"One." He watched her. "Now she's going to spend some time deciding which cookie is the biggest."

"It's the ones Mary Katherine makes. Maybe you should tell her."

His mouth quirked into a grin. "I'll tell her."

He started to walk past her, and then he stopped and became serious. "Thank you for what you did. Sarah Rose obviously needs a friend right now."

More than you? she wanted to ask, but she didn't.

6

$\mathcal{N}$aomi yawned as she walked into the back room where Anna was working on an order.

"I came to get some coffee to wake up," she admitted as she sat down with a mug. I stayed up too late last night."

"Wedding plans?"

"I was sewing my dress."

Anna bit her lip and then looked at her cousin. "I'd like to make it up to you."

"Make up what?" Naomi sipped her coffee and tried to stifle another yawn.

"I've felt terrible since I didn't pay attention while you were telling me about your wedding plans the other day."

Naomi shrugged. "It's okay. Wedding plans are interesting only to the person who's getting married."

Anna reached for the cookie jar and set it before Naomi. "Have some. You're getting thin."

"Nick said that, too," she admitted, reaching into the jar and taking out a couple of Snickerdoodles. "It's not deliberate. Sometimes I just get busy lately. I'm not trying to lose weight for the wedding."

"You're sure?"

Naomi nodded. "Nick was asking me that the other day. He says he knew some *Englisch* friend who made herself really sick doing that, and he wanted to make sure I didn't."

Anna smiled as she selected a cookie. "I never thought Nick would be the *mann* God set aside for you, but now I can't see you marrying anyone else."

Silence stretched between them, and the room grew so quiet the ticking of the kitchen clock could be heard.

"I can almost feel you wanting to ask something."

"It might be too personal," Naomi said at last.

"That's never stopped me," Anna told her.

Naomi laughed, then her expression grew serious. "I saw Gideon leaving the shop with his daughter when I came back from running errands."

Anna set the cookie jar back on the counter. "He was taking the knitting class with Sarah Rose."

"You've seen a lot of him lately."

"No, I haven't. He's come to the shop to buy the kits and then for a lesson."

"And you went to his house after church one day to help him get the dye off his hands."

Anna regarded her. "Keeping track?"

Naomi colored, but she kept her gaze level. "He's the first man you've even looked at since Samuel died."

Rising, Anna put her mug in the kitchen sink, and Naomi did the same. "It hasn't been personal. It's been business. Shop business."

"I see."

Laughing, Anna gave her cousin an impulsive hug. "No, you don't. You're in love so you think everyone else should be."

"They should," Naomi said staunchly.

"I remember how it felt," she said. "I know how it is to feel like everything's wonderful and you want it to be that way for everyone else."

She stopped, not wanting to sound bitter or unhappy.

Her gaze went to the window. The day was gray and chilly. If she wasn't careful, it would be too easy to let it put her in a melancholy mood. She tried to watch those when she was at work and out in the community. People tended to try to cheer you up or tell you how it was God's will. Her grief—her coping . . . well, it was her business.

She knew her moods still went up and down like one of those amusement park roller coasters the *Englisch* were fond of. Best to keep it all inside and deal with it in the privacy of her home.

"Who knows what God has planned?" she said, keeping her voice level.

"Maybe He's sending Gideon to you."

Anna saw the hope in Naomi's expression. She loved her cousin for her eagerness to believe that Anna might have a second chance at love, but hope was a dangerous thing. Gideon had been in love with Mary as deeply as she had been with Samuel. She doubted he was any more ready to become interested in her than she was with him.

And he had a troubled little girl to deal with, one who had so recently acted a bit . . . jealous of her father for being friends with her.

Unless God showed her very clearly that He was sending Gideon to her for more than friendship, Anna felt it was just friendship that Gideon or his daughter were intended to have with her.

Naomi just had romance on her mind. Brides wanted it for everyone.

Especially her cousin.

❧

Lunch was over and Anna seldom lingered at the table in the back room, but something compelled her to sit there, thinking.

"Don't worry about cleaning up," she told her cousins. "I'll take care of it."

"What is it?" Mary Katherine wanted to know. "You seem distracted."

Frowning, Anna shook her head. "Is it my imagination, or is there something different about Grandmother today?"

"I didn't notice anything," Naomi said. "What's different? She's not looking sick or losing weight, is she?"

"She seems a little distracted. Happier. Lighter. I just heard her humming."

Naomi laughed. "That's not a bad thing."

Anna stood and began gathering the dishes. "I didn't say it was. What do you suppose is making her look that way?"

"I'm the one who got accused of wanting everyone to be in love," Naomi told Mary Katherine.

"Comes from being in love," Mary Katherine told her. "I was like that before my wedding, too."

She put the carton of potato salad back in the refrigerator. "And that's why I'm looking that way," she said quickly. "Not because I'm expecting."

"We didn't ask."

"Yet today. Do you know how often the two of you've done it lately?"

Anna cast a guilty glance at Naomi, but she was staring at the ceiling.

"You two!" Mary Katherine shook her head and laughed. "I'm going back to work."

They made quick work of cleaning up, and then Anna pulled out the order information and sat down to complete the paperwork.

"Need any help?" Leah asked when she walked into the room a short time later.

"No, I'm nearly done." She glanced over when Leah poured herself a cup of coffee. "You don't usually drink coffee in the afternoon. You say it keeps you awake."

"I need it to stay awake this afternoon," she said. "I was up later than usual."

"Oh?"

"Mmmhmm," she said noncommittally and walked out of the room, humming a hymn under her breath.

Maybe we've had a better month than usual with shop business, Anna thought. *That might explain things.*

"Anna! Guess who's here?"

She looked up and saw Naomi fairly dancing in the doorway. "Who?"

"Nick!"

"Okay," she said slowly. She liked Nick but didn't think a surprise visit was something to be so excited about. Maybe for Naomi, but not her.

"He has something to show us."

She pulled Anna's jacket off the nearby peg, thrust it at her, then grabbed one of her hands to draw her along toward the front of the shop. "Come on, Grandmother said we can go with him."

"Where are we going?" Anna asked.

"It's not *where*. It's *how*."

Leah gave them an indulgent smile, but Mary Katherine was nowhere to be seen. The minute they stepped out of the shop, however, Anna saw her cousin climbing into a buggy parked at the curb.

Nick had always dressed in a businesslike but unobtrusive way—simple dark slacks, a white dress shirt, and a black tie—for his work as a driver serving the Amish community and tourists.

Today, he wore a blue shirt and dark pants like the Amish men as well as a black wide-brimmed felt hat and a jacket.

Anna hung back and waited while Mary Katherine got in, watching Naomi look with pure adoration at Nick until she could climb inside.

This was more than seeing two people in love and so happy that their marriage was drawing near. Nick had been born *Englisch*, and this was the culmination of his work to become Naomi's husband: classes in becoming a member of the church, with all the requisite learning of the *Ordnung* and the many rules that guided the community. He'd stepped up his study of German and Pennsylvania *Deitsch* that he'd picked up in his work with the Amish.

And most of all, he'd shown such eagerness to be the *mann* Naomi—and those close to her—had come to feel God had sent to her.

"I wanted to take you ladies out for one of my first official tours," he said, grinning as he gestured grandly toward the buggy.

All Anna's warm and fuzzy feelings as she'd watched him with Naomi plummeted. It was one thing to be supportive of Nick's switch from driving a car to driving a buggy. While she knew there was more horsepower under the metal hood of Nick's SUV, a horse was a challenge for anyone who didn't have experience.

He must have sensed her ambivalence because his grin faded, and he took a step toward her. "I know you must be feeling a little anxious about riding with a beginner like me," he said seriously. "But I've been working with Abe Harshberger for weeks now. I wouldn't take a chance with the woman I love and the family she loves."

She felt the affection that had grown for him the longer she knew him—especially as she saw how he adored Naomi as much as she did him—and nodded. "I know. And I know that you realize that a horse isn't a predictable machine as well."

He glanced toward the cars that occasionally passed them. "Especially with tourists around here, right?"

"I always knew you were a smart man," she told him and climbed into the backseat.

Nick helped Naomi into the front seat and walked around to climb into his own seat. He took the reins and called to Ike with authority, careful to check for traffic and guide the rig out onto the road.

He didn't seem quite as comfortable as other men—Amish men she knew—driving the buggy, but then again, he hadn't been doing this since he was a *kind*.

As they rode along, he talked easily about the area like Abe did. When Naomi turned to her, lifting her eyebrows, Anna nodded. When Nick gave up driving a car, he'd be giving up his livelihood. It was extremely important that the business of buggy tours do well.

"I'm picking up the brochures we designed this afternoon," he told Naomi. "Right after I drop you ladies off at the shop."

Anna had ridden in a buggy behind Ike before. She watched with admiration as Nick dealt with the horse's little behavior quirks. Abe had told her his horse let little bother him—a wonderful trait for a horse that traveled so much around traffic—but let a paper take-out food bag or something similar blow across the road toward him and he'd become skittish as if someone had planted land mines in his path.

Anna relaxed and let herself enjoy the clip-clop of the horse's hooves and the brisk air as they turned back to town. She knew she should be thinking about getting back, but this ride was an unaccustomed pleasure in the middle of the afternoon.

She was thinking about how Gideon and his daughter would be stopping by that afternoon for a knitting lesson when she became aware that a car was following too closely behind the buggy.

Nick had noticed it, too, and had commanded Ike to speed up a little and began looking to the right for a place to pull over to let the driver pass.

That wasn't good enough for the driver, though. He drew even closer and, when Anna glanced behind, made an angry gesture at them.

"It's not safe to pull over here," Nick muttered. "The shoulder of the road isn't wide enough." He stuck his hand out his window and gestured for the driver to pass him.

The driver zoomed past, and Anna watched the way that Nick kept calm, even waved at the driver as he passed with an annoyed glance.

The buggy swayed a little as the backwash of air pushed out by the car hit it.

Nick sighed. "It's going to take some getting used to."

Naomi reached over to pat his hands on the reins. "You're doing so well. Are you still certain this is what you want?"

He turned to look at her. "Please don't ask me that again." His tone was quiet but firm.

She bit her bottom lip and nodded. Nick transferred the reins to his left hand and lifted Naomi's and brought it to his lips to kiss it. Anna looked away quickly, feeling his gesture too intimate for her to witness, and found Mary Katherine watching her.

Anna started to roll her eyes and make a joke the way she'd done when she saw Mary Katherine and Jacob do something romantic.

Then she stopped. *Let them be*, she told herself. *They're all so happy. Are you sure you're not teasing them because you envy them for being in love right now when you aren't?*

It was a sobering thought. She'd have to think about it later. For now, the way the day was growing darker concerned her. She peered out her window.

"Looks like it's going to rain soon, Nick. Maybe we should head back?"

⸎

Jamie stood cutting fabric for a customer when they returned to the shop.

Anna smiled with pleasure when she saw that the customer was Jenny Bontrager.

"Starting a quilt?" she asked after she hugged her friend.

Jenny laughed. "Not me. You know quilting isn't among my skills."

"You're not required to be an award-winning quilter to just sew and enjoy," Anna said gently. "Stop being so hard on yourself."

"This is for Hannah," Jenny told her. "She's watching my *kinner* for me so I can run some errands. I said I'd pick up fabric for her."

"If you have time, maybe you'd like to stay for a knitting class," Anna said casually as she picked up a bolt of fabric and returned it to its display table.

"Yeah, that might be fun," said Jamie, folding a fat quarter of fabric and placing it atop the stack of others she'd just cut. "You just never know who might show up."

Anna reached over and pulled at one of Jamie's long pigtails. It was tied with lavender ribbon today.

"I liked it when you dyed your hair this color."

Jamie grinned. "Am I getting too tame?" She glanced down at her outfit of scarlet shirt and short black skirt worn with black boots. Mismatched polka-dot knee-high socks showed above her black boots.

She turned to Jenny. "But Anna's changing the subject. She doesn't want to talk about who's coming to the class."

Jenny straightened. "Who?"

"She just wants to gossip," Anna told Jenny.

"It's not gossip. It's keeping up with community news."

"Matthew calls it the Amish grapevine. Now you've got my curiosity up. You know I used to be a reporter."

Anna gathered up the remaining bolts of fabric and walked off to put them on their tables. She didn't have to turn to know that Jenny followed. Her friend might look unassuming in her gray Plain dress that matched her eyes and her serious manner, but Anna knew that she was as stubborn and determined as a person could be. If she hadn't been, she'd never have survived the bomb blast in a war zone overseas or the grueling surgeries and physical therapy that had left her with only a mild limp.

It wasn't easy to be accepted as a convert to the Amish faith, either, but years after she married the boy-next-to-grandmother's house, Anna didn't think most people even thought of her life before she'd returned to stay here forever.

The shop door opened, and Gideon walked in with Sarah Rose.

Who didn't look particularly happy.

Jenny glanced at Anna and raised her eyebrows. Anna gave her a shrug and went to greet her students.

Everyone seemed to stream in the door at the same time.

"Whoa," said Jamie. "Did the school bus just let out?"

Maybe it was Anna's imagination, but the scowl on Sarah Rose's face grew darker. She threw herself in a chair and crossed her arms over her chest.

Anna glanced at Gideon, who'd taken the chair next to his daughter. He shook his head in a subtle message that it was best not to ask any questions right now.

"Sarah Rose, would you like some hot chocolate?"

She stuck her bottom lip out and then must have thought better of it. Straightening, she looked at him hopefully. "Can I have some?"

"May I?" he corrected.

She frowned but then amended her question, smiling when he nodded.

"*Schur.* Remember to thank Anna."

"Hot chocolate sounds good," Jenny said. "Could I have some?"

"Oh, sorry, I should have asked you if you'd like something warm to drink on a rainy day like today." Anna gestured at the back room. "You can come with me if you want or stay here by the fire."

They both followed her and took seats at the table.

"So, Sarah Rose, how is *schul*?"

Anna held up the packet of hot chocolate mix to Jenny. "This or coffee?"

"You have the kind with marshmallows!" Jenny cried. "That goes so fast at our house I hardly ever get it."

"A cup of hot chocolate then." The teakettle had just been used to boil water so it only took a few minutes to get the water boiling again and make the two cups of chocolate.

Anna set the cups before Jenny and Sarah Rose, then took a seat at the table.

"So, how's *schul*?"

Sarah Rose glared into her cup. "Fine." She looked up. "Why do people always ask that?"

"Because it's a kid's job." Jenny blew on her chocolate and then carefully took a sip. "People ask me the same kind of question, only about what I do for my job."

"What do you do?"

"I'm a writer."

Sarah Rose didn't look impressed. "I hate writing. Teacher makes us write things all the time, and it's hard."

Jenny nodded. "Sometimes it's not easy even for a person who writes for a job."

"Then why do you do it?"

"Because I like it when something's a challenge."

"*Schul* is hard."

"Tell me what your hardest subject is."

"I'm going to go out and get the class started," Anna said, rising. "Sarah Rose, take your time with the hot chocolate, and I'll help you when you're ready."

She left them talking and as she reached the doorway, she glanced back and smiled when she saw how easily Jenny chatted with the child. Jenny had four *kinner* now—three widower Matthew had shared with her when they married, and a little boy she hadn't expected to become pregnant with after her internal injuries from the bombing.

Gideon gave her a questioning look when she walked up to the knitting class. Anna told him that Sarah Rose was finishing her hot chocolate with Jenny, and he nodded. She noted that he seemed more comfortable holding the knitting needles in his big hands.

"I've been practicing," he said in a low voice as she looked at the muffler he was knitting.

Once again several of the ladies watched their interaction with interest. Anna saw them exchanging looks. They'd obviously decided a romance might be brewing. They lived locally, so she would have thought they'd be more aware that such things weren't conducted out in public, but she knew they meant no harm.

Sarah Rose came out a few minutes later, her canvas tote bag filled with knitting stuff on her thin little shoulder. She climbed up into a rocking chair, got out her materials, and began knitting.

"Why, Sarah Rose, you look like you've been doing this forever," Thelma remarked. "Pretty soon you'll be able to help Anna teach."

Demut—humility—was practiced in the Amish community, but Sarah Rose reacted as any *kind* would: she glowed. "*Daedi* and I have been practicing," she said, echoing his words.

Jenny came out and sat in a chair in the circle of students. She watched for a few minutes. When Anna walked past her a few minutes later to check the progress of her knitting, she looked up. "This looks relaxing," she said. "Maybe I should try it. If I can do something simple to start out with."

Gideon looked up and grinned. "Can't get any simpler than this," he said, holding up the long muffler he was knitting. "I recommend it."

"I'll try it," Jenny said. "As long as I don't have to go around with Smurf blue hands."

Gideon grimaced. "How long will it take me to live that down?"

"Let's get you some supplies," Anna said.

"Said the spider to the fly," Jenny murmured. "How much is this going to cost me?"

"I'll give you the class discount," Anna said with a smile.

"So who did you fall for first?"

"Excuse me?"

"Who'd you fall for first: the daughter or the father?" Jenny asked as they stood in front of the display of yarn.

"I don't know what you're talking about. Sarah Rose and her father are just taking knitting lessons to do something together."

"Uh-huh," Jenny said, nodding. She picked up a skein of yarn. "This would look good made into a muffler for Matthew, don't you think?"

Anna nodded. "And you could get it done by Christmas."

"Perfect."

Anna chose a pair of knitting needles for her, and they walked to the cash register.

"I think I'll join you next week for my first lesson," Jenny told her as she pulled money from her purse. "I still have another errand to run. But I'll ask Hannah if she can babysit for me this time next week."

Anna handed her the bag with her supplies and her change. "That would be wonderful. I'll enjoy having you in the class."

"Looks like fun." Jenny started to walk toward the door, then turned back. "And just for the record, I fell for the daughter first. Sarah Rose is a challenge, not like Matthew's sweet little Annie was when I met her. But she needs you just as much, maybe more."

She smiled. "And I suspect you're like me, and you don't mind a challenge."

The bell jangled over the door as she left the shop, making Anna stare after her.

7

$\mathcal{H}$e saw her before she saw him.

She walked separate from the other *kinner*, and his heart ached when he saw the way her shoulders slumped and her feet dragged. Something was wrong with his little girl lately, and he just didn't know what to do about it.

Had he been so busy with the farm and getting through the past year and a half that he hadn't paid enough attention to her? Mary had been ill for months before she died, and even though Sarah Rose had been surrounded and cared for by a large and loving family, it hadn't been her mother and father. In a way, with all the time her mother spent at the hospital with treatment, Sarah Rose had begun losing her before she was actually gone.

It had rained earlier, and the minute Sarah Rose saw the puddle on the side of the road he saw her expression brighten and her shoulders straighten. She glanced at the others, but they were already walking on and turning down their drive.

She bit her lip and stared at it, clearly torn.

Gideon felt the corners of his mouth twitch. He found himself moving forward, calling her name, and tried not to feel hurt that her expression wavered—she obviously felt disappointed that he'd shown up when she wanted to jump in the puddle.

So he beat her to it.

He jumped in and splashed and laughed when she squealed as the muddy water sprayed over her shoes.

"*Daedi*! What are you doing?" she cried, staring at him as if he'd grown two heads.

"Jumping in a puddle. What does it look like?"

"*Daedis* don't do that!"

"Well, maybe they should," he said, giving it one more big jump and splash. "You should do it."

She tilted her head and studied him. "Really?"

"Really," he said.

He took her books from her and stood back. "Go for it. Clothes can be washed."

Sarah Rose didn't wait for a further invitation. She jumped; she splashed; she stomped around in circles until nearly all the water was gone.

The sound of a buggy approached. Gideon turned and saw Anna in the front seat. He got a feeling in his chest not unlike what Sarah Rose must have felt when she stomped in the puddle. Well, okay, it had been fun for him, too.

She stopped and looked at his muddy legs. "Having fun?"

"*Ya*. Aren't we, Sarah Rose?"

She nodded vigorously. "He did it first," his daughter informed her with wonder in her voice.

Gideon loved seeing the sparkle in her eyes. He held out his hand to Anna. "Want to join us? There's still some water in the puddle."

A laugh slipped out. "No," she said, shaking her head. "I have on my favorite shoes. Maybe next time."

Gideon elbowed his daughter. "Says she wants a rain check."

"What's a rain check?"

"She can have another chance later."

"Oh." Sarah Rose considered that. "Can I?"

"May I?"

"*Schur* you can," she said grandly, as if she were a queen granting a royal favor.

Anna laughed. "I think he meant you should say, 'May I?'"

"Oh. *May I?*" she said with great emphasis.

"We'll see. Depends on if we get the mud out of those sneakers."

"I'll go take them off right now and put them in a bucket of water."

"Good idea." He handed her the books he'd been holding. "Put yourself in a big tub of water and see if you can get the mud off you, too. Then—"

"I know. I know. Chores."

"Chores. I'll be inside in a minute."

He debated asking Anna if she wanted a cup of coffee. It had been years since he'd dated. How did he get restarted?

"Gonna take a big tub of water to get you clean," Sarah Rose said, smirking.

She started to turn, then apparently thought better of it. "Anna, can you stay for supper?"

"Sarah Rose, Anna might have plans." But he hoped not. He didn't have any idea what he'd make if she said yes, but he'd like the chance to try.

Anna glanced at Gideon, then back at her. "I have to take Annie B. some yarn."

"Couldn't you to do that and come back?"

He decided on the spot that his daughter could jump in puddles every day since she'd come up with such a great question.

"Couldn't you?" he asked, and their eyes met. He saw Anna's widen, and she shifted the reins in her hands in what seemed like a nervous gesture.

"I—suppose so. I'll go do that now and be back in about a half hour."

"You really think you'll get away from her that quickly?"

She laughed again and shook her head. "Probably not. I was being optimistic."

"See you when you get here. It'll give me time to get the mud off and start something for supper."

"See you soon."

She got the buggy moving. Once she was a few yards away, she glanced back over her shoulder and waved at him. He waved back.

The afternoon that had seemed so gray and bleak as he watched his little girl walking home had suddenly become very bright indeed.

❧

A delicious aroma hit her the moment she stepped onto the porch.

Gideon answered the door and ushered her in, inviting her to sit at the kitchen table while he finished supper.

"You're here," said Sarah Rose as she walked into the room. "I thought you'd never get here."

Anna smiled at how it came out part complaint, part delight. How nice it felt to be looked forward to. She bent to hug her. "I'm sorry. I was talking to Annie B."

"You don't need to apologize," Gideon said, giving his daughter a stern look. "You were on your way to see her when we invited you to supper. Sarah Rose, you need to wash your hands and set the table."

"But they're clean," she protested. "I just took a bath."

"And then got dressed and put your shoes on and tied them. So wash your hands, please."

"How can I help?"

"Everything's ready," Gideon told her. "I should have asked if you like macaroni and cheese. We have it often here since it's Sarah Rose's favorite. And it's easy for me to make."

"It's Jacob's recipe," Sarah Rose told her as she placed a plate on the table before Anna. "You know, Jacob who's married to Mary Katherine, your cousin."

Gideon drew on a pair of oven mitts, opened the oven, and pulled out a casserole. "He's given me a couple of recipes," Gideon told her.

Anna remembered how Jacob had told her he'd been forced to learn how to cook when he offended one of his sisters by saying there wasn't anything to cooking. His supply of home-delivered meals from his sisters and mother had immediately dried up.

She wondered if Gideon had experienced the same experience learning to cook that Jacob had: he'd told them a funny story about how the first time cooking supper for himself he'd managed to cut a finger chopping vegetables, burn his hand, and set fire to a kitchen towel set too close to the gas stove. Exhausted from a long day of farming chores, he'd fallen asleep at the kitchen table and only awakened when the macaroni and cheese casserole had started burning.

Now Jacob's practice had paid off, and Mary Katherine enjoyed occasional help in the kitchen. She helped him with the farm when she could, just as many Amish wives did.

Had Gideon helped Mary in the kitchen? If not, he'd had to learn when he lost his wife. He'd learned how to take care of his little girl as well.

She, on the other hand, hadn't had to take on another role like Gideon. She'd started working full-time instead of part-time to support herself, but it hadn't been a hardship. Working in the shop would be a dream for anyone but especially someone who loved crafts as much as she. But she hadn't taken on any of the roles of the other partner in the marriage the way he had. She didn't do any carpentry or any of the maintenance to speak of. Her attempt to fix a pipe had shown her how woeful her skills were in taking care of her home. And Eli leased part of the land and farmed it.

She hadn't had to raise a child by herself.

Sarah Rose added paper napkins to each plate and then sat down. Anna spread hers on her lap and frowned when her skinned knuckles stung a little. She pulled one of her hands from her lap and stared at the abused skin.

"How'd you hurt your hand?" Sarah Rose asked her.

"I was trying to fix a leaky pipe. But I'm no plumber."

Gideon set a bowl of green beans on the table and leaned over to study her hand. "Did you clean it good?"

"The pipe?"

"Your hand," he said patiently.

She smiled. "I knew what you meant. Yes. Put some antibiotic cream on it, too. I'm not a plumber, but I know about first aid."

"I'll come over and take a look at it tomorrow," he told her as he took a seat. "The pipe, not the hand."

"No need. I'm sure I can ask one of my brothers to do it."

"You tried to fix it instead of calling them. Why?"

She shrugged. "Well, they're so busy. I hate to bother them."

They said a silent prayer over their meal and then began filling their plates. Gideon had duplicated Jacob's recipe exactly—it was cheesy and warming and perfect for a simple supper.

"It's good, isn't it?" Sarah Jane asked around a mouthful. When he saw her father frown, she shut her mouth and chewed. "*Daedi* cooks good."

"I have a few things I cook well but not many," he said with a shrug. "I'm working at getting better. Jacob and I have swapped recipes. But that's not for public knowledge."

Anna tried to keep a straight face. "Are you afraid the other men in the community will think you're less manly?"

"It's not funny. You know some of them think men and women have certain roles."

"Do you think that's really true these days? If it ever was? We've always worked together as partners in the community. And when we're—" she stopped, glanced at Sarah Rose who was finishing up the last of her supper, and she hesitated.

"Sarah Rose, do you want more macaroni and cheese, or are you ready for dessert?"

"Dessert!"

Gideon grinned. "Well, what a surprise."

"Can I pick?"

"Maybe we should let our guest decide."

Sarah Rose considered that, and although Anna could tell she wanted to choose, she nodded. The *kind* might be having some problems, but her good manners prevailed.

"I'd rather you choose," Anna said. "I don't know what you have."

"Two kinds of ice cream and some chocolate chip cookies *Daedi* and I made last night." She thought about that for a moment. "We could make ice-cream sandwiches!"

"I would never have thought of that," Anna told her. "I'd like one."

"Vanilla or chocolate chip ice cream?"

"Can't have enough chocolate chips. I'll have the chocolate chip ice cream."

Sarah Rose looked to her father and got the same order. She went off happily to make the requested desserts.

"Now, what did you start to say?" Gideon asked, turning back to her.

Anna bit her lip. "When we're widowed, things often change. You had to start taking care of Sarah Rose, and that involved doing things you hadn't before—things that a *mamm* usually does. And you've done them well. Some men would have just gotten remarried quickly so they didn't have to do things that weren't easy."

His eyes searched hers. "Well, *danki*. That's very nice of you to say."

"I'm not trying to be nice," she said, straightening. "I'm not that nice."

"What?"

Her face flamed. Why had she blurted that out? She sounded like an insecure teen. But she was feeling a little off-kilter lately, realizing that she was still trapped in a self-prison of grief that left her with conflicting emotions.

And this attraction she felt for Gideon. She'd never been interested in anyone but Samuel. He'd been her friend at school and then the boy she went with to singings and other church functions and then the one she'd exchanged that first tentative kiss with . . . and then her husband. It felt strange . . . and a little unnerving to be around a man who seemed interested in her. She didn't know how to act.

"What about you?"

"What do you mean?"

"What have you learned to do since Samuel died?"

Her gaze fell to her plate. "Well, I haven't had to raise a *kind* on my own. And I certainly haven't learned how to do home maintenance very well."

"But you've learned how to support yourself. And you're a great teacher. Sarah Rose and I have learned how to knit, and your class is so much fun she looks forward to it."

"That's nice to hear."

He frowned. "She doesn't seem to like school very much."

"Jenny talked to her at the shop, and that's what she said. Mary Katherine didn't like school very much. She was so creative and just wanted to daydream and sketch designs for her weaving once she got interested in it. Everyone's not the same. Maybe Sarah Rose just hasn't discovered what she'd like to do yet and doesn't think school will help her with it."

"I never thought about it that way." He looked at the kitchen window, but Anna felt he was looking inward. Then he shook his head and got up to pour them more coffee.

Sarah Rose walked in with a plate of cookie sandwiches with enormous scoops of ice cream in the middle. Anna didn't know how she was going to get one in her mouth, but there was no way she was going to say that. The child was wearing an enormous grin.

"Look what I made!"

"I can't wait to try one."

She was offered the first choice as the guest and chose the smallest, but still, the cookies were big, there were two of them, and they were stuffed with an enormous gob of chocolate chip ice cream. By the time she finished eating it on top of the macaroni and cheese supper, she was stuffed.

"I'm just going to roll home," she said with a satisfied sigh. "I won't even need the buggy." Anna glanced at the window. "And speaking of getting home, I hate to eat and run, but I need to get home soon."

She stood and began picking up the empty plates.

"Guests shouldn't—"

"Don't be silly," she told him. "You cooked, and Sarah Rose set the table and made dessert. I should do the dishes."

"She's right, *Daedi*," Sarah Rose said, clearly liking Anna's statement.

"We don't take advantage of friends," he chided. "Now, how about you wash and I'll dry and put away, and then we'll follow Anna home to make sure she gets there safely."

"Oh, you don't have to—"

"We do," he said firmly. "It's getting dark."

She wanted to argue with him, but Sarah Rose watched them avidly and she sensed it wasn't a good thing to do in front of her.

It felt good to sit and relax in the warm, cozy kitchen and rest after a busy day on her feet. But as she watched this handsome man as he moved around so comfortably in a room many Amish men shied away from working in, she couldn't help envying his easy relationship with his daughter.

They'd talked about how their lives, their roles, had changed after the deaths of their spouses. She wondered if it had been easier for him or harder that he'd had Sarah Rose to care for after Mary died. In a way, it meant that he'd had to push himself to look out for someone else rather than dwell in grief the way she'd done for so long. Then again, he had someone to live for, someone who obviously loved him.

It was wrong to envy, but she felt that emotion. She'd waited and hoped for some sign that Samuel would leave her a part of himself after he died, but God hadn't had that in His plan for her.

She wondered what He did have planned for her. Widows and widowers often remarried without a long wait here. Some reasoned that God didn't want you to do without love and companionship . . . He wanted you to add to your family if you were still in your childbearing years. Samuel had even talked to Anna just before he died about hoping God would send another *mann* to love and care for her and protect her after he was gone.

"Anna, can I get you anything? More coffee?"

"Maybe you want another ice-cream sandwich?" Sarah Rose asked with a note of hopefulness in her voice.

"Sounds like someone else does."

She just grinned.

Anna couldn't help smiling. Sarah Rose was a sweet girl, but she certainly had a gift for winding people around her little finger.

"I couldn't eat another thing," she said. "Not even a tiny little chocolate chip. Maybe some other time."

"*Daedi*, she could come back for supper, can't she?"

Gideon dried a dish and put it in the cupboard, then closed the door and hung the dish towel up to dry. His eyes met hers. "Anna can come back for supper any time she wants."

Something passed between them, something warm and wonderful and suddenly a little bit frightening. She hadn't felt like this with anyone but Samuel. But what he asked—the step he wanted her to take—she wasn't ready for that yet.

"I—thank you very much," she said quickly. "I'll have to let you know."

⁓❧

She'd let him know?

Gideon reached for his jacket and handed Sarah Rose hers. "I'll go hitch up the buggy. You ladies get your jackets on and join me when you're ready."

Sarah Rose giggled. "*Daedi* called me a lady."

"He called me one, too," Anna told her with a grin.

Gideon walked out to the barn and set about hitching up the buggies, thinking about what she'd said. He didn't know what to think of her reaction, not having much experience with women. After all, he and Mary had fallen in love almost before they had left school, and they'd married when they were barely twenty. Now he was twenty-eight and looking at starting all over, and he didn't know how to do that.

Not that there was a shortage of women. They approached him and struck up conversations at church services and Sarah Rose's school activities and social events and shops. They brought food. He and Jacob had discussed how often unmarried young women and sometimes widows showed up with casseroles and cakes and pies and desserts and bread still warm from the oven.

Well, that had stopped some time ago at Jacob's house. When he was a bachelor, his mother and sisters had worked out a schedule to keep him fed so that the single young women would stop coming. And then, Jacob had thoughtlessly let it slip to one of his sisters that really, cooking couldn't be that hard. She'd handed him a saltshaker to season the foot he'd put into his mouth and told him he better learn because she and the women of the family weren't feeding him anymore.

After they talked about their mutual experience with ladies bearing food, Jacob gave Gideon a couple of recipes. The macaroni and cheese tonight was one of them. He'd found Mary's recipe box and worked on making some of his favorites from it as well.

Sarah Rose ran down the back stairs, followed by Anna. As usual, she hadn't buttoned her jacket, and one side of her collar stood up and the other was tucked inside the jacket.

"Can I ride with Anna on the way to her house?"

"Long as you don't ask to ride back with her."

"What?" she stared at him, then she laughed. "Oh, you were being silly."

He started to help her into the passenger side of the buggy, but she'd already climbed into it with the agility of a monkey.

Once again, he wondered if Mary would want him to work more on making sure Sarah Rose wasn't a tomboy.

He followed Anna's buggy and wondered if his daughter was talking Anna's leg off.

The trip to Anna's didn't take that long, and soon they were saying good-bye to Anna and traveling back to their own house. Sarah Rose began to wind down by the time they pulled into the drive.

He sent her inside while he put the buggy and horse in the barn. After he gave the barn one last look, he picked up the lantern and headed out the door.

Outside, the night was crisp and cool. The wind blew a rag of a cloud away and stars began winking on.

When he stepped into the kitchen, he saw Sarah Rose standing before the freezer, staring longingly at the little plastic baggies of leftover ice-cream sandwiches she'd made for dessert after tonight's supper.

She turned when she heard him enter. "*Daedi* —"

"One," he said. "And you eat it quickly so you can study your spelling words before you go to bed."

"I still get a bedtime story," she said, sounding like she expected an argument.

"Of course. But a short one. It's almost bedtime."

He watched her compare several of the sandwiches before choosing one she evidently decided was the biggest. She reminded him of Mary so much at that moment with her determination to get what she wanted—he'd teased her once that she'd done that with him and she'd laughed and agreed.

She had a quiet way of getting her way, but she always got it. Sarah Rose was smart like her mother had been about that.

There wasn't much of himself he could find in his daughter unless you considered that she was a tomboy and wanted to do things most boys enjoyed.

He poured a cup of coffee and watched her unwrap the sandwich, then bite into it.

That memory of teasing Mary that she'd gone after him and not stopped until she'd gotten what she wanted. She'd laughed and agreed.

Maybe I need to do that with Anna, he thought. Maybe he needed to convince her that they should see if they were the pair God meant them to be. So what if he'd been pursued the first time. This was a different woman. That she was different than Mary was a good thing. It wouldn't be fair to her to be thought of as a copy of Mary.

Sarah Rose had finished the treat and was looking longingly at the freezer. Did she have a hollow leg? Then he chuckled to himself. *Maybe there is something of me in my daughter after all*, he thought, and hustled her upstairs before she could persuade him to give her another treat.

8

Naomi made a beautiful bride, dressed in sky blue as she stood beside Nick at their wedding.

Anna sat watching them exchange their vows, and she wondered if anyone else thought of their own as they watched.

She felt a slight movement and turned to look at her grandmother in the next row of seats. Leah glanced at her as she did and smiled. When she turned to her left, she found Mary Katherine blinking back tears. Her cousin slipped her hand into Anna's and squeezed it. Nothing was said, but the gesture spoke volumes.

Her wedding had been the happiest day of her life. She'd lain awake for hours thinking about how she and Samuel would never be separated again. While she might have been younger than her parents wanted her to be when she married, they had been as convinced as she that Samuel was indeed the man God had set aside just for her. Kind, steady, generous. Thoughtful. He'd been the boy she'd had her first crush on and grown into the kind of man everyone loved.

Other girls had wanted him, but Samuel had eyes only for her. She'd worn a blue dress the color of the sky at twilight, Samuel's favorite color on her.

Samuel had drawn her outside that day as soon as he could and whispered words of love, told her she'd never looked lovelier, and made her blush when he said he couldn't wait to get her alone.

He'd had to wait a long time, though. An Amish wedding day began before the sun came up with the same daily chores as any other day, followed by a quick, simple breakfast often no more than a quickly grabbed cup of coffee and a piece of bread or whatever was at hand. Guests began arriving at the house soon after, and the wedding—three hours just like a regular every-other-week church service—began at 8:30 a.m.

No wonder Samuel had been so ready to eat. Of course, all the aromas of food that had been prepared in the house and been kept warm waiting for the ceremony to end hadn't helped. Roast chicken with filling was one of his favorites although there were so many weddings in the fall after harvest everyone would be heartily sick of the dish by Christmas. Her mother might have suggested that Anna and Samuel wait another year before they married, but she'd been the one to quietly plant the celery that was a staple at Lancaster County weddings.

She'd grown celery this season, too, in between some corn, so that it couldn't be seen and start rumors there was an engagement. Naomi's mother still had to be careful of overdoing after her heart attack.

When those seated around her stood and voices lifted in song, Anna realized that she'd been daydreaming a bit. She stood and sang along, loving the sound of Mary Katherine's clear soprano. Weaving wasn't the only thing her cousin did well. That baby she'd be having would love being soothed by her lullabies.

Naomi and Nick sat while a visiting bishop stood to tell the story they had all heard many times. Anna knew the story well and had enjoyed hearing it before. Nearly ninety and frail, he had a stern look about him until he looked out at the congregation.

It was a story she'd heard before, but today, at the spiritual joining of two of her favorite people, the telling seemed new and fresh and caught her attention.

"Many of you may know by now that Linda is my second wife," he said, and almost as one being, the congregants nodded.

"My first wife was young and died giving birth prematurely," he said solemnly. "And my son died a day later. I thought that my life was over. But God showed me that it wasn't, that I had to have faith in His will, and two years later, He sent the woman He created and set aside for me, my Linda. This month we celebrate fifty years together."

Was God sending her the message that He had a plan for her? That He had set aside another *mann* for her so that she would walk through the rest of her life knowing a beloved partner's love and spiritual support?

Several people around her shifted—three hours on a hard wooden bench weren't easy, after all. But Anna became aware of something else that caught her attention. The hair prickled on the back of her neck . . . she thought she saw movement in the periphery of her vision. A slight turn of her head and she was staring into Gideon's eyes.

She looked away quickly, uncomfortable with him possibly guessing her reaction to the bishop's story. It was, after all, her business, and she also didn't know how she felt about seeing more of him. She just didn't know how she felt about taking that step with him.

There was a quiet rustling at the back of the room as Sadie carried her fussy baby into the bedroom to feed it. Anna watched Mary Katherine's gaze follow her, watched as her cousin's lips curved into a smile. Her gaze moved on, and as it did, Anna followed it, curious but not surprised when it landed on Jacob.

When he smiled at her as if nothing existed but her, Anna's heart turned over. They were going to have a *boppli*; she was sure of it. When Mary Katherine glanced back, Anna looked away, feeling guilty as if she'd invaded their privacy. But it was so hard not to jump for joy.

She wondered why they hadn't told the family yet and, in the next moment, decided it must have been because they'd just found out—or because they didn't want to take any attention from Naomi and her wedding. Anna suspected it was the second; it was just like Mary Katherine to think of others.

Her grandmother sat in the next row, and Anna tilted her head, studying her. Something was different. Her grandmother gazed in the direction of Naomi and Nick, but it seemed that her attention turned inward.

Was she remembering her own wedding day? She'd shown Anna her own wedding dress—a midnight blue, darker than Anna's. Blue was a favorite color for brides in the community, and when she held it up before her, Anna had seen how the color had favored her grandmother's fair skin. Actually, it wasn't the color so much as the way her skin warmed and her eyes grew gentle and far away as she talked about the day she'd married her husband.

She heard sniffling and saw Jenny Bontrager wiping her nose with a tissue. When she realized Anna watched her, she shrugged and mouthed, "Weddings!"

People always said that the wedding couple never looked happier, but it was true of Naomi and Nick. *Their journey to walking together to stand before the congregation and take their vows hadn't been easy*, Anna thought. Naomi had fallen in love with a man who said he loved her but hurt her with his words and his hands. She had believed she had to stay with him—if

God had put them together, then she needed to prove her love and keep trying to stay together.

Her cousins, her grandmother and even Nick had tried to convince her otherwise. In the end, Naomi finally realized that love wasn't supposed to come with battered emotions and her love being used against her to manipulate her to John's will.

Nick had started off being their driver and became their friend, then a close personal friend. And then slowly, showing he cared for her and not for his own selfish reasons, he'd become more . . . he'd become the man who loved her and wanted to protect her.

Naomi and Nick were pronounced man and wife and turned to walk back down the aisle. And the journey continued.

∽⌾

Tables groaned under the weight of all the food.

Later in the month, some might complain that they were tired of roast chicken and filling after so many post-harvest weddings, but for now, they were eagerly anticipating the meal. Vegetables that many in the congregation had planted, nurtured, and harvested accompanied the chicken. Celery both raw and creamed was often served at the wedding meal here in Lancaster County.

And desserts by the dozens scented the air with sugar and spice.

Jenny nudged Anna as she helped serve. "Look over there."

Hannah's youngest, an angelic little girl, stood in front of the cake table, gazing with wonder at the wedding cake. Anna turned to glance over at Hannah and tilted her head at the child. Hannah's smile became a grimace as her daughter swiped her finger through the icing at the bottom of the cake and popped it into her mouth. Just as she did, she caught sight of her mother and bolted from the room.

With a sigh, Hannah picked up a knife and a napkin and went to repair the slight damage. Then she headed in the direction her daughter had gone.

Anna and Mary Katherine looked at each other, and then, hard as they tried, they couldn't keep from laughing.

Leah walked up and wanted to know what they were laughing about. Mary Katherine was telling her, and then Anna saw that Gideon had walked into the room. Her smile faded, and she looked away before he could catch her staring.

"Are you *allrecht*?" her grandmother asked quietly.

Anna nodded, careful to keep her eyes on her.

"Has something happened between you and Gideon?"

"It's—not going to start," she said finally.

"Let's have something to eat," Leah said.

"But I'm helping—"

"There's plenty of help, and there'll be more opportunities all day."

Anna sighed and nodded. They got their plates and then sat at a table that had been set up after the ceremony was over.

"You looked like you were lost in thought during part of the wedding," Anna said, hoping to start the conversation in the direction she wanted it to go. Couples kept matters of the heart private. Not that she and Gideon were a couple . . .

"I did think about something else for a few moments," Leah admitted. "Mmm, try the green beans that Ruth brought."

"The wedding made me think of my grandfather. Your Ben, I mean."

Leah set down her fork. "Really? You weren't at our wedding."

Anna laughed and then she sobered. "Of course not. It just made me think of how you've never married again."

"*Nee.* I haven't." Leah stared off into the distance again. "God never sent me another *mann.* He——" she stopped and shook her head.

"He?"

Leah shook her head. "Nothing."

Thoughtful, Anna stirred her mashed potatoes. "Are you sorry?"

"Sorry? I wasn't happy at first," Leah admitted. "But I grew to be content." She eyed Anna. "But it hasn't happened for you yet, has it, *kind*? It doesn't take the same amount of time for everyone, does it?"

"I'm fine," Anna assured her quickly.

"More coffee?" one of the servers asked her.

"*Danki,*" she replied and held up her cup.

"No more for me," Anna said. "*Danki.*"

Leah smiled at the server and watched her move on. "You were thinking about your grandfather Ben because you wondered if I missed him? Or because we both lost our husbands at a young age?"

It wasn't a surprising question since Anna had wondered if others thought of their own weddings or the weddings of someone dear to them. "I did think of Samuel. Who wouldn't at a time like that?"

She straightened. "But I thought about him today because——" she stopped, biting her lower lip.

"You don't have to be careful of what you say to me," Leah told her. "You know that."

Anna looked at Naomi and Nick sitting at the *eck*, the corner of the table reserved for the bride and groom.

"I just wondered what might have happened if he hadn't died. You know, how different life might have been for you."

She took a deep breath. "And for Mary Katherine and Naomi and me."

"How so?"

"I guess I wondered whether you hadn't needed to support yourself if Mary Katherine, Naomi, and I would have ended up helping you with the shop. If we'd ended up doing the things we do—the weaving, the quilting, the knitting in the shop."

"Interesting thought, eh?" Leah asked, and Anna watched as a smile bloomed on her face. "I've often wondered myself. I think I might still have done so. He always encouraged me in what I wanted to do. I'd like to think that he would have urged me to do more after our *kinner* were grown."

Anna wanted to talk to her more but now wasn't the time. The usual games and activities were about to start.

"You didn't eat much," Leah remarked as she looked at Anna's plate.

"Don't worry. All we'll do today is eat."

"True. Oh, there's Fannie. I think I'll go see how her mother's doing in the hospital if you don't mind."

"Not at all. Leave your plate. I'm going to take yours and mine to the kitchen and help with cleaning up."

Before she could rise, someone walked up to her and stood there. She looked up . . . and up . . . Gideon was staring at her intently.

"Are you enjoying the day?" he asked politely.

"Very much," she responded just as politely, wondering if men did the same thing. "You?"

Gideon glanced at Naomi and Nick receiving hugs from their friends. Some of the *newhockers*, the single attendants, were laughing and gathering around the bride and groom.

He turned back to look at her, and in his eyes she didn't see the past, with memories of his wedding to his late wife, but the present, and a question about the future with her. He obviously wanted an answer to the question he'd asked the other day: if she would be interested in seeing him.

Terror was the last thing she'd have imagined she'd feel.

She'd felt indecision, some trepidation, maybe even some awkwardness about once again being involved with a man who wasn't her childhood sweetheart. But terror? Never.

She got to her feet so quickly that she bumped the table, and he quickly reached out to steady it.

"I have to get to the kitchen to help," she said, gathering the dishes and flatware. "Nice to see you again."

"But—" she heard him begin as she rushed to the kitchen. "Everything all right?"

Mary Katherine had been standing at the kitchen door, and her gaze went past Anna's shoulder.

"Fine," Anna said.

Apparently, she denied it too quickly because Mary Katherine's eyes narrowed.

"Did Gideon say something upsetting?" she asked, her hands on her hips.

"What, are you going to be a mama tiger and go after him for me?"

Laughing, Mary Katherine shook her head. "I can't imagine Gideon doing or saying anything that you need protection from."

Just my heart, Anna thought, and surprised herself.

"On the other hand, I found it hard to believe at first that John could hurt Naomi," she heard Mary Katherine mutter before looking back at Anna.

Her emotions about what Gideon had said were too new, too private to share even with her cousin who had always felt like a sister to her. She wanted to go home, think about that startling emotion that she'd never felt before. Life with Samuel had been one of joy and happiness but also of contentment and serenity.

Gideon and terror. That seemed cause for backing away.

Running, even.

She was grateful for the time in the kitchen. She didn't have to think. She didn't have to feel. The other women were chatting around her, with her. Weddings were joyful, daylong occasions where the whole community got involved helping with cooking and cleaning and sharing the joy of the day.

"I love weddings here," Jenny told her as she handed Anna a dish to dry. "It's like the forever thing is expected, not hoped for."

"The what?" Anna asked, puzzled.

"You know, that you expect to be together forever."

"Don't the *Englisch* expect that?"

"Well, yes, but I don't think these days they believe it so much." Jenny stopped, and her forehead crinkled in thought. "They even toss around this supposed statistic that half of all marriages end in divorce. I looked it up. One out of eight isn't as good as I'd like to see it, but it sure isn't half end in divorce."

She shook her head and glanced around. "I'm sorry, I shouldn't even be talking like this on such a day."

"*Mamm*? *Daedi* said please come look at Johnny. He says his tummy hurts."

Jenny wiped her hands on a dish towel. "Probably just ate too much cake. I'll be back in a minute."

Emma moved into place at the sink and began washing dishes, rinsing them, and handing them to Anna to dry.

"She's something else," said Emma.

"Excuse me?"

"That Jenny." Emma rubbed at something stuck on the plate until Anna thought she'd rub off a hole in it. "Did you see what she brought today? The mashed potatoes were lumpy, and the cake was lopsided."

"Well, to be fair, that's how you know the potatoes aren't from a box," Anna told her, drying a plate and putting it into the cupboard. "The lumps tell you that the potatoes are fresh, not flakes from a box."

"You'd think she'd be better by now," Emma responded. She glanced at Waneta, who nodded. "Maybe if she didn't spend so much time writing—"

"Did you ever think maybe she's doing the best she can?"

Everyone turned to see Sarah Rose standing in the doorway, arms folded across her chest, a scowl on her face.

"And she writes good stories, about kids who need people to help them. I read one of them. I liked it."

She spun on her heel and ran from them.

"Well, wait until I tell her father about that behavior!" Emma huffed.

Anna set the plate she'd been drying on the counter and tossed the dishcloth on top of it. "I'm going to go talk to her."

"Oh?" Emma perked up, her eyes avid on Anna. "So you're seeing her father?"

Her breath caught in her throat. Anna started to respond sharply, and then she remembered her manners. Even if Emma had none. She took a deep breath and counted to ten, and when she thought she could be polite, she smiled at her.

"No," she said. "Although that sort of thing is private, Emma."

She left the room and went in search of Sarah Rose.

∽❧∾

Gideon happened to be standing with a clear line of vision of the front door when he saw his daughter rush outside, followed a few steps behind by Anna.

What is up? he wondered, excusing himself politely and stopping in the bedroom to retrieve coats for the three of them.

Something must be up for Sarah Rose and Anna not to get their coats before they went outside.

He shrugged into his jacket and walked outside, finding them almost immediately in a corner of the porch protected a little from the wind.

Anna glanced up in surprise when she heard him walk toward them. Tucking her jacket under her arm, she took Sarah Rose's jacket to slip it on her. She gave her a reassuring pat, then smiled slightly at Gideon.

"Aren't you going to put your jacket on?"

"I need to get back inside."

Gideon frowned. "What's going on? You two just came out here."

Anna looked at Sarah Rose, and it seemed to Gideon that some unspoken message passed between them. Sarah Rose studied her shoes for a long moment, and Anna bent to whisper something in her ear. She looked up and nodded at Anna, then turned her attention to him.

"I guess I said something I shouldn't have to Emma," she confessed.

"You guess?" He looked from his daughter to Anna and back again. "You don't know? I think you're acting like you know you shouldn't have. What did you say?"

Sarah Rose chewed on her thumbnail, then sighed. "I sorta told her that she shouldn't say bad things about Jenny."

Gideon looked to Anna for confirmation and watched her straighten. "Well, she shouldn't."

"What did she say?" he asked her, hoping it wasn't as bad as it sounded.

"Who? Emma or Sarah Rose?"

"Both."

"Emma was criticizing Jenny's cooking."

"Jenny says things about her own cooking," he reminded her.

"Yes, well, it wasn't nice of Emma to say it, and then she said if Jenny didn't spend so much time writing, she'd be better at her cooking."

Emma's words hadn't been nice, but they also hadn't been appropriate in front of others. Gideon knew Sarah Rose liked Jenny—after the day Jenny had briefly shown up at the knitting lesson at the Stitches in Time shop and she and his daughter had talked in the kitchen Sarah Rose had asked if he'd get something Jenny wrote. They'd read it one night and Sarah Rose had been thoughtful and they discussed how Jenny tried to get people to help little kids being hurt by wars.

Sarah Rose had obviously been defending someone she liked and respected. He wasn't sure his independent and increasingly verbal daughter might not have been too outspoken this time.

"So what did you say to Emma, Sarah Rose?"

Her bottom lip jutted out. "I asked her if she thought about maybe Jenny was doing the best she could."

Gideon felt Anna's movement more than saw it. When he pulled his gaze from Sarah Rose, he saw the flash of indignation in Anna's eyes.

"She's right," Anna blurted out. "It's not right the way Emma talked, the way she gossiped, especially when other people could hear."

"Like me," Sarah Rose said, nodding righteously.

He considered that for a long moment, biting back a smile. It wouldn't do to minimize Sarah Rose being disrespectful to an older woman from the community, even though nearly everyone thought Emma was a gossip and tended to poke her nose into the business of others. He suspected there was one in every community.

A chill wind blew past, and Anna shivered. She glanced at the door. "I should get back inside."

"No, don't go," Sarah Rose pleaded and stepped closer to her.

Gideon took Anna's coat from her and held it out to her, and she slid her arms into it and pulled it closer. "Stay for just a few more minutes," he said. "Maybe you can help me decide what to do with Sarah Rose."

She wavered and then looked at his daughter. "Maybe Sarah Rose should decide what she should do."

Wonderful idea, he thought. *Why didn't I think of it?*

She thrust her bottom lip out again. "She did wrong." She hesitated. "But I did, too."

"That's right."

Sarah Rose rolled her eyes. "So, I guess I should go 'pologize." She looked at Anna, who looked impressed and nodded.

"I think that's an excellent idea," he agreed. "And the sooner the better."

With another eye-roll, she scuffed her shoes as she walked inside.

"You'd think she was walking to the gallows, wouldn't you?" he asked, grinning now that she was gone.

"It's not easy apologizing."

"No," he agreed, wondering where this was leading.

She looked at him, her brown eyes clear and steady on his, but full of uncertainty. In a gesture that seemed nervous, she licked her lips. "I've been avoiding you."

"I noticed," he said, moving closer as some people walked past. Moving closer because he wanted to be nearer her and study the way the moisture on her lips glistened in the light. "Why was that?"

9

Anna looked away for a moment, then back at him. "This isn't really the place for this discussion, is it?"

Gideon hesitated, then shook his head. "But if you don't want to date, all you have to do is say so. I wouldn't be happy, but I wouldn't bother you again."

She held his eyes. "It's not that. And you wouldn't be bothering me."

He tilted his head and studied her. "Then what—" he stopped. "Sorry."

"What are you sorry for?" Sarah Rose asked, startling him.

Looking down, Gideon frowned. "I didn't hear you walk up."

"I didn't sneak," she said. "I couldn't find Emma. I think she prob'ly went home."

"Then we'll have to go see her at her house. We should do that now."

"And leave the wedding?" Aghast, Sarah Rose stared at him. "They were just going to have games and snacks for us kids!"

"It would be the right thing to do to go apologize," he told her. "The Bible says we should apologize quickly and then forgive."

Sarah Rose gave a big sigh. "I'll go look again."

"Try the kitchen," he called after her.

Gideon heard a muffled sound and glanced at Anna. "It's not funny," he said, trying to sound stern as she fought to suppress her mirth. But he had to admit that even he saw the humor.

"Don't be mad at her. She's just going through a stage."

"I'm praying that I survive it."

Her smile faded. "Some of it's a stage, and some of it is she's working her way through grief. It takes some people longer."

"Does that include you?" he asked quietly.

"We're not talking about me. We're talking about your daughter." She hesitated. "She's a child. Jenny said—" She stopped, unsure of how much Jenny had said about losing her mother she should repeat. It could be something Jenny didn't want shared with everyone. "Talk to Jenny someday and ask her about her mother, okay?"

He nodded. "It feels bad not being able to protect your child from pain."

But God's will was God's will. He knew what He was doing. There was a reason He'd taken Mary to be with Him and had left Sarah Rose here with him.

As for working through grief, all he knew was that he'd started feeling like he'd come out of a fog recently and begun to feel like he was beginning to come to life again. But he didn't really know how she felt, he realized. Was she trying to tell him that she hadn't gotten to the place he had?

"Jenny lost her mother when she was young," Anna said quietly. "She told me she never really got over it. She just learned to cope—especially when her father was too lost in his own grief to help her. I can see that you're trying hard to help her. That should mean something."

She shivered. "I need to go inside."

"Can we talk later?"

She hesitated and then she nodded. "Maybe we can have coffee tomorrow morning? Around ten?"

"Sounds good."

Sarah Rose came back out onto the porch. She looked aggrieved.

"I found her."

"I thought you would."

"She wasn't real nice about me 'pologizing. Said I wasn't polite to an older person."

His heart went out to his little girl who looked disappointed that her attempt to make up for her impetuous words hadn't gone better.

"And what did you say to her?"

"I told her she was right, and I would try to do better."

Gideon let out the breath he didn't realize he'd been holding and smiled. "*Gut.* Don't you feel better now?"

She stared up at him with wide eyes. "I guess. Can I go play games and have snacks now?"

He smiled at the nasal way she pronounced *snack* as *snahk* with a flat, nasal tone like so many *kinner* her age did. "*Schur.*"

She spun, sending her skirts swirling, and ran back into the house. He called out to her to slow down, but she was already inside.

"Looks like someone's enjoying the wedding." Chris climbed the steps to the house.

"Chris, good to see you." The two men shook hands. "*Ya,* Sarah Rose is quite happy. There's games and *snahks.*"

"That's how my kids say it, too."

Gideon jerked his head toward Chris's buggy parked in front of the house. "You're leaving?"

"Hannah's not feeling well. We're going home."

The front door opened and their son poked his blond head out. "*Mamm* says she'll be out in a minute. She's getting the dish she brought."

He mirrored Sarah Rose's behavior of a little while ago with his shoulders slumped and his chin tucked down.

"Someone isn't happy," Gideon murmured. "Why don't you leave him, and I'll bring him home later?"

"You sure?"

"Of course."

Hannah walked out carrying an empty serving dish. Chris held out his hand to her, and she took it, smiling at Gideon.

"Gideon here says he'll bring Jonah home later. That way he can stay and have fun."

"Why, that's nice of you," Hannah said.

"Saw him out here talking quite a while with Anna," Chris told Hannah. "Wonder if there's going to be another wedding?"

"Chris! You know that's private! Don't be a gossip!" she chided. Looking at Gideon, she shook her head. "Don't feel you have to tell this former *Englischman* about your plans." She bit her lip and then gave him a mischievous smile. "Unless of course you want to tell me."

"There's nothing to tell," he said.

And regretted having to say that.

Anna felt herself hugged from behind as she walked down the front hall to the room that had been set up for the reception.

For a split second she wondered if was Gideon, but he wouldn't do something like that and besides, the person was a woman and she was laughing.

Turning, she saw that it was Naomi. "I'm so happy!"

Anna grinned. "Really?"

"Giving away another hug?" Nick asked, coming up to join them. "Save some for me."

Naomi blushed. "Nick!"

His eyebrows went up. "Too much? Sorry, love." He wrapped his arms around her waist. "I'm trying to be more circumspect now that I've joined the church."

"Really?" she asked, glancing down at his arms.

"It's our wedding reception," he told her. "You're not saying a *mann* can't show his love and affection for his *fraa*, are you?"

"There's appropriate and there's . . . not," she said sternly.

But Anna saw her cousin's lips curve in a smile.

"Keep working with him," Anna advised. "He'll make a good Amish *mann*."

"I've already shown her that, or she wouldn't have married me," Nick said with a grin.

She'd never seen him so happy and lighthearted.

"What a day!" he said, looking around him. "Look, it's time to eat again."

Naomi rolled her eyes. "It's Nick's kind of day. Two all-you-can-eat meals and snacks and desserts as well."

He took her by the hand. "C'mon, people will expect us to be at the—what's it called? The neck of the table?"

Laughing, shaking her head, she let him lead her away. "You know very well that it's the *eck*. You just have to tease."

"Nick! Can I pull you away from your bride for a moment?"

Naomi let him go with a smile and took a seat next to Anna. "Did you hear the news about Daniel in Florida?"

"No, what?"

"I just heard he's getting married. Isn't that a wonderful surprise? I can't wait to tell Nick. They got to be friends when we were in Florida."

"You're just happy someone else you know is getting married."

Naomi smiled and nodded. "I'm working on you next."

"I'm invited to three weddings this week. That's enough for me. I don't need my own."

Gideon looked directly at Anna as he reentered the room.

"Oh," Naomi whispered. "Oh, my. I had no idea."

"Don't start getting them," Anna hissed. "Stop looking at him."

"How long have you been dating him?"

"I haven't," Anna told her, giving her a quelling glance.

Naomi made a humming noise. "Well, I'd say he's sure interested in dating you."

Anna opened her mouth to say she knew that, but then she shut it. She didn't need to give Naomi any more information. Naomi wouldn't gossip, but she didn't want any questions.

"Nick's waiting for you."

Naomi laughed. "He's waiting for me so he can eat again." But she joined him, and they exchanged such a look of love Anna knew that Naomi was very sure of his feelings for her.

❧

Later that night, Anna lay on her side, thinking about meeting Gideon for coffee the next day as she looked up at the stars through her bedroom window.

She pressed a hand to her stomach. Butterflies were competing with the food she'd eaten at the evening meal at the wedding reception. It was so silly to be feeling like a *maedel* about to go out on her first date. My goodness, she was in her midtwenties, and she was a widow.

But she'd dated only one man—loved only one man—since they were youngsters at school. Only one.

And Gideon had been giving her those . . . looks that reminded her that she was a woman and he was a handsome and—dare she say it to herself—sexy man attracted to her.

It was enough to make any woman have butterflies just thinking about it.

Reminding herself that it was just coffee didn't seem to be helping. Sleep just wasn't coming.

She sat up and reached for the basket with her knitting that she kept by the bed, hoping that it would soothe her. Maybe she just hadn't allowed herself enough time to slow down and relax from the excitement and busyness of the wedding before she got into bed . . .

Of course, she knew that wasn't it. The long day and the physical work of helping to serve and wash up had made her so tired she'd found climbing the stairs to the bedroom a chore.

It was meeting Gideon for coffee. And it didn't help to remind herself that it was just coffee.

So she told herself if she wasn't ready to date yet or if she decided Gideon wasn't the man God had set aside for her, well, then she didn't have to see him again.

Dating was, at least, a little easier than what Jamie had told her it was like in the *Englisch* community. Couples who dated here almost always knew each other from childhood, and dating was kept private, which took some of the pressure off. Dating itself consisted of attending singings and other structured, often chaperoned activities that were still fun.

Less "drama" as Jamie called it, and Anna liked that she and Samuel had known each other so well by the time they got married.

As for Gideon, there was so much she already knew about him. It should have made it easier. But it didn't. He'd been a friend before, but now that he was asking to date, it changed everything.

She rubbed at her forehead, feeling a bit of a headache coming on.

No, this was getting way too worked up. It was just coffee. And a relationship wasn't supposed to be something you stressed over. Hers with Samuel had been loving and deep, but it had been so much fun, a partnership of working together to build a marriage and a home. She'd never lain awake and found herself stressing about things—not even the first date.

You were so young then, though, she reminded herself. Dating then—the older people in the community still sometimes called it courting—was just an innocent evening at a singing or a drive with Samuel, and a starry-eyed hope they'd get married one day.

Now she and Gideon were widowed. They both were at a stage where they knew life could be short, that the person that they built all their hopes and dreams on could be called away. That they could be left alone, so very alone.

Her knitting needles stilled. She stared at the baby hat that she was knitting. Neither of them would have children without getting married. Gideon was fortunate—he had a *kind* already, but if he wanted more—she had no doubt he wanted more. *Kinner* were God's gift to couples. Large families were encouraged . . . expected. If Mary had lived, it was likely that she and Gideon would have had at least another *kind* or two by now.

Just as she and Samuel would have had a baby or two. She'd so hoped that she would get pregnant quickly, but it hadn't happened and then before they knew it, Samuel became so sick, his disease draining the life from him before the chemo weakened him. Pneumonia had swept in, and he was gone.

Anna looked down at the baby hat in her hands and dumped it into the basket beside the bed. Even if she failed to get to sleep the rest of the night, she didn't want to think about the *kind* she'd never had with Samuel and now would never have.

She lay down again and placed her hand on the empty side of the bed. This was the time of day she always missed Samuel the most. She felt warmth flood into her cheeks as the thought came to her that Gideon could change that. It was best for a widow not to think of that part of life when she didn't have a *mann* . . .

Drawing the quilt up over her shoulders, she felt her body warming, relaxing, and her eyelids drifted shut. She'd sleep now and maybe she'd dream.

❧

Gideon pulled up in front of Anna's house.

The place looked neat as a pin, the walk neatly swept with nary a leaf blowing across it. Bright orange and yellow mums gave a last hurrah to the season from planters on the porch. A wreath decorated with bittersweet hung on the front door.

All of it looked more welcoming than his own. Mary had been better at that kind of thing than he was. He raised the crops on the farm and raised their daughter and helped Mary where he could when she was alive, just as she'd done with him.

He climbed the stairs, knocked on the front door, and waited.

A woman was the heart of a home, and Mary wasn't there anymore. He'd tried to make it a home for Sarah Rose and himself, but he didn't think he'd done all that good of a job. Maybe when his daughter got old enough, she'd do some of the things that her mother had done that made a house a home. That wasn't fair to her, though. And it wasn't fair to him as a man who wanted to love and be loved again. He'd had a good marriage and hoped it was God's will that another *fraa* had been set aside for him.

Mary had believed there would be. She'd told him he was a good *mann* and made him promise that he would marry again. He'd been in too much pain to even think about it, but Mary had insisted. It hadn't been just to ease his loneliness, she'd assured him. Sarah Rose deserved to have a *mamm,* and she also deserved to have *bruders* and *schweschders.* Mary had grown agitated, and he'd finally promised to ease her mind.

The door opened, startling him from his thoughts.

"I'm so sorry," Anna said quickly. "I was taking care of something." She dabbed at her hands with a damp dish towel that was spotted with drops of blood.

He reached out and took her hand, studying her scraped knuckles. "You hurt your hand again?"

"A little plumbing emergency," she said, shrugging. "I fixed it. For now."

"What kind of plumbing emergency?"

Anna stepped outside, pulling her coat on and turning to lock the door behind her. "The pipe under the kitchen sink again. It was leaking."

She started toward the steps, but when he didn't follow, she turned, raising her eyebrows.

"How did you fix it?"

"You think I don't know how?"

"How did you fix it?" he repeated, curious.

She lifted her chin. "You don't think a woman can do such a thing?"

"I think you can do anything you want to do. Amish women are capable of doing many things," he said and was relieved when she began descending the stairs. "Just as Amish men can do many things."

"Like cook?"

He nodded.

She turned as she reached his buggy. "I put a bucket under the leak," she said, and she laughed. "It's only a slow leak so I decided not to go crawling around under the sink getting my good dress dirty when you were due here."

"You're sure?"

She nodded.

Speaking of crawling around, he glanced at her. "You look very nice," he told her and was rewarded with a smile.

"I'm looking forward to coffee. It's a treat to have it out."

"I agree." He walked around and climbed into the driver's side of the buggy. "Especially since Fannie supplies their baked goods, and mine aren't anywhere as good."

They traveled a ways, but the silence didn't feel awkward.

"Sarah Rose has been getting interested in baking some things," he said after a time. "Chocolate chip cookies are her favorite. We've even put chocolate chips into pumpkin bread."

"I used to love chocolate chip pancakes."

"That sounds sweet."

"Makes up for my tart personality."

He glanced at her. "You've never been anything but pleasant to me."

"I have my moments." She glanced at him. "I'm nothing like Mary."

Surprised, he stared at her. "I didn't think that you were. But I wouldn't want you to be. You deserve to be yourself."

She searched his eyes and finally appeared to believe him. "I just thought maybe you were hoping to meet another woman like her."

"I do if you mean one who loves God and her family," he said slowly. "One who is generous with that love and compassion. Who is a partner with her *mann* and loves his *kind* and hopes with him that they'll have a *boppli* or two or three—however many God gives them."

He drew up in front of the parking lot of the small restaurant favored by the locals, and when he turned to look at her his eyes were intense.

"Is that you, Anna? Are you that woman?"

10

$\mathcal{H}$is words shocked Anna speechless.

"Never knew you to be at a loss for words." He grinned.

"I'm not," she said, and she got out of the buggy.

They walked into the restaurant, found a table, and ordered coffee and some of the coffee cake that the place was known for. Actually, Gideon ordered two slices for himself.

Anna stared at his plate. "I'd forgotten how much a man can eat." Then she blushed—*that hadn't really been polite*, she chided herself.

"It's okay," he said, washing down the bite he'd taken with his coffee. "Nothing wrong with an honest appetite and appreciation for fine food."

She smiled. "True."

"From what I remember, Samuel loved a good meal. I remember him talking about your cooking more than once as we ate a meal after church."

That is an advantage of living in a small community for so many years, she thought. *They all knew each other for years and shared memories, worked together, and relationships—especially those between married couples—were kept private.* But Anna had seen how Gideon treated his wife with care and love in public, and most of the time, when a man misbehaved, word got around and the bishop visited his home to talk to him.

Anna couldn't finish her coffee cake and offered it to him. She wasn't surprised when he took it and scraped the plate clean.

Looking satisfied, Gideon leaned back in his chair to sip his coffee. "So what about you, Anna? It's a two-way street. I don't expect you to be another Mary. I'm sure you aren't looking for another Samuel."

"Of course not. But he certainly was a man few others have measured up to."

"So you've dated?"

"No," she said firmly, setting her cup down with a snap. "You're the first man I've gone out with since Samuel died."

He raised his eyebrows. "Well, I'm glad you went out with me today."

The waitress came to top off their cups, and Anna raised hers as she looked at Gideon. "It's coffee. Just coffee."

"It's a date," he said. "I'm serious about wanting to be with you, Anna."

She swallowed, suddenly a little nervous. "You're with me right now."

"And I want to be with you again. How do you feel about that?"

It felt a little unnerving to have things be so serious so quickly, but as she'd thought earlier, dating a boy, getting married so soon, well, that was a different thing entirely than marrying a grown man who was obviously interested in getting married again.

He reached across the table and touched her fingertips with his, lightly, teasingly. "We're not the young kids we were when we married the first time. It means more this time. We know how it can be, don't we?"

Then, as if he'd gotten too serious, he withdrew his hand and sat straight. "Let's go for a little drive, and then later, after Sarah Rose comes home from school, I'll stop over and fix that little plumbing problem for you."

"You don't have to," she began, but he was standing and pulling out some bills to pay the check.

"I don't mind," he told her.

They went for a drive, enjoying the bright blue sky, the cool air, and the scenery. The leaves were almost gone, but a few drifted across the road. Time always seemed to go by so quickly this season. The days would become busier and busier as more customers visited the shops in the area, buying gifts for Christmas and doing last-minute visits before the weather became worse.

Their conversation became lighter. She wasn't sure if it was because Gideon felt he'd asked what he needed to or if the serious tone would have been too much in the more intimate space of the buggy.

The horse's hooves clip-clopped at a pleasant, relaxed pace on the road. The drive was the perfect way to talk and get to know each other without pressure.

So when they arrived back at her house and he leaned in as if he was about to kiss her, she drew back and frowned. Surely, he wasn't going to rush her into a kiss on the first date?

But just when she thought he'd try to kiss her on the lips, he kissed her cheek. "See you later."

"Later," she said, trying to look and sound unaffected. But her heart raced and her cheeks felt warm.

He came around to her side of the buggy and helped her down, then stroked his hands up and down her arms once, twice. "I'll bring Sarah Rose."

"It'll be nice to see her."

"I was thinking more like she could be a chaperone," he said, looking at her meaningfully.

Then, as he turned, he stopped and touched her arm.

"Someone's on your porch."

⁂

"It's Grace. Her husband farms part of my property."

"Were you expecting her?" Gideon asked her.

Anna peered at Grace. "No. Looks like she's asleep."

"Make sure she's okay before I leave. I could be wrong, but it looks like she's—" he paused, "expecting."

She laughed. "There's nothing wrong with her if she's pregnant."

He reddened. "I just mean make sure she's not sick."

"I'll do that." She turned and smiled at him. "I had a good time today."

"Me, too. I'll see you later with Sarah Rose."

Anna felt a little self-conscious walking away, but when she glanced back, he stood looking down the road, his hand on his horse.

Grace sat up and blinked as Anna started climbing the steps to the front porch.

"Everything all right?"

Nodding, Grace yawned. "I'm just so tired lately."

Anna turned and waved at Gideon, who climbed into his buggy and left.

"Did I forget that you were coming today?" Anna asked Grace.

Grace pulled her shawl closer around her shoulders. "Eli's out in the barn. I just wanted to get out of the house for a little while. The fresh air's doing me good."

"It's making you cold," Anna fussed. "Why didn't you go inside? You know where I hide the key."

"I'm fine. And it didn't seem right to go inside when you weren't here."

She ushered her into the house.

"Such a beautiful home," Grace said, removing her shawl and thin coat, revealing thin shoulders and a burgeoning belly.

"Here, sit down at the table. When are you due?"

"Middle of February."

"I'm ready for something warm to drink," Anna said, washing her hands. "And lunch. I'm ready for lunch."

She didn't usually have much of an appetite. Must have been the fresh air, she decided, and a few hours' break from work and cares.

There was no way she was going to get all in a tizzy because she'd been out with an attractive man who was interested in her. And she in him. No, that would be shallow, and she wasn't a shallow woman.

She opened the refrigerator and considered her choices. "I have some vegetable beef soup. Will you have some with me?"

Grace withdrew a wrapped sandwich from her purse. "No, thank you. I made us lunch. Eli took his sandwich and a thermos of coffee with him to the barn. I think he's making up his seed orders for spring. He doesn't expect to be here long today."

"I have plenty of soup." She poured the contents of the container into a pan and set it on the stove to warm. "Do you want to call him in?"

"I will, but I think he enjoys spending time in your barn." She smiled as she unwrapped the sandwich. "I'm looking forward to the time we have our own farm. It feels like we've been saving forever. Thank goodness we've been able to live with Eli's parents to save more."

Anna watched as Grace's hands stopped, and she frowned. Then with a shrug, she finished pulling the waxed paper from the two slices of bread with just a thin slice of ham in the middle. She stared for a moment at the sandwich, then took a bite.

The soup smelled heavenly as Anna turned off the flame under the pan and poured some in a bowl. She set it near Grace, served herself a bowl, and sat down at the table.

"Have some. Otherwise I'll end up eating it for a week."

"Only if you'll share my sandwich."

Anna shook her head. "Aren't you supposed to be eating for two? Besides, I'm not real fond of ham. I made this mistake of baking one when Samuel and I first married. A very big ham. I served it to him in some form for nearly a week."

She smiled at the memory. "Neither of us could eat ham after that."

Grace laid her hand over Anna's. "He was a special man." She glanced around her. "I pray God will send another to you to share this beautiful home and have *kinner* and fill it with love."

Incredibly touched, Anna stared at Grace, her spoon halfway to her mouth. "Thank you," she finally managed to say.

She curled her fingers around Grace's hand and squeezed it. "I appreciated everyone helping me get the crop in that last harvest he was alive."

"Everyone helped," Grace said simply.

"But Eli went on to plant the fields again as Samuel would have wanted the next season, and that was on top of his work with his father on his farm."

Thoughtful, Anna stirred her soup, watching the chunks of vegetables and beef swirl around the spoon. Then she set down her spoon and stood. "I'm going to see if Eli would like to come in and have some soup with us."

"I can go—"

Anna shook her head. "You stay put and stay warm. I'll be right back."

She grabbed her shawl and went out the back door before Grace could insist on going.

Grace had been right: when she opened the barn door she found him poring over a pad of paper and making notes. He looked up and smiled. "Anna! You're home!"

"Took a day off," she said, rubbing her hands together. "It's cold out here. Thought I'd see if I could get you to come inside and have some hot soup."

"Maybe you can get Grace to go inside."

"I already did. But of course she's worrying about you being cold out here. I know you don't want that."

She knew the right words. He got up immediately and followed her.

When he bent over his wife to kiss her cheek, she shivered. "Your beard is cold!" she told him, laughing.

"Did you want to talk about the spring planting?" Eli asked Anna as he shed his jacket and black felt hat.

Anna noted the time and shook her head. "We'll have to do that another time. I have someone coming to fix the sink."

He glanced at it. "I'd have fixed it if I knew. You should have called me."

"You do too much," she said, setting a steaming bowl of soup before him. "And it just started this morning."

They were chatting over coffee—Grace sipped decaffeinated tea—when there was a knock on the door. Anna went to answer it and saw Eli and Grace look surprised and exchange looks when she returned with Gideon and Sarah Rose.

The men shook hands, and then as if they were partners, they went to confer under the sink.

Sarah Rose settled at the table with some homework. "I have to write an essay," she complained, rolling her eyes. "I hate to write essays."

"That wasn't my favorite," Grace confided. "I loved math. Now I'm keeping the books for several businesses in town."

Anna was looking over the shoulders of the men, and she straightened when she heard Grace's voice. "Really? Grandmother's looking for a part-time bookkeeper. Would you have time to work maybe ten hours a week for us?"

"That would be *wunderbaar*!" Grace exclaimed. Her cheeks pinked and she became animated. "Did you hear that, Eli?"

He mumbled something from under the sink.

"What?"

"Yes, dear," Gideon said, leaning back on his heels to give her a wink.

Grace, always shy, blushed and laughed.

Not long after, the two men proclaimed victory over the leak under the sink. Eli and Grace left, saying they had to get home to help his parents with chores.

"Can I get you some coffee, Gideon?"

"We should go."

"I'm almost done." Sarah Rose scribbled furiously.

"I'll take the coffee, thanks," Gideon said, and he sat down at the table.

"Thanks for fixing the sink."

"You're welcome."

Sarah Rose looked up, her eyes going from her father to Anna and back again. "What?"

"Nothing," her father said, waving a hand at her paper. "Get done so we can go home."

"Maybe we can stay for supper."

"We don't ask ourselves to supper," he told her sternly.

Sarah Rose sent Anna a crafty look. "Maybe we'll get asked to supper."

Anna laughed. "Maybe you will. But it might not be a good time. I'll have to ask your *daedi*."

Resting her elbows on the table, Sarah Rose gazed at her hopefully. "Maybe you could do that now."

Gideon opened his mouth to say something, but Anna waved her hand at him. "Maybe I could. Gideon, would you and Sarah Rose like to have supper with me?"

He met her eyes and she felt her heart race. "I think I can speak for my daughter in saying we'd love to."

The daughter in question grinned and returned to her essay, looking much happier.

"I'm not sure what I have to offer," Anna said, rising to look through her supplies.

"Maybe *Daedi* can show you how to make macaroni and cheese."

"Sounds like a good idea, "Anna agreed, her gaze going to Gideon.

"The dish, I mean. I know how to make it. Let me see if I have everything I need."

Sarah Rose made a production of jabbing her pencil in a final, big period on the essay paper. "Done!"

❧

It was business as usual at Stitches in Time a few days later.

Except every time Anna glanced at Naomi she saw that her cousin wore a quiet smile as she worked on a quilt.

Naomi looked up then and blinked at Anna. "What?"

Anna laughed and shook her head. "I don't think you've stopped smiling since you got married."

Her cousin's smile grew wider. "You're probably right. Nick's been grumbling a bit, though. He thinks it's a little strange that we don't go on honeymoons."

"You'll have to show him that staying home is better," Mary Katherine said, and then she looked up and put her hand over her mouth. "I didn't mean to say that out loud."

Leah gave her an arch look as she stood and put her sewing down on a nearby table. "But you thought it."

She started toward the back room and then, a few steps away, turned and fanned herself with her hand and grinned.

The three of them looked at each other, and then they collapsed in giggles.

Naomi knotted a thread and clipped it with scissors. "So, Anna, how was your date with Gideon?"

"Date?" Mary Katherine looked up from her weaving. "You had a date? When did this happen? Why didn't I know?"

"Coffee," Anna said. "It was coffee."

"Why didn't I know about coffee?" Mary Katherine walked over to sit beside Anna in a chair in the circle before the fire. "When did you have coffee with Gideon?"

"I feel like I'm back in *schul*," Anna said, shaking her head. "Aren't you both a little old to be teasing me like I have a new boyfriend?"

"You should have seen the way they were looking at each other at the wedding," Naomi told her cousin.

Anna rolled her eyes.

"You can't blame us," Mary Katherine told her. "You teased us unmercifully when we were dating Jacob and Nick. And nosy? Oh, my."

"If I was as nosy as you say—" she broke off as Mary Katherine shook her head.

"Yes?" Naomi looked up from rethreading her needle. "Finish what you were going to say."

"I'd be wondering why Grandmother's making a big fuss with lunch today."

Naomi looked at Mary Katherine. "I don't think that's what she was going to say."

"Sure it was. You know Anna's always interested in her stomach." Mary Katherine checked the clock and got up to walk across the room to lock the door and turn the sign to "Back in an Hour."

They filed into the back room and found it filled with the delicious scent of baked ham and scalloped potatoes.

"What was all that I heard out there?" Leah asked as she set the ham on the table.

"Naomi was teasing Anna," Mary Katherine said, sneaking a sliver of ham.

"I was not!" Naomi denied. "I just asked her about her having coffee with Gideon."

"Now the two of you need to stop teasing Anna," their grandmother chided. "You're sounding like teenagers again."

She tilted her head and studied Anna. "You had coffee with Gideon?"

Anna started to protest that her grandmother was behaving no better than her cousins when they heard a knock on the shop door. Anna started for it, but her grandmother passed her the oven mitts in her hand. "You get the potatoes out. I'll get the door."

"Ignore them and they'll go away."

But Leah was hurrying out of the room.

Mary Katherine took dishes from the cupboard. "Is she expecting someone?"

"I don't know any more than you do," Naomi said.

When it had been a few minutes and their grandmother hadn't returned, Anna walked to the doorway and looked out into the shop.

"Grandmother!" she gasped, and the mitts fell from her fingers.

"What's the matter? Is someone robbing her?"

Her cousins pushed her out of the way, then stopped dead in their tracks and stared.

She stood there just a few feet from the doorway, Henry's arms encircling her waist. Lifting her chin, she smiled at them. "Henry and I have something to tell you."

11

"Married? You're getting married?"

Feeling as if someone had pulled the rug out from under her feet, Anna looked from her grandmother to Henry. "This is a surprise!"

Leah smiled at him. "We've known each other since we were in school. He was even one of the attendants at my wedding to your grandfather."

"I guess we thought the two of you were just friends," Mary Katherine said.

Henry patted Leah's hand lying on the table. "We were. We are. The best marriages start with friendship, don't you think?"

Anna had to agree with that and not just because that was what had happened between her and Samuel. You became friends with each other in school, went to singings and other activities, and started feeling deeper emotions, falling in love with each other.

Leah helped herself to a slice of ham and passed the platter to Henry. Anna watched them smile and exchange a look of love. *Well*, she thought, *they had certainly not shown this when I saw them together before.*

The platter came to Anna. She speared a small slice of meat and put it on her plate, then turned to pass it to Naomi.

All the while Anna kept thinking how she never expected her grandmother to get remarried. Why, she wasn't elderly but she was . . . old. Her grandfather had died so many years ago.

Scalloped potatoes and bread were passed around, and then they bent their heads in prayer.

Anna chewed her ham and thought about how she and her grandmother now had more than being a widow in common— God seemed to be sending other men to them. He hadn't set aside just one for them. She hadn't been certain how she felt about dating Gideon, but now that she'd tried it, she was glad she had.

"Are you planning on getting married this year?" Mary Katherine asked.

Leah exchanged a look with Henry. "We're not sure yet."

They aren't sure after they've known each other so long? Anna wondered.

"There's no rush," said Henry. "If Leah wants to wait, I'm fine with that." He gazed at her, adoring. "I'm not going anywhere."

If—If—things progress with Gideon, it will be next autumn before we marry as well, Anna thought. She didn't think he was the kind of man to behave so impulsively that he'd ask her to marry him this month. And certainly she didn't see herself going from that panic about dating him to marrying him just weeks later.

"Anna?"

She blinked and looked into Naomi's amused face. "What?"

"I was just saying that this is such a wonderful surprise. I wonder if there'll be any others this month?"

"Well, no one can accuse you of being *sub-tle*," Anna said, emphasizing the pronunciation of the word.

Naomi didn't take offense but instead just laughed and elbowed Anna the way they'd always done when they were young girls teasing each other. "That's no answer."

"Okay. Here's my answer: don't look at me."

"What?"

"You heard me."

Their meal was full of conversation and good food and warmth on a cold day. They'd known Henry all their lives so once past her surprise, Anna felt comfortable with the news and even wondered why she'd never thought of him as a possibility for a second husband for her grandmother.

"Have you told anyone else?" Mary Katherine asked.

Leah shook her head. "I wanted to tell you three first. Henry and I will be stopping by to see your parents later this afternoon.

Finally, after a glance at the clock, Leah sighed, wiped her lips on her napkin, and set it beside her empty plate. "Back to work. We'll have a busy afternoon with the holidays coming."

Leah turned to Henry. "I'm so glad you could come have lunch with us today." She slipped her arm inside his and smiled up at him. "I'll walk you to the door."

"Mary Katherine, if you and Anna don't mind doing the dishes, I'll go open up with Grandmother," Naomi suggested.

Anna saw the expression of disappointment flash across her grandmother's face before it was quickly changed.

"Naomi, we need your help in here," Anna said quickly.

"Three people are needed to help clean up lunch dishes?" she asked with disbelief, but she began clearing the table.

Mary Katherine tilted her head in the direction of Leah and Henry as they left the room. She pursed her lips and mimed making kisses. Anna laughed.

And her face froze as their grandmother walked back into the room.

Leah lifted her brows. "What's going on?"

Biting back laughter, Anna turned to put dishes in the sink. "Mary Katherine was just telling us a story about when she and Jacob got engaged."

"Anna, I'm going to go out and get ready for class," Mary Katherine said, backing out of the room. "If you and Naomi don't mind doing the cleanup."

Leah stared after her for a moment, shook her head, and then reached for a roll of aluminum foil and wrapped up the leftover ham. "This'll make some nice sandwiches for a soup and sandwich supper tonight." She hummed a hymn while she finished putting the leftovers in the refrigerator.

"You were looking thoughtful during lunch," Naomi said the minute their grandmother left the room.

"I seem to be missing a lot lately," Anna said after a moment. "I didn't pay attention when we talked about your wedding plans, and now I didn't see this coming with Grandmother and Henry."

Naomi accepted the plate Anna handed her and began drying it with a dish towel. "Didn't you notice that Mary Katherine and I were just as surprised?"

Anna considered that. "No, I didn't think you were."

"He'll be a good *mann* for Grandmother," Naomi said. "He always showed he loved his wife before she died. Both he and Grandmother have been alone for a long time. I think it's wonderful that God has brought them together now. "

She wiped the dish and put it away. "Love's not just for the young."

Anna put her hands on her hips and pretended to glare. "What are you saying?"

Naomi just threw her arms around her and hugged her. "You're hardly old."

She'd been so impulsive, so in love with Samuel, that she'd married before Mary Katherine and Naomi. So then she'd become a young widow.

Calling herself a widow made her feel old no matter how young anyone else thought she was. Everyone thought of widows as being women who lost their husbands after a long marriage. But life wasn't like that. Husbands and wives died young as well as old. Samuel wasn't the only proof of that or Gideon's wife, Mary. There were other widows and widowers in the community.

Calling herself a widow also made her feel lonely. Being alone didn't automatically mean being lonely, but the word *widow* sure did. Most young women in her community went from their parents' home to the one they'd share with their husband—sometimes with time spent with her husband's parents while the newlyweds built their home. So living by yourself as a woman wasn't done as often as she'd heard it was done in the *Englisch* community.

Sometimes people in her community tried to get those who'd lost their spouse to look at another in a similar situation to remarry. It seemed like a good idea for widows and widowers to remarry. After all, if you'd been happily married, of course you'd want to be again. And with the shared experiences of marriage, you had many things in common.

They finished the dishes, and Anna was hanging up the dish towel to dry when a she heard Naomi make a low sound of approval. She glanced at Naomi and then followed her gaze to the doorway.

Gideon stood there, and when she looked at him, he smiled slowly at her.

Naomi left the room, but Anna never saw her go.

Gideon glanced around at the décor in the Italian restaurant he'd taken Anna to. There were framed posters of scenes of the Italian countryside on the walls, vases of big, fat sunflowers on the tables, and the aromas in the place were incredible.

"How's your chicken parmigiana?" she asked him.

"Delicious. Your gnocchi?"

"I love it. Reminds me of the little dumplings my *mamm* makes of leftover mashed potatoes. These taste like little potato and cheese pillows."

She sighed. "But we didn't need to come to someplace so expensive. It's crazy to charge the prices they do here."

"Is that why you chose the cheapest thing on the menu?" he asked quietly, setting his fork down on his plate. "There's no need to worry about my wallet."

"I think we should go Dutch," she said. "Isn't that what people do these days?"

"A modern woman, eh?"

"It just seems fair," she said, putting another gnocchi into her mouth.

"Did you split checks when you and Samuel dated?"

Her laugh was rueful. "We never went anywhere that cost us. We went to church stuff, singings, you know. You were there at those kinds of things with Mary."

"We got out for a special night now and then."

"Samuel and I were saving for our own house," she said, her expression becoming faraway. "He wanted us to have our own place, not live with his parents or mine until could buy one. So he worked all the time. When he wasn't doing that, he was building the house. You know the story. It seemed like everyone we knew came and helped with something."

Gideon nodded. "I was happy to help. Mary and I would have had to do the same thing if my parents hadn't decided to sell us the farm and move into the *dawdi haus* of my brother's place. They're older than your parents, and *Dat's* arthritis was getting too bad to take care of the farm."

He buttered a roll and took a bite. "Later they decided to move in with one of my brothers since they have a special needs child and they could use the help."

"Grace and Eli are living with his parents right now," Anna said. "Working their fingers to the bone and wanting to put their roots down . . ." she trailed off, looking down at her plate.

"But they have each other," he said. "And they'll value what they build together more, don't you think?"

"I guess." She lifted her gaze. "If you get to live to enjoy it." She set down her fork. "I'm sorry, I didn't mean to say something like that. It sounded bitter, and I'm not bitter anymore. Or angry at God."

"That's good," he said with a grin. "I'm sure He appreciates that."

She laughed and nodded. "Well, I was pretty angry that after all that waiting for marriage with Samuel, I got so few years with him."

"I don't know anyone who isn't angry at God after they lose someone they love." He looked up as the waitress came to refill their coffee cups, thanked her, and waited for her to leave. "We don't always understand God's will but we just have to go on faith that He knows what He's doing."

"True." She straightened and smiled at him. "So let's talk about something more pleasant. How's Sarah Rose?"

"She wasn't happy she couldn't come tonight."

"Maybe she could join us next time we go to a restaurant."

He studied her, liking the way she looked at him with a directness that had always been a trait of hers even when she was a young girl. He didn't know her as well as he wanted to yet and suspected that she wouldn't be the calm woman Mary had been—even a little shy and reserved years after they'd been married.

"Would you like there to be a next time, Anna?" He reached across the table to touch her fingertips with his.

She nodded. "I like her. She reminds me a little of myself at that age."

"I think you're right." He considered what it might be like to live with two strong-willed females in the house. It might not be quiet and easy. But it would certainly be interesting.

He thought he might like that a lot.

"How about some dessert, folks?" the waitress returned to ask.

"I saw brownie sundaes on the menu," Gideon told Anna. "Isn't that one of your favorites? You bring brownies to church a lot."

Surprised, she nodded.

"We'll both have one," he said to the waitress.

"One for the two of you?"

"No, one for each of us," he corrected.

"Be right back with them," she said and took their plates with her.

"We could have shared one," Anna said.

"I don't dare come between you and a brownie sundae," he told her seriously. "I need all my fingers to do my work."

"I'm not quite that bad."

"I saw you get after Samuel for stealing a bite of your brownie once at a church lunch," he said.

She grinned. "I'm surprised that we're seeing each other with what we know."

"What can you possibly know that's negative about me?" he asked, pretending to be offended.

"I heard about that incident when you and a couple of your friends sneaked off to drink a keg of beer during your *rumschpringe*."

"Got deathly sick and could never look at a beer again," he said, laughing. "That was the extent of my wildness. I didn't really want or like the beer. It was just something I think we thought we needed to do then."

Shared memories. They had so many of them growing up in their tight-knit community, bonds that came from attending school together, holding church services in each other's homes, and having a common belief in hard work and putting God and family first.

But it wasn't all about traditional values and responsibility. She knew Gideon was a steady, dependable man who obviously loved and cared for his daughter like he'd always done for her and his wife. But she was like any other woman: she'd had a warm, loving marriage and true happiness with one man.

She wouldn't take less with another.

There was a full moon out, bright and white, lighting their way home. Gideon took the long way home, and she didn't point out that fact to him. He switched on the small battery heater, but she didn't feel she needed it. Sitting so close to him, she could feel the warmth his body projected, and whenever he glanced at her, the look in his eyes made her temperature rise and shivers race over her skin all at the same time.

He must have seen or felt her shiver because he frowned and reached for a blanket kept on the backseat. She took it and spread it over her lap, not needing it but grateful for his consideration.

Gideon was a handsome, vital . . . *sexy* man. The single women in the community had tried to attract his attention but hadn't. She was smaller than her cousins and felt more feminine, almost delicate next to Gideon's tall, muscular body.

The skin on her hand tingled when he touched it lying between them on the seat. She looked at him, saw the heat in his eyes, and her heart beat faster in her chest as she thought about venturing down this road to discovering if they had a future together.

❦

"Ready?"

Anna looked up as her grandmother entered the storage room, attached a mailing label to the box in front of her, and nodded. "That's the last one. You know I could drop this shipment off by myself. You don't have to go with me."

Leah placed it on top of the packages in the cart and wheeled it out of the room. "I know. But it won't take long, and it'll give us a chance to talk."

Hmm, thought Anna. She pulled on her coat, grabbed the handle of the cart, and followed her grandmother out of the shop.

"It's beginning to look a lot like Christmas," played from a nearby speaker over a shop.

The air felt a little nippy, but they moved briskly so Anna didn't feel chilled. The weather forecasters predicted cooler temperatures the following week. Stores up and down the street were festive, decorated for the holidays with swags of pine greenery, shiny ribbon, and ornaments.

A tiny fireplace with a battery-operated fake flame set a warm scene in their shop window. Several of Leah's dolls sat near it, covered with one of Naomi's warm and comfy Christmas-patterned quilts, Anna's baby hats that looked like fanciful little forest creatures, and Mary Katherine's pillows woven of red-, white-, and green-colored wools.

And since the Amish believed in making gifts for each other for the holiday, one corner of the window was devoted to all the kits that customers could buy to sew or knit or cross-stitch to give to friends and family.

Some store owners had used a light dusting of fake snow to give windows a wintry look since the real stuff hadn't shown up yet. Signs in windows advertised specials and sales. It was proving to be a good season for retail judging by all the shoppers crowding the sidewalks, carrying shopping bags loaded with their purchases.

Jamie, Mary Katherine, and Naomi were back at the shop taking care of the customers, but it wasn't like her grandmother to take a break in the day. Anna wondered what was going on but waited until she chose to reveal why she'd asked her to take the packages to ship.

Finished with their chore, Leah turned to Anna. "How about some pumpkin spice coffee?"

"It's expensive," Anna said.

"We only get it this time of year. It'll be my treat. Let's have ours here and take some back for the others."

Anna nodded, and they went inside the coffee shop. The line moved quickly as the baristas created the specialty coffees with holiday flavors like pumpkin, eggnog, cinnamon, and peppermint.

They ordered their coffee and found a small table near the front window.

"I know Henry and I didn't let any of you know that our relationship had changed from just being friends," Leah said. "But it really seemed to surprise you."

"It's not that I don't like Henry," Anna said. "He's a very nice man. I guess I just hadn't thought you might end up getting remarried."

"Because I'm old?"

"No! You're not old!"

"Well, I'm not young," Leah said with a smile. "But I'd gotten to where I didn't think God was going to send along another *mann.*" She paused to take a sip of coffee. "How about you?"

"How about me?" She looked at her grandmother. "What do you mean?"

"Thelma asked me how you and Gideon were doing."

Anna rolled her eyes. "She's such a matchmaker. We're just friends. But that doesn't mean it'll turn into more like you and Henry."

"Of course not," Leah said, giving her a sage nod. "But how would you feel if it did?"

Life seemed . . . heightened, she thought. Everything seemed a little bit brighter, a little bit more interesting. And when they weren't together, he came to mind constantly. Like now. He and Sarah Rose would be coming to the shop for a knitting lesson, and then they'd be having supper afterward.

She couldn't wait.

Aware that her grandmother watched her, waiting for some reaction, Anna dug in her purse for her wallet. "I like him," she said finally.

"I'm getting the coffee," Leah objected, reaching for her purse.

"It's fine. It's my treat."

"If you don't want to talk about Gideon, just say so," Leah said, a smile lurking around her lips.

Anna turned back and took her seat. "It's still too new. He's a really nice man and I like him a lot. But I was happily married for—"

"And you don't want to settle for less. I understand."

She patted her grandmother's hand. "I know you do." She sighed. "I'm not sure I'm ready for more than friendship right now."

"That's fine." Leah's smile grew wider. "*Gut* things come from friendship." Then her smile faded. "You've grown up a lot in the last year. Your moods have settled down a lot, and you seem happier, less wanting to be by yourself." She paused and sipped her coffee. "More mature."

Anna made a face. "Oh, goodness," she said, pretending horror. "Mature?"

Leah laughed. "Maybe not. I've been known to be wrong." She patted Anna's hand. "Whenever you want to talk, let me know, *liebschen*."

12

"We're here!"

Anna looked up from stocking a shelf and saw Sarah Rose skipping down the store aisle. "I see that."

Gideon was right behind her, his smile warm. "Hello."

She glanced at the clock. "You're a little early."

"We couldn't wait," Sarah Rose told her.

"Really?"

Gideon winked at Anna and she blushed.

Sarah Rose dug her hands into the skeins of yarn in the box Anna was stocking in bins built into the wall of the shop. "Pretty. And soft. Can I help?"

"That would be wonderful." Anna handed her the box of yarn. "Just put each color in the bin there with others the same color." She turned to Gideon. "There's fresh coffee in the back room."

"That sounds good." He strolled off toward the room with a nod at Mary Katherine, Naomi, and Leah.

"Maybe there's some hot chocolate in there, too?" Sarah Rose asked her.

Anna noticed that she asked after her father was out of earshot. "I think there is. You can go in and ask your *daedi* if you can have some. He can make it while I finish this box."

Sarah Rose's face fell. "He won't let me have any. He brought me a snack in case I got hungry before we ate supper."

"I see," Anna said seriously. "What kind of snack?"

"An apple and a carton of milk."

Her expression was so disgusted you'd have thought he'd packed sawdust and water. Anna barely suppressed her smile. Careful not to promise anything, she said, "Why don't you finish this, and I'll go have a talk with him?"

With a grin that nearly split her face, Sarah Rose began putting the yarn into the proper bins.

Anna was aware that she'd allowed herself to be manipulated, but she figured it wasn't such a bad thing. A cup of hot chocolate sounded *gut* to her right now, too. Besides, she hadn't promised . . .

Gideon stood at the stove, pouring a mug of coffee. He turned when she walked into the room and held out the mug to her. "Want some?"

"Thanks, but I think I'll have some hot chocolate. Okay if I make Sarah Rose some as well? I have her hard at work helping me out there."

"Did she complain to you about the apple and the milk?"

Anna laughed. "How'd you guess?" She filled the teakettle and set it on the stove. "But think about it. She's already having milk—hot chocolate is just warmed up and has some chocolate in it. And didn't I read somewhere that chocolate is good for you?"

"My daughter is becoming too good at getting what she wants."

"I know. It's what *kinner* do."

Gideon stirred some sugar into his coffee and took a sip. "You know, eh?"

She frowned. "I might not have had a *kind* of my own, but I've had a lot of them around."

He reached out and touched her hand. "I didn't mean that."

She glanced down at his hand on hers and then raised her eyes to his, seeing only kindness and compassion. "I know."

"No, but careless words can hurt. I know I hurt Mary more than once that way. Not because I wanted to or meant to. But I'm no more perfect than the next man."

Anna stared at him. "That's quite an admission."

"Marriage teaches you some things."

"That you can be wrong?"

Gideon grinned. "I was thinking more like you learn that even if you think you're perfect, you're not. Even if you're right, the marriage is more important than who's right or wrong."

He paused. "Why are you looking at me like that?"

"I'm just wondering what it would be like to—" she broke off.

He lifted her hand and held it to his cheek. "What?"

"To be—" she tugged at her hand while she glanced over her shoulder.

"Go on."

"Stop that!" she hissed when he pressed his lips to her fingers.

"I will when you finish your thought." His eyes were warm with desire.

Anna glanced at the open door, hoping no one saw, then shook her head and gave him a quelling glance. His touch was having a powerful effect on her. They'd been dating for several weeks, and she knew the time when his touch would become more direct was coming. She just felt a little unnerved now that it had.

"Anna, your class is here."

She stepped back quickly and looked at her grandmother, who'd just walked into the room.

The teakettle began to whistle, a jarring noise in the silence as the three of them stood there.

Leah glanced at Gideon, then Anna, and pressed her lips together. "I'll tell them you'll be a minute."

"I—okay." She watched her grandmother leave the room. And told herself that it was her imagination that she thought she heard a chuckle.

Flustered, Anna turned to the cupboard, opened it, and found a packet of hot chocolate and a mug. She quickly made the drink, stirring it, watching the marshmallows bob merrily so that she didn't have to look at Gideon.

She started for the door, but when he touched her arm, she stopped and glanced back at him.

"We'll continue our discussion later."

She straightened and met his gaze directly. "Yes, we will."

Sarah Rose was seated in a chair, knitting on her project when Anna walked out with the mug of hot chocolate and set it on a table near her.

"Thank you. Where's yours?"

"I changed my mind." She forced herself to look stern. "Don't let it ruin your appetite for supper."

"I won't."

Anna glanced around at her students who were already seated and working on their projects. "Welcome."

She walked around to check progress.

"So, any news for us?" Thelma inquired in a low voice.

"News?"

She jerked her head in a not-so-subtle motion at Gideon on the other side of the circle of chairs near the fireplace. "Has he popped the question yet?"

Anna's face flamed. "Uh, no, I told you before. He's just a friend."

"Uh-huh." Thelma squinted at her work. "Sarah Rose is such a darling. So well behaved."

Anna couldn't wait to share that with Gideon. Other than taking that thimble—which no one outside the shop knew about—Sarah Rose had indeed been wonderfully behaved here.

"Of course, I wouldn't have expected anything different, seeing as how she's Amish."

"Children are children whatever and wherever they are," she disagreed gently. "They're not perfect."

"Well, you should see how some children I know behave." She held up the infinity scarf she was knitting. "He's a nice man, and it's time for him to look for a mother for his daughter."

Anna froze. It had never occurred to her that Gideon might be interested in her just to get a mother for his daughter, maybe a mother for more children he might want.

"As I said, he's just a friend," she stammered and moved on, forcing her to look at another student's work so that she didn't look like Thelma had upset her.

Agnes got up to stretch. She had to get up and move around every hour or so because her back hurt when she sat for too long.

"Oh, these are so darling," she said, holding up one of the baby hats that Anna knitted. "I've got to get it for my new granddaughter."

Sarah Rose looked up. "Will you make one of those for our baby when you have one?" she asked in a high, clear voice that carried. "After you and *Daedi* are married?"

Anna's gaze flew to Gideon. He looked as shocked as she felt.

The room was so quiet she could hear the crackle of the fire in the fireplace.

Gideon watched his daughter approaching the table in the family-style restaurant with her plate. "Wait 'til you see what she gets," he told Anna. "Her idea of a wonderful meal is cottage cheese, macaroni and cheese, and cheesecake for dessert."

"And I was worried about her spoiling her appetite with hot chocolate."

"What?" Sarah Rose asked them when she got to the table and noticed they were watching her.

"Nothing," he said. "I was telling Anna you liked cheese."

They bent their heads over their meal, asking a blessing for it. Then Sarah Rose made quick work of the macaroni and cheese. "It's really good. Want some?"

"No, thanks. And don't talk with your mouth full."

She rolled her eyes. "Can I go get some more from the buffet?"

"*Schur.* Get a vegetable this time as well." He turned to Anna after she left the table. "I thought the rolling of the eyeballs didn't start until they got to be teenagers."

"Don't ask me," she said. "I'm a bad example."

"Why do you say that?"

"I did it a lot at that age. And quite a bit beyond."

She told him how she'd always been a little impatient—first to be allowed to date Samuel, then to get married.

"I think I was a little immature. Maybe a lot immature. I didn't want to listen to their rules or advice. After Samuel died, I wouldn't listen to anyone wanting to help me with grief. Even my grandmother. I pushed them away—"

She stopped as Sarah Rose approached the table with a small bowl of macaroni in one hand and a slice of cheesecake in the other.

Two green beans decorated the top of the macaroni and cheese. Gideon wanted to roll his own eyes at his daughter.

"So you like this restaurant?" Anna asked her.

Sarah Rose nodded. "*Mamm* and *Daedi* brought me here for my birthday before she died."

"Excuse me," Gideon said. "I'm going back for some more meat loaf."

"Do you like this place or the Italian one *Daedi* took you to better?" Sarah Rose asked her.

"They're both nice," Anna said. "This is more the kind of food I'm used to." She put down her fork and told Sarah Rose about the entrée she'd had that hadn't been much different than her mother's potato dumplings. And the price!

"Can you help me make something for *Daedi*?" Sarah Rose asked quickly, keeping her eyes on her father at the buffet.

"Sure. What do you want to make?"

"A muffler but a dark one, something nice. And it's gotta be easy. Oh, here he comes. Can we talk about it later?"

Anna nodded.

Gideon lifted his eyebrows. "What did the two of you have your heads together about?"

"Nothing," Sarah Rose said, her eyes wide and innocent. "I was just talking to Anna."

Gideon looked from one to the other. "Okay," he said slowly. "Sarah Rose, would you get me a slice of apple pie from the buffet?"

She nodded and got up from the table. Then she stopped and turned to look at him. "Don't go asking Anna about what we were talking about."

He turned to Anna when she was out of earshot. "Are you two keeping secrets?"

"Christmas is coming," she told him. "Don't ask questions."

He tilted his head and studied her. "It seems my little girl and you are getting along better than I expected."

When she stiffened, he frowned. "What is it?"

She shook her head and dropped her gaze to her plate.

"Anna? What is it?"

"Nothing."

He touched her chin, lifting it with his finger so that she was forced to look at him.

Shrugging, she shook her head and started to repeat what she'd said. And then she realized that she might as well find out if Thelma was right.

"Are you interested in me just to have a mother for Sarah Rose?"

Gideon dropped his hand and stared at her. "Where did you get an idea like that? No, of course not."

He leaned forward. "Don't you know how attracted I am to you?" He sighed. "One of us must be very rusty at dating to have signals crossed so much."

"Look at this," Sarah Rose said, her voice almost squeaking with excitement as she held out the plate of pie. "I put some of the soft ice cream in that machine on top."

Gideon took the plate from her and examined it carefully. She'd evidently let the ice cream swirl around and around from the machine until it was several inches high and ended in a point at the top.

"Well, this is a work of art. It's too beautiful to eat." He showed it to Anna. "What do you think?"

"I think you're not going to be able not to eat it." She glanced at Sarah Rose. "What do you think?"

She giggled. "I think he'll eat it all. *Daedi*, could I go look at the fish tank over there?"

"Sure." He waited until she'd walked away and then looked at Anna again. "I'm surprised you'd go out with me again if you thought I only wanted you to be a mother to my daughter, however charming she might be at times."

He was a little relieved when she smiled slightly.

Pretending an interest in his pie, he cut a bite and tried it. "How long have you been thinking that way?"

"Just today," she admitted. "I—someone said something. I shouldn't have believed her." She sighed, picked up her own fork, and scooped up a bite of his pie. "It was Thelma who made me wonder."

"I thought she was being a bit of a matchmaker. I'd see her talking to you, then looking at me when we had a lesson."

"I don't think she was thinking when she said it. Maybe she didn't think we Amish cared about—"

"About love as much as we do?" he asked, enjoying her blush.

He laughed when she swatted at him. "Funny how the *Englisch* think we're stern and serious. Where do they think all our *kinner* come from?"

Sarah Rose reappeared at the table. "What are you talking about kids for? Are you talking about babies?"

Anna's fork clattered to the table.

"Sit down," Gideon said. "Let's talk about that question you asked at the shop."

Her eyebrows drew together, and she bit her lip. "Am I in trouble?"

Gideon felt someone nudge his foot under the table and, for a moment, thought his daughter had done it. Then he glanced at Anna and saw the warning look in her eyes.

He looked back at his daughter, thinking about how Anna must be feeling like a part of his family or she wouldn't care if he was too strict with Sarah Rose.

"Well, we need to talk about that question you asked about a baby back at the shop earlier," Gideon began, choosing his words carefully. "There are some questions we don't ask in public."

"Oh," said Sarah Rose. She reached over with a spoon and snitched some of his ice cream. "So, this isn't public, is it?"

Gideon glanced at Anna and picked up his coffee. "Uh, no."

Sarah Rose gave him a wide-eyed, innocent look. "Are you two going to have a baby after you're married?"

Gideon exchanged a look with Anna. He caught the attention of their waitress. "Check please."

⟞♋⟝

Anna walked into the back room to get her things and found Naomi huddled over a small sampler in her hands.

"What are you doing?" she asked as she reached toward the peg where her coat hung.

Naomi turned around the sampler she was sewing on to show Anna. "It's one of Nick's Christmas gifts. It's hard to find time to work on it at home when he's around."

Anna studied the sampler, a square of off-white muslin surrounded by small patchwork squares, enclosed in a round embroidery hoop. She'd never been able to stitch twelve stitches per inch like Naomi and some other experienced quilters Anna knew. The cross-stitch had the same tiny, evenly spaced stitches. With those precise stitches, in multicolored thread, Naomi had spelled out: *Ask, and it shall be given you; seek, and ye shall find; knock, and it shall be opened unto you. Matthew 7:7.*

"It's beautiful."

"I hope he'll like it," Naomi said with a smile. "He's made such a journey to find his way to God. To me."

Suddenly, she straightened, tilting her head as if listening to something Anna couldn't hear. "Is that him?"

Anna walked to the doorway and saw Leah unlocking the door to let him in. "Yes." Amused, she walked over to the cabinet, unlocked it, and pulled out her purse.

Naomi jumped to her feet and quickly shoved the sampler behind her back. "Hi!" she said when Nick strolled into the room. "You're early."

"Just a few minutes. "

He leaned down to kiss her on the cheek, looking at her curiously when she backed up slightly.

Anna lifted the strap of her purse onto her shoulder, and the movement caused Nick to glance over at her, as if he'd just realized she was in the room. "Hey, Anna, how are you?"

"Well, thanks. You?"

He looked at his wife, and his smile grew and grew. "Just fine now. Ready to go?"

"Okay."

"Okay." Then he tilted his head. "Then let's go."

Naomi looked at Anna. "I have to talk to Anna about something. Why don't you wait for me outside?"

"You won't be long, right? It's cold out."

"I'll be right there. Promise."

"Okay." He backed up. "See you in a minute."

Turning, he started for the door. "Don't know what it is you're hiding, but it must be for me," he tossed over his shoulder with a chuckle.

Naomi glanced at Anna. "See how hard it's been to keep a secret?" She started to bring her hand from behind her back, but something was stuck. "Oh no. The needle must have gotten caught on my dress. Help me."

Laughing and shaking her head, Anna crossed the room and gently pulled the sampler until she found the place where the needle had become entangled with the fabric of her cousin's dress.

Christmas secrets. It seemed that it wasn't just her and Sarah Rose who were keeping them.

Jamie walked in, pulled a Diet Coke from the refrigerator, and popped the top. She sat down and put her feet up on a chair. "Feet are killing me. It was a long day, and they're not going to get any easier until Christmas is over.

"Going home . . . or out on a date?" she asked with a mischievous grin.

"Home."

"Sometimes I envy Amish women. You really know the guy before you date them. I mean, you've grown up in the same neighborhood, gone to the same school. They think commitment's important."

Anna saw Jamie's bottom lip tremble. She pulled out a chair and sat down. "What's wrong? Has something happened?"

"Steven says he's not ready to get married."

"But he gave you an engagement ring a couple of months ago." Anna looked at Jamie's hand. There was no ring.

Jamie shrugged. "He saw a bridal magazine on my coffee table, and I guess he panicked."

Leah poked her head in. "Anna, our driver's here. Jamie, can we give you a ride?"

"Yeah, thanks," Jamie said, taking her feet from the chair and standing. She took a last sip of the soft drink and tossed the can in the recycling bin.

Anna made an impulsive decision. "Why don't you come over to my house? I thought I'd make Christmas cookies tonight. Sarah Rose will be there for a while so Gideon can help one of his friends with something."

"I dunno—"

"What's your favorite cookie?"

"Snickerdoodles. Well, this time of year, maybe gingerbread men."

"We'll make Snickerdoodles *and* gingerbread. And hot chocolate."

Anna slipped her arm through Jamie's. "And we'll have sandwiches for supper first, so we have plenty of room for the cookies. It'll be fun to talk. We haven't done that in ages. You can sleep over so you don't have to find a ride back to town after. I miss Girls' Night Out," she confessed.

"Me, too. We haven't had one since Mary Katherine and Naomi got married." She looked at Anna. "You're not getting married for a while, right?"

Anna stopped in her tracks. "Who said I'm getting married?"

"C'mon," said Jamie, pulling her along. "I've seen the way you two look at each other every time he's in the shop."

Was it that obvious? Anna wondered and blushed. She might be a grown woman, but she still sometimes wondered if he felt the way she was growing to feel about him.

Best to take it slow, she cautioned herself as she got into the van. Marriage was forever . . . well, unless your partner died. And there was a child involved. Anna didn't want Sarah Rose hurt if marriage didn't happen. And weddings didn't take place until next fall. There was plenty of time to decide—and for all to be revealed by God, whose will would be done.

13

"Interesting cookies."

Gideon held one up and looked at Anna through the heart-shaped hole in the middle of the chest of the gingerbread man.

"Jamie made those," Anna told him quickly. She glanced over in the direction of the living room and lowered her voice. "She's—rather upset right now. Steven broke off their engagement."

"I'm sorry to hear that," he said. "Jamie's a nice woman." He watched her box up the gingerbread men. "May I have one?"

She offered the plastic container, and he chose several. "Coffee?"

"Yes, thanks. Didn't Sarah Rose help make the cookies? I thought that was why she wanted to come."

"She helped with the first batch of Snickerdoodles."

"Then what did she do?"

"Gideon? Don't ask questions I can't answer this time of year."

"Oh," he said, realization dawning. "Christmas secrets?"

She gave him a mysterious smile and said nothing. Handing him a mug of coffee, she gestured at the table. "Have a seat and I'll get Sarah Rose."

He grasped her hand and pulled her over to the table with him. "In a minute." He clasped her hand with hers and sat there, studying her, until she fidgeted.

"*Daedi!*"

He glanced up just as his daughter threw her arms around his neck and hugged him. "I heard you come in. You're early."

"Not very."

She reached for a cookie and stuffed it into her mouth.

"Sarah Rose!"

"What?" she mumbled, scattering crumbs.

"Let's not make Anna think I haven't taught you manners."

She accepted the glass of milk Anna got up to pour for her. "Thank you!" She turned to him. "See? I have manners."

Then she used the back of her hand to wipe away her milk mustache.

"*Ya*, I see," he said dryly.

"I had such fun! Did you have fun with your friend tonight?"

"I did. Ready to go?"

She frowned and thrust her bottom lip out. "I don't want to go. Can't I stay overnight?"

"Maybe some other time. It's a school night, remember?"

"You could pick me up here and take me to school tomorrow."

"Some other time," he said more firmly. "Go put your coat on, and let's say thank you to Anna for having you."

Anna held out Sarah Rose's coat and helped her into it. "I need some help baking more cookies day after tomorrow. Would you like to come back?"

Sarah Rose turned to look at him hopefully. "Can I?"

"May I?" he corrected.

"May I?"

He nodded. That would give him some time to finish the gift he was making for Anna.

"Be right back," Sarah Rose said suddenly. She ran down the hall, and Gideon heard the guest bathroom door slam.

Gideon pulled Anna into his arms. "Got you to myself again. There's something I want to ask—"

"Wow, I fell asleep," Jamie said as she shuffled into the room. "Oh, hi." She patted at her hair, but one side stood up like a rooster tail, evidence that it was the side she'd slept on. "Long day," she said, then slapped a hand over her mouth as she yawned. "Had two finals this morning and worked in the afternoon."

She walked over to the stove and turned the gas flame up under the teakettle. "One more final to study for tonight and I'll be done." She looked around the kitchen. "Where are the cookies I made?" she asked Anna.

"They're hidden from impressionable little girls."

Jamie made a face. "Sorry." Shrugging, she turned and looked a little sheepish at Gideon. "I got a little carried away. Hey, at least I didn't do it to Steven."

Gideon nodded gravely. "He's lucky. You could have lopped off his head. The gingerbread man's, I mean."

"I was being childish."

"You're entitled," Anna told her, slipping an arm around her waist and hugging her. "I know you're hurting. Do you want me to fix you a sandwich to eat while you're studying?"

Jamie made a face. "Food won't fix this." She sighed as she fixed her cup of tea. "See you later." She padded off to the living room.

Gideon turned to Anna. "Now, back to my—"

"Aren't you ready yet?" Sarah Rose asked, putting her hands on her hips. "I thought you said we had to go home. I coulda had another cookie."

Anna laughed. "If you had another cookie, you'd pop." She picked up a plastic container from the counter and handed it to her. "Here, some cookies to take with your lunch tomorrow."

Sarah Rose hugged Anna around her waist and turned to slip her hand into Gideon's. "Let's go."

Gideon had hoped to get a good-night kiss as he left but didn't want to do it in front of his daughter. Disappointed, he followed her to the door.

And as she walked out onto the porch, he felt Anna tug on his arm so that he turned to see what she wanted.

And she kissed his cheek.

Grinning, he followed Sarah Rose to the buggy and lifted her inside for the ride home.

❧

Anna held the van door open and watched her grandmother slide across the seat. Bless her, she still had energy at the end of one of their busiest days ever.

Collapsing onto the seat, Anna reached for the door handle and pulled it shut. She was so tired, buckling her seat belt felt like a chore.

Adam, their driver, dropped Leah off first and then drove on to take Anna to her house. Anna's eyes widened as she saw the buggy sitting in the drive.

Gideon stepped out.

"Someone you know?" Adam asked her, giving her a grin.

"I didn't know you were coming over." Anna found she was breathless.

Gideon waved at Adam as he backed the van out of the drive, then he turned to Anna. "Sarah Rose got invited to her grandparents' house tonight."

He bent his head, and their breath mingled. And then he kissed her, tentatively at first and then with more passion until she put her gloved hands on his chest and broke the kiss.

"I thought I'd see if you were free," he said, his breath coming in little ragged puffs of white.

When she shivered, he ran his own gloved hands up and down her arms. "You're cold."

"We can't go inside."

"I know, I know." He touched his forehead to hers, and then he gestured at his buggy. "I have a surprise for you."

"I may fall asleep on you," she warned as they walked toward it. "It's been a very long week."

"I don't think you'll fall asleep." He helped her into the buggy, then went around to climb inside and get it moving.

"Where are we going?"

"You'll see," he said mysteriously.

He watched her face as he pulled into the drive of his friend Ira's farm. A horse was hitched to a sleigh, and when he pranced and pawed the snowy ground, the sleigh bells on his collar jingled.

Anna turned to him and her eyes glowed. "Oh, what a perfect surprise!"

Ira held the horse's reins until they climbed aboard, and Gideon tucked a woolen blanket around their laps. Then Ira handed the reins to Gideon, and they were off, gliding over the snow-covered ground, through the silent woods lit by the full moon rising in the sky.

"Warm enough?" he asked, holding one of her hands on top of the blanket.

"Mmm."

"Hungry?"

"A little. But I don't want to go. This is so lovely."

"Ira's wife packed a basket for us." He gestured at the basket on the floor of the sleigh.

Anna reached down for it and lifted it onto the seat beside her. Inside she found a thermos and cups, several sandwiches wrapped in waxed paper, and a plastic container of Katie's fruitcake cookies.

They stopped in a clearing and feasted on the sandwiches and drank the hot chocolate they found in the thermos. The wind blew gently through the bare branches of the trees and sent the ice on them tinkling like nature's wind chimes.

"This is so romantic," she said with a sigh, relaxing against his arm around her as she gazed up at the velvety night sky. "Did you arrange for the moon to be full tonight, too?"

"Absolutely. I wanted to show you a little romance after what you said the other night. About how you wondered if I just wanted to date you so I'd have a mother for my daughter."

"That," she said, shaking her head. "Sorry."

"No, it's my fault," he told her. "I was trying not to rush you, and maybe I was moving too slow. I didn't want to scare you off."

Gideon looked down at her hand resting in his, then back up at her. "Anna, marry me. I love you, and I want to spend the rest of my life loving you, God willing."

Evidently, he'd shocked her speechless. She stared at him for the longest moment.

"It was an awkward time when we started dating. Marriage season," he explained. "I wanted us to have the time we needed to get to know each other properly."

He took her cold hands in his. "What do you say, Anna? Will you marry me? Can we start our lives together in the fall as man and wife?"

Anna opened the front door to her grandmother's house and felt she stepped back in time to when she was a little girl attending her Christmas Eve gatherings.

Nothing had changed about the warm, delicious scents coming from the kitchen, the laughter and the welcomes she heard from the family and friends assembled within. She set her plate of cookies on the counter and surveyed the bounty of casseroles, breads, and desserts that would be eaten that evening. Then she walked into the living room.

Her *mamm* and *dat* were already there along with Mary Katherine and Jacob and Naomi and Nick and many of her other cousins and other relatives. She went to hug her grandfather, who sat by the fire cradling his newest great-grandchild.

Pine boughs tied with red ribbon and small pots of poinsettias adorned the mantel. There were candles everywhere lending a warm glow. They were the modern flameless ones with batteries hidden in them, Anna noticed, looking like real ones but so much safer with so many *kinner* running around the room.

She said her hellos and gave and received hugs. But as the room filled with those she loved, she wished for the one—actually, two—who weren't there. Gideon and Sarah Rose had their own family to visit, and she wouldn't see them until the next day.

Leah asked everyone to take a seat, and quiet settled over the room. The great-grandchild was taken off for a nap. Grandfather made himself comfortable in the big armchair, opened his worn Bible, and found the story of the birth of the Christ Child.

It was her favorite part of Christmas, this story of that long-ago night when there was no room at the inn and a very special baby had been born.

The room was quiet but for the occasional pop from the sap as the wood burned in the fireplace while her grandfather quietly read the story. His body might be old and feeble, but his voice sounded strong and commanding, filling the room. Anna glanced around and saw that every person there—child to adult—listened, rapt.

Afterwards, Anna helped the other women set out the many dishes that had been brought: ham and turkey and sandwiches and casseroles and cookies . . . my, she'd never seen so many cookies. Her frosted sugar cookies went fast. They always did.

Hours later, after the last Christmas memory had been retold, the last crumb had been eaten, the last wish for a wonderful Second Christmas had been made, the last dish washed, Anna watched the last buggy roll down the road. She closed the door and gazed out at the snow beginning to fall gently.

"Shall we have a cup of tea before bed?"

"That would be nice." She stayed at the window, looking out.

"Missing someone?" her grandmother asked, coming to slip her arm around Anna's waist. "Or maybe two someones?"

"Gideon needed to spend tonight with his parents. They're not really able to get out much these days. Not in the cold weather, anyway."

"But next year . . . maybe you'll be spending it with Gideon and Sarah Rose and his parents."

Anna smiled. Her grandmother wasn't fishing for information—she would ask if she wanted to know something.

The teakettle whistled, and Anna moved quickly to turn off the flame beneath it and pour them both a cup of hot water. Anna breathed in the soothing scent of chamomile as she sat at the table and tried to relax.

"So tell me what's troubling you."

It was a statement, not a question. Her grandmother knew her so well.

"What makes you think I'm troubled?" she asked, bluffing.

Her grandmother just looked at her. "All day today while you've been helping me you've had that little line between your eyebrows, the one you get when you're thinking about something troubling. And you were very quiet. That's not like you."

"Are you saying I talk too much?" Anna asked in what she hoped was a teasing voice.

Leah reached over to take her hand. "You were almost withdrawn tonight."

"I'm just tired. We've been so busy at the shop and then all the cleaning and cooking."

"True. But I also know that anniversary dates of when we lost our husbands are hard, too." She paused, looking at Anna with sympathy. "Especially when they're near a holiday."

Anna pushed her mug away. "Bless Samuel," she said after a moment. "He held on until after Christmas. Tammy, the hospice nurse, was amazed. Said he told her he didn't want Christmas ruined for me if he died that day."

She sighed and rubbed at her forehead, feeling a headache coming on. "Samuel didn't consider that I'd think about him every day. Especially near Christmas. After all, how could I not remember that was the season our dreams died?"

Her grandmother reached over and grasped her hand. "Samuel had a will of iron, and he wanted to live for you even more than for himself. But just before he died he told me he wondered if it was God's will for him to go."

"I know. You told me." That had happened on one of the days when her grandmother and some of her friends had come to the house and insisted Anna take a break. She hadn't wanted to but, under their kind, yet firm insistence, had taken their buggy and gone into town for a few hours. She'd come home to find Samuel talking with her grandmother and noticed that he seemed more at peace than he'd been in a long while.

The other women had fussed over her, making her eat some soup they'd prepared and waved away her thanks for them cleaning up the house and putting some meals in the freezer.

"That's what I figured it was." Still, Leah watched her. "Is everything all right with you and Gideon?"

Anna lifted her chin. "Everything's fine." More than fine, she wanted to say. *He asked me to marry him and I said yes.*

So why didn't I say that? Anna wondered. *And why didn't I say yes to Gideon?*

"You're sure?"

"I'm positive. I'm just tired. And, of course, I'm a little disappointed that he couldn't come tonight. But I'll see him tomorrow."

She yawned and covered her mouth with her hand. "I'm glad you invited me to spend the night. I think I've got just enough energy to climb the steps and fall into your guest bed."

Getting up, she walked to the sink to wash her cup, then did the same when her grandmother handed her the cup she'd used. Together they climbed the stairs to their rooms and exchanged a hug before going into them.

But long after she climbed into the narrow bed in her grandmother's guest room, Anna lay there, exhausted from her day but totally unable to sleep.

⨳

Second Christmas dawned cold and clear.

Visitors began arriving after breakfast bearing good wishes and presents. Last night they had celebrated the birth of Christ, the gift of God to man.

Today was a day to celebrate the joy of the season and the gifts friends and family had made, gifts made from the heart and hands.

Gideon and Sarah Rose showed up at 9:00 a.m. dressed in their Sunday best.

"Hope it's not too early," he said, looking sheepish. "Someone here couldn't wait."

"Merry Christmas!" Sarah Rose cried, holding out a package covered a bit clumsily with wrinkled wrapping paper and a lot of tape. A package almost bigger than she was.

"Thank you!" Anna accepted the gift and bent to hug her. "Come inside. It's cold out!" She carried the box and surreptitiously shook it to see if she could guess what it was, an action that didn't go unnoticed by Gideon.

He grinned at her and took the box. "No guessing."

Sarah Rose bounded into the house. "Leah! I have a present for you!"

Anna smiled at him. "How about some coffee to warm you up?"

His eyes darkened. "How about a kiss?" he asked in a lowered voice.

"Hey, Gideon, are you coming or going?"

John slapped him on the back and eased past him to enter the house.

Shrugging, Gideon stepped inside and slapped the other man on the back. "Coming," he said. "Not letting you eat all the food!"

Anna shook her head and smiled as she shut the door and followed Gideon inside. Like Sarah Rose, he carried packages. Unfortunately, he hadn't put tags on any of them so that she could tell which was meant for her.

"Are you feeling better?" he asked quietly, leaning forward so no one could hear.

Not that anyone paid them any attention. John talked animatedly with Lizzie in the kitchen, gesturing with the cookie in his hand as he spoke. Leah sat with several friends in the kitchen, enjoying tea and plates of goodies.

She nodded. "Why don't you two go into the living room and I'll get your coffee? Sarah Rose, someone gave me a package of white hot chocolate mix. Shall we try it?"

"White hot chocolate?" Gideon asked, looking interested.

"Sorry, should I have asked if you wanted that instead of coffee?"

"I guess men can't drink white hot chocolate."

"We'll still think you're a manly man," Anna teased him. "How about I bring you a cup of each?"

"Sounds great."

Sarah Rose leaned against the counter in the kitchen as Anna heated water in the teakettle. "How can it be chocolate if it's white?"

"I don't know. But it is." Anna poured the hot water into mugs and, on a whim, reached for candy canes sitting in a jar nearby. "To stir with," she told Sarah Rose. "Help me pull the cellophane off them."

Anna had never seen the *kind's* eyes so big. She watched as Anna put the mugs on a tray and pouted only a little when Anna said she couldn't carry the tray because the chocolate was hot and she didn't want to risk Sarah Rose burning herself. When Anna handed her a plate of sugar cookies, the little girl was pacified and proudly carried it into the other room.

Sarah Rose sat on the sofa, took one look at the presents piled on a nearby table, and immediately forgot about the white chocolate.

"Can we open our presents first?" she asked her father.

"Drink your chocolate first. But blow on it to cool it down before you drink it."

"Just one?" Dutifully she blew on the chocolate.

"After."

Sarah Rose looked to Anna, but Anna quickly picked up the plate of cookies and offered it to Gideon. She didn't want to interfere in his parenting . . . well, she'd convinced him to change his decisions regarding his daughter before, but she couldn't do it all the time.

Oh, but it *was* Christmas.

She pushed the plate closer to Gideon.

"Thanks, I have one."

"Have another," she said and, with a tilt of her head in Sarah Rose's direction, raised her eyebrows and sent him a silent message. She saw him look at his daughter, and his lips quirked as he studied her little cheeks puffing in and out as she blew like mad on the hot drink.

"An ice cube would probably make that cool off faster," Anna said casually.

Sarah Rose looked up, her eyes widening. "It would."

"Maybe if you went into the kitchen and asked Leah very nicely she'd give you an ice cube."

The child bounded up and started out of the room, then raced back and hugged Anna, almost making her spill her drink. "*Danki*, Anna!"

She watched her head for the kitchen and then looked at Gideon. She found him watching her.

"I wasn't sure you'd come."

"Why wouldn't I? You said you needed more time. You didn't say no."

Anna nodded. "No, I didn't."

Sarah Rose returned with a cup with two ice cubes. Anna saw Leah peeking out from the kitchen, a mischievous smile dancing on her lips. Apparently, Sarah Rose had a coconspirator in the cooling off the hot chocolate so she could open presents faster.

Anna had wondered if Sarah Rose would like her present of a book on knitting, but the child unwrapped it and immediately became excited, flipping through the pages of projects for children. She chattered with Anna about which project they'd do first while Gideon unwrapped his present, a navy blue cardigan sweater Anna had designed and knitted for him. He took off his suit jacket and immediately put it on, exclaiming over its workmanship and warmth. Anna felt warmed by his appreciation and thought he'd never looked more handsome.

"Now it's your turn," Sarah Rose announced and set her book down. She pushed the box she'd put near Anna's feet closer to her. "This is from *Daedi* and me."

Anna tore at the paper, pulled open the flaps of the box, and dug through wadded up tissue paper to reveal a footstool, the wooden legs beautifully carved, the top covered with a simple cross-stitch pattern with slightly crooked letters.

"*Daedi* made the stool and I did the top," Sarah Rose told her, kneeling beside her on the floor and running a hand over it. "He said you have to be on your feet all day at work so you can put your feet up on this. You can take it to work or keep it at your house."

Anna felt tears well up in her eyes.

"*Daedi*, she doesn't like it!" Sarah Rose cried, distressed.

"I love it," Anna said, reaching to hug her. "I love it so much." She looked at Gideon and saw that he was watching her with that quiet air of his, but the expression in his eyes spoke volumes.

He loved her. She had no doubt of that. And his child sitting beside him, looking at her so expectantly—she loved her, too.

It was the best gift she could have been given.

14

Jamie walked into Stitches in Time frowning, her mouth downturned, and her shoulders slumped.

Curious, Anna followed her into the back room and watched her put away her things.

"Something wrong?"

"I didn't have a very good Christmas." She poured herself a mug of coffee from the percolator on the stove and sat down, wrapping her hands around the mug to warm them. "I know we're supposed to tell ourselves it's the thought that counts but I don't think a lot of thought went into the things I got for Christmas."

Then she looked stricken. "Oh, I didn't mean you or anyone from the shop. I loved my presents I got from all of you."

Her hand went to the purple beret on her head. "I love this. You know I do. And the throw that Mary Katherine made for my sofa is so nice to wrap around me when I study. The quilted placemats Naomi sewed make my hand-me-down wood table look so cute.

"And the little doll that Leah sewed that looked like me . . .", she trailed off. "Well, that was the sweetest, most unexpected present." She frowned. "Okay, that's why I was so disappointed in the other gifts I got. They weren't as thoughtful."

Anna patted her shoulder and reached over to the counter for the box of cinnamon rolls she'd brought to work. She opened the box and held it open under Jamie's nose. "Not everyone has the time or interest in making a gift."

Jamie chose a roll, took a healthy bite of it, and closed her eyes in appreciation. "Yeah, well, one aunt gave me a boxed set of perfume and bath oil. Half of it had evaporated because the box sat in the local drugstore for so long. I told my mom I needed a plain cardigan I could wear with everything, and she got me a ski sweater with reindeer on it for goodness' sake."

Anna sat down. It was early, and the front door was still locked. Once the sign on the door was flipped to "open" there would be a big after-Christmas sale rush. "What are you really upset about?" she asked gently.

"How'd you know it wasn't the gifts?" Jamie asked, staring into the coffee with a glum expression.

"Because I know you."

"I went to my parents for Christmas supper, and all they did was argue. Mom had to tell everyone how hard she'd worked since sunup on the big supper and Dad—well, never mind. Both of them kinda ruined things by bickering."

She sighed. "I was just hoping it would be different this year. That everyone would remember the reason for the season, you know? Sometimes it can be hard to be around family during the holidays."

Then she gasped. "I'm sorry! Talk about putting my foot in my mouth! I didn't mean—"

Anna bent down and hugged her. "It's all right. I know what you meant. You've told me about your family and how they've hurt you, especially during the holidays. You'll change that."

"Oh yeah? How?"

"One day you'll have a family of your own, and you'll make the holiday what it should be. You're already starting by wanting things to be better."

Jamie bit her lip, and then when Anna nodded encouragement, a slow smile bloomed on her face. "You're right. It's when we stay content with what we don't want that things don't change."

She tilted her head and studied Anna. "Love looks good on you."

Anna blinked. "Excuse me?"

"I know the Amish are quiet about dating and getting engaged. But it's sure no secret the way you feel about Gideon and Sarah Rose."

Anna felt a blush steal over her. "No?"

"No," Jamie said definitely. She rose and put her cup on the counter, then turned and hugged Anna. "I'm happy for you."

Tilting her head, she gave Anna a sly look. "I don't suppose you got engaged at Christmas?"

"No."

"Would you tell me?"

Anna grinned. "Maybe."

Mary Katherine rushed into the room, breathless. She shed her coat and put her purse away in a cupboard, then turned back to the others, her expression happy and expectant. "Glad you're all here early. Got something to tell you. Let me get the others."

She walked over to the doorway. "Naomi? Get Grandmother and come back here."

When everyone gathered in the room, she grinned at their expectant faces. "I have an announcement. Jacob and I are going to have a baby!"

"That's your announcement?" Anna couldn't resist asking. "We all guessed that at least a month ago."

Mary Katherine's face fell. "You knew? How did you know?"

"The usual signs," Naomi said dryly. "The secret looks you and Jacob exchange when you think no one's looking. No coffee. The constant eating and the way you've been drinking milk at every meal—especially the drinking of glasses and glasses of milk. And you haven't complained about that monthly visitor that has given you such trouble for ages now."

"I see," Mary Katherine said after a moment. "I had no idea you were so observant."

Leah hugged her. "We're happy for you."

Naomi and Anna and Jamie gathered her in a group hug. "Us, too."

"I don't understand why you waited to tell us," Jamie told her, finishing her coffee and setting her mug in the sink.

Mary Katherine shrugged. "I remember my *mamm* had several miscarriages. I just felt I wanted to wait until we were sure things were okay."

Leah looped her arm around Mary Katherine's waist and hugged her. "You'll be just fine." She glanced at the clock, then at everyone. "It's that time. Are you all ready for the after-Christmas sale?"

Jamie took a deep breath and nodded. "As ready as I'll ever be."

◈

The trees were stark and bare against the gray winter sky. A light snow fell, swirling through the branches and softening them, piling softly against the sharp edges of the tombstones.

Anna carefully picked her way along the path between the stones, noting new ones among the old ones. Up ahead she saw a particularly poignant grave—one that still made her sad—was the grave of Lina, a cousin of hers, who'd died just days after her tenth birthday from a buggy accident.

And just ahead, the simple, unadorned grave of her husband, Samuel.

The sight brought a pang of grief as it always did. She knelt in the snow and brushed the flakes that had accumulated in the letters carved into the stone with her gloved hand: "Husband." Not "Husband" and "Father." She regretted that almost as much as his death. How she'd longed to have a child with this man so full of life and laughter.

How she'd struggled with God's will. Why give her the gift of this *mann* He'd set aside for her only to yank him back to heaven such a short time later?

Yes, heaven. That was where she knew Samuel dwelled now. She knew he was in a better place, but for so long she'd fought against that. She'd wanted him to be with her. She *needed* him to be with her.

Schur, she'd learned to live without him. She didn't know how a person did that when her heart had been ripped out of her body, but somehow she'd learned to do without it.

Until a certain man and his little girl who'd been acting out because she missed her mother came along.

"I've been seeing this man," Anna began. "You remember Gideon. I think it started because we both lost our spouses."

She frowned. "Well, maybe a little. For me it began with a little girl who lost her mother. You see, I didn't just lose you, Samuel. I lost that little girl and that little boy I always wanted to have with you when you died."

She found herself telling Samuel about Sarah Rose, about how she misbehaved to get attention, but what a sweet child she was.

"Jenny said that she fell in love with Matthew's *kinner* before she fell in love with him," she told Samuel. "I fell in love with that little girl before I fell in love with Gideon."

She looked up at the sky and watched snowflakes falling to the ground without a sound. She felt such peace here.

"Yes, I finally did what you insisted I must." She sighed. "Remember, we never argued. Well, except when you wanted to be too protective. I did as you asked. I hope you're happy. I didn't care if I ever met someone else and fell in love."

She frowned and wiped away more of the snow that had fallen on the gravestone. "You remember Gideon. You always liked him. He and Mary were like you and me. We were so involved with each other that we barely saw anyone else." She sighed. "Maybe that was good. You and Mary are already gone. At least we had those years."

Out of the corner of her eye, she saw someone moving in the cemetery. She looked up and realized that Gideon was walking between rows of headstones with Sarah Rose, who couldn't be heard but was clearly chattering a mile a minute.

Then she caught sight of Anna, tugged on her father's hand, and made him look in Anna's direction. Gideon stared at her across the distance that separated them, his gaze serious. He bent his head to listen to Sarah Rose, and then he nodded.

Sarah Rose hurried across the cemetery, careful of stepping on a grave, and stopped in front of Anna. "Hi."

"Hi."

"We came to give this to my *mamm*." She held out a card she'd made, and Anna took it to study it. Sarah Rose had lettered "Happy Birthday" on a piece of folded construction paper and pasted some sparkly fake gems from the craft store on it.

Anna felt her throat tighten as she studied the card. The printing was uneven, the jewels gaudy, the block lettering uneven. But the card showed such love.

She felt tears burn at the back of her eyelids, but she blinked them away and looked up to smile at Sarah Rose. "It's beautiful."

"*Daedi* says *Mamm* can see it up in heaven."

"He's right." Anna looked up at Gideon and found him staring at her.

Sarah Rose grinned, revealing two missing teeth. "I'm going to go give it to her." She looked to her father for permission and, when he nodded, ran off in the direction Anna knew Mary was buried.

"Beautiful afternoon," Gideon said. He shoved his hands in his pockets and gazed around them, then looked back at her. "Aren't you cold?"

Anna nodded. "A little."

He bent and offered his hand to help her up. After a moment's hesitation she took it and, when she rose, was glad for it. The cold ground she'd been sitting on had made her stiff and awkward. She stumbled when she took a step, and his hand tightened, steadying her.

"How come you're holding Anna's hand?" Sarah Rose asked, suddenly at their side.

"Your *daedi* was just helping me up," Anna said quickly. She brushed the snow from her skirts. "I'd better be on my way."

"We got hot stuff with us," Sarah Rose piped up. "It was a special 'casion to come here. Want some?"

The corners of Gideon's mouth quirked. "Special occasion. Coffee for me, hot chocolate for her. Why don't you have some before you leave?"

Anna started to make an excuse but saw the expression in the child's eyes—bright hope. It was Sarah Rose's late mother's birthday, and she wanted to share it. *How can I leave?* Anna asked herself.

"I'd like that," she said and smiled when Sarah Rose slipped her mittened hand into hers. The three of them—Sarah Rose in the middle—walked to Gideon's buggy.

They sat inside it, a quilt covering their legs, and Anna drank coffee from a plastic cup Gideon had brought in the picnic basket. A small handful of tiny marshmallows floated atop the hot chocolate Sarah Rose held. Anna sipped her coffee and felt something thaw in her a little.

❦

"Well, some people say, 'Thank goodness for Friday.' I say, Thank goodness for the New Year." Jamie set the take-out pizza box in the center of the table in the back room, threw herself into a chair, and sighed dramatically. "I had a real hoo doo here today."

"A 'hoo doo'?" Anna asked as she joined her at the table and opened the box. "Mmm, pepperoni." She sat down, picked up a slice, and took a bite.

"You know, it's someone who is so rude and obnoxious you want to say, 'Who do you think you are?'"

Mary Katherine laughed. "You know you wouldn't do that."

"I guess I'm still not in the best of moods," Jamie admitted. She looked at the spread of food on the table: pizza, dips and chips, soft drinks. Even cookies for dessert. "This doesn't quite replace Girls' Night Out. I so wish we could do one again."

She looked at Mary Katherine and then Naomi. "You two had to go and get married. And Anna's next."

"We don't know that," Anna told her. She dug a taco chip into the spinach and artichoke dip.

Leaning over, Jamie opened up a drawer and pulled out a pad of paper and a pencil and began scribbling on it.

"What are you doing?" Naomi leaned forward to pick up her can of Diet Coke.

"Making a list." Jamie chewed on the pencil. "We could still do it sometime."

"And watch a movie and eat pizza and sleep over?"

"Sure we could," Mary Katherine said. "The husbands could do without us one night."

"That would be so great." She scribbled on the pad some more. "I'm sorry to sound like I'm in such a bad mood." She stopped. "It's not been a good last few months. You know I had trouble with the college messing up my student loan. Steven dumped me. I tell you, I'm staying up late to make sure this year leaves for *good.*" She picked up her soft drink. "This is one year I'll really be toasting a New Year."

They lifted their drinks—Mary Katherine's was a bottle of grape juice in deference to her pregnancy—and Jamie made a toast to the New Year being a good one.

Then she set her soft drink can down on the table and frowned.

"What's the matter?" Naomi asked her.

"I'm just thinking of adding another resolution." She studied her list, then looked up. "I've never heard any of you talk about making resolutions."

"I barely know what they are," Anna told her and shrugged. "I do sometimes pray to change how I think about something, but that's not the same thing, is it?"

Jamie laughed and shook her head. "No. A lot of people make a resolution to lose weight, and they eat less and go to the gym. Then they lose their determination. Sometimes that starts about the end of January."

"Why make resolutions then?" Mary Katherine asked.

"Every year you think it'll be different," Jamie told her.

"Do you want to share yours with us?"

Jamie smiled at Naomi's question. "When I get them finished. You know Anna will just drive me crazy asking until I do."

"I will not!" Anna protested. "I've been much better about that sort of thing the past few months."

"She has," Mary Katherine agreed, looking thoughtful. "I think true love has made Anna more mellow."

Anna snorted. She glanced at her cousins, and they were laughing, too, and shaking their heads.

Mary Katherine was the first to stop laughing, and she sat there, regarding Anna with a sober face. "Seriously, you do seem different somehow lately."

"True love," Naomi teased. "It's softened her."

Rolling her eyes, Anna reached for another slice of pizza. "Maybe I've just matured a little." She put the slice on her plate but didn't eat it. "I know it hasn't been easy sometimes to be around me while I've grieved over Samuel."

Mary Katherine's expression softened, and she reached across the table to touch Anna's hand. "We love you. It hurt to watch you grieving. We never minded anything you said or did even when you lashed out. You hurt, so we hurt."

Anna knew she didn't dare take a bite of pizza. She'd never get it around the lump in her throat.

"You know we're just teasing you because we love you." Naomi got up to peek out the door when they heard the bell over it tinkle as someone came in. "It's Grandmother."

"I shudder to think how they'd be if they didn't love me," Anna told Jamie.

"I think it's so neat that you guys are such good friends," Jamie said. "Most of my cousins are scattered around the country. I've barely seen some of them, and there's two I haven't even met. Their families moved, and we never got together."

Jamie reached for the cookie jar and pulled out an oatmeal raisin cookie. She looked at Mary Katherine and grinned. "I think I just got into a good mood."

"All it took was one of my oatmeal raisin cookies?"

"That's it." Jamie looked around the table. "And having lunch with the three of you. Did you know there's a saying that cousins are your first friends?"

"That's true," Naomi agreed.

"Everyone done with this?" Jamie asked. When they all nodded, she pulled a plastic container from a cupboard, filled it with the leftover pizza, and put it in the refrigerator.

"What are you guys whispering about behind my back?"

"We thought we'd see if you'd like to be our honorary cousin," Mary Katherine told her.

Jamie's eyes filled with tears. "Oh, guys, that is so sweet." She went around the table and hugged each of them. "Thank you."

Anna accepted Jamie's hug and watched her return to her seat.

"So, did you all have a nice lunch party?" Leah asked, walking in to put up her jacket and purse.

"The best," Jamie told her. "I'm an honorary cousin."

Leah smiled. "Well, that's wonderful. Does that mean I get to call you my granddaughter?"

"Look at that," Anna said, grinning. "I don't think I've ever seen Jamie speechless."

"Oh, stop," Jamie finally managed to say. "My grandmothers died when I was young. I've always felt I missed out. I would love to have you as a grandmother!"

Leah leaned down to hug her. "I have a surprise for the four of you." She reached into her purse, withdrew four envelopes, and passed them out.

"What's this?" Naomi asked, frowning as she pulled out a check.

"Bonuses," Leah announced. "We had a very good year."

"Wow! Oh wow! This'll cover my last semester tuition. I think you're the fairy godmother," Jamie exclaimed. She jumped up and hugged Leah, then did a little happy dance.

They heard a knock on the shop door.

"I'll get that," Jamie said. "Suddenly I'm in a really good mood!"

"I imagine if I said we're going to close a half hour early that mood would get even better," Leah mused, her eyes alight with mischief.

"Wow! Double wow!" She stopped in front of Leah, gave her a smacking kiss on her cheek, and fairly danced out of the room.

"This is going in savings," Mary Katherine said, tucking the check into a pocket of her dress. "It'll help pay for the hospital if I decide to have the baby there."

"I need to talk with Nick. See if we should put it in the bank or in the business he bought." She looked down at the check, then up at them. "It was expensive for him to buy Abe Harshberger's tour company. I thought it was a big sacrifice for him to stop driving a van, but he looks so happy taking tourists around in a buggy. Maybe it was a good decision after all."

"It's not just his work that makes him happy," Leah told her, setting the teakettle on the stove. "It's you and the church he joined." She turned to Anna. "And what will you do with your bonus?"

"I don't know." Anna fingered the check. "I don't need anything."

Leah walked over and hugged her. "Of course you don't. You've always had everything, even when you thought you didn't. He's watched over you and seen to that."

Anna didn't have to ask who her grandmother meant. She knew the *He* her grandmother referred to was God. She'd forgotten sometimes when she was angry at Him after Samuel died, in her pain of losing the man she loved more than anything.

But now she was beginning to see that God had sent someone else to her, someone who loved her, someone who wanted to walk the path of life with her.

What else could she possibly need?

15

Gideon had always considered himself a patient man.

After all, the work he did required him to take a tiny seed and nurture it for months, hoping that God would help him with a fruitful harvest. The longer that he did the work the more he trusted that God worked with him and all would be well.

But lately, he noticed a growing restlessness in himself. He was so used to working hard, and winter was a time of rest—not just for the fields, but the farmer himself. But after weeks of doing maintenance on equipment in the barn, building new bookshelves for Sarah Rose, and taking care of assorted other winter projects, Gideon still had pent-up energy and wanted to be outside.

There was a change in the weather. He noticed it the moment he stepped outside. Long experience had him scanning the sky—lightening a little earlier each day. He stood there, listening to a whippoorwill call. Some said there would be no frost after you heard a whipporwill. Avid birders—and many of his friends in the community were—said so. He only knew that he'd seen a flock of Canadian geese fly north the day before, and that was a sure sign, one he knew to be true.

Oh, and the reappearance of his elderly neighbor who was just home from Pinecraft, Florida. *Snowbird*, he thought, and smiled. The man said his arthritic old bones couldn't take Pennsylvania winters any longer and so he basked in the Florida sunshine with his wife.

Gideon bent to scoop up a handful of the rich earth beneath his feet. He sniffed it, formed a ball with it to test its texture, then let it drift through his fingers.

"Are you playing in the dirt?" Sarah Rose said behind him.

He turned and saw her nightgown peeking out from under the hem of her coat. Rubbing his hands together, he reached for her. "I'm going to get some dirt on you, little one!"

Sarah Rose shrieked and backed up, but when she tried to run, one slipper got caught in a muddy patch and she landed on her fanny. Laughing, she held out her arms. "Help me up!"

He bent and let her climb on his back like the little limber monkey that she was and began walking the fields with her. She looped her arms around his neck and pressed her cheek to his. "Are we gonna go see Anna today?"

"*Ya*," he said, watching where he was going. He knew the fields like the back of his hand, but you never knew what could have dropped or blown into them overnight. And he had precious cargo hanging on his back.

"What are we gonna do?"

"What would you like to do?"

"Go on a picnic."

He considered that. It was still a little cool for a picnic, but they could bundle up. "Okay. After we do our chores, we'll make up a picnic lunch."

Gideon knew without looking that she probably made a face at the mention of chores. Sarah Rose didn't particularly care for the ones at the start of the day. But his agreeing with her plans kept her from objecting about doing them. That, and the knowledge that they both had chores and everyone had to do their part.

"Maybe we should just put some carrot sticks in the picnic basket for you today. I think you've gained some weight since we did this." He reached behind him and tickled her at the waist.

She giggled and wriggled away, causing him to grab her so he wouldn't drop her. "I'm a growing girl," she said. "That's what my grandmother says."

"A growing dumpling," he pretended to complain.

"Oh, a squirrel!" she cried. "Let me down! Let me down!"

He did as she asked and watched her scamper after the bushy-tailed animal. "Don't get too close! I don't want it to bite you!"

"I won't!" she called back over her shoulder. But at the rate she was running, Gideon figured she could overtake the squirrel if she wanted.

She vanished into the woods that bordered the field, and he felt a moment's unease. Then she yelped, and he took off after her, his heart in his throat. Had she caught the squirrel? Were snakes out yet?

When he drew closer, she stepped out of the woods, clutching something white in her hands. "Lookit this!" she cried, holding out her hands. "Snowdrops! You told me once they were *Mamm's* favorite!"

"They were," he agreed quietly, seeing so much of Mary in her face then—the glow in her eyes, the pink in her cheeks. The sweet lift of her lips in her smile.

"Can we take them to her on the way to the picnic? Anna won't mind. I see her in the cemetery sometimes. She goes to see Samuel, remember?"

He nodded. Indeed, he remembered. His thoughts went back to the last time he'd seen her there, when he and Sarah Rose had gone to leave the birthday card for her mother.

"When did you see her there?" he asked casually. It was wrong to pump the child, but he couldn't help it. He'd been troubled by seeing Anna sitting on the cold ground that day and wondered how long she'd been there.

"Other day," Sarah Rose said, lifting the flowers to her nose to sniff at them.

Gideon thought about that as he walked. Normally, he wasn't a person who tried to rush things. That kind of personality couldn't be a farmer. Whoever heard of a farmer who waited impatiently for a seed to sprout, who dug it up to see how it was going?

No, he was a patient, steady man. Mary had even teased him for how he was patient to a fault.

Yet he knew part of his restlessness came from wanting things to move along a little faster with Anna. They spent as much time together as they could, but he wanted more than that. He wanted them to share a roof, share a life, not this seeing each other for an hour or two every other day or so.

He wanted more with her. The trouble was, along with that restlessness he still had a niggling doubt that she was as ready as he was for marriage.

Together, he and Sarah Rose took care of the morning chores, and after washing up, they put together a picnic lunch in the kitchen. Leftover roast beef sandwiches on thick slices of bread, some tart Granny Smith apples, peanut butter cookies they had made the day before. He tucked in a carton of milk for Sarah Rose and a thermos of coffee for himself and Anna.

"*Daedi* said he wanted to wait to get you," Sarah Rose said when Anna opened her door.

"It's not polite to show up early," Gideon said, giving his daughter a stern look. "After all, when we made our plans earlier in the week we said eleven o'clock."

"It's all right," Anna said with a smile. "I was waiting for you."

She turned to put the knitting she held in her hands in a basket on a table near the door. "Do you want to come in?"

"A kitten!" Sarah Rose cried as one wound itself around her feet. "It's a kitten! When did you get a kitten?"

"It's not mine. She showed up one day, and she's been sleeping in the barn at night. I was about to feed her. Do you want to do it?"

"Can I?" Sarah Rose looked at Gideon with a pleading expression.

"So long as you're careful and don't let it scratch you. It's a wild thing, remember?"

"I didn't get scratched by the squirrel this morning," she reminded him and followed Anna into the kitchen, accidentally bumping into her when she followed too closely and Anna stopped to get a can of tuna from the kitchen cupboard.

"And don't get any ideas about asking if you can take her home," he warned.

The two females exchanged a look, and then Anna handed Sarah Rose a saucer to put the tuna in. She carried it outside and carefully put it down, then sat on the porch watching the kitten wolf the food down.

"Gideon," Anna began.

"No," he told her, not taking his eyes off his daughter's hand reaching tentatively toward the kitten's head.

"You don't even know what I was going to say."

He turned to look at her. "Sure I do."

"But—"

"No," he said mildly.

"Every child should have a cat or a dog."

"No."

"But it's so little trouble."

"Are you going to take care of it?"

"I'm not living at your house."

"Exactly." He watched her blush.

"You know I can't come there too often or people will talk."

He stepped closer to her and watched the soft rose deepen in her cheeks. "And you know people would be happy to see the widow and the widower getting together."

Anna stepped back, indicating with her glance toward Sarah Rose that she could see and hear them.

"She hasn't noticed anything since that kitten walked up to her," he said, reaching for her hand. He stroked it with his. It felt so good to hold it. "Fireworks could be going off and all she'd see is a little gray kitten."

"She's going to work on you," she warned. "And I notice that she usually gets her way with you."

He shook his head. "That's not true." He watched her press her lips together to keep from smiling. "Well, only when it's something that's good for her."

"*Schur*," she said, drawing out the word.

They pulled Sarah Rose away from the kitten with the promise she could feed her again later when they brought Anna home, and then it was off to the picnic with a side trip to the cemetery first.

And all the way there Gideon wondered if there was a way to find out whether Anna was any more ready to become engaged than the last time they'd talked about it.

"You're sure you don't mind stopping here?"

Gideon brought the buggy to a stop at the cemetery, then got out and helped Sarah Rose down.

"Of course not." Anna watched the child scamper off to her mother's grave, the snowdrops clutched in one hand. "I think it's so sweet that she wants to do things like this."

He got back into his seat and searched for the right words. "Did you want to go see Samuel?"

She smiled slightly. "That would be a little hard."

Feeling his face redden, he cleared his throat. "Of course. I meant his grave."

"No." She turned to him. "Why would I want to do that?"

"I don't know," he said, and he shrugged. "We're here." He wanted to look away, but she was studying him and looking puzzled.

Sarah Rose came racing back. "I gave Samuel some flowers," she told Anna as she clambered into the backseat. "I didn't think *Mamm* would mind if I gave him some of hers."

"Of course, she wouldn't," Anna hurried to say. "That was a very nice thing to do for Samuel." She turned from smiling at Sarah Rose and stared straight ahead, her mind swirling with questions about why Gideon asked if she wanted to visit Samuel's grave. It didn't seem like a casual question . . .

Sarah Rose chattered nonstop about the picnic on their way. It was a blessing in a way because Anna didn't have to talk to Gideon.

They spread an old quilt on the ground in a little park overlooking a pond. They ate the sandwiches, the apples, the cookies, and though she made a face at drinking milk, Sarah Rose did so while Anna and her father drank coffee.

Then, after a quick promise to her father that she'd be careful and not fall into the pond, she ran down to the water's edge clutching a leftover sandwich for the ducks.

"Why did you ask me if I wanted to visit Samuel's grave?"

Gideon looked up from packing the remains of the picnic. "It was just a simple question. I know you visit."

It was just a feeling, something she couldn't explain. There was something bothering him, and she couldn't let it go. "Are you concerned about me visiting it?"

"Of course not. I visit Mary's grave."

"For yourself—or for Sarah Rose's sake?"

He jerked his head up, and the lid slammed on the picnic basket. "What kind of question is that?"

"It's just a question. If we have them, we should be able to ask them, shouldn't we?"

Gideon stared at her for a long, long moment. And then he sighed and nodded.

"So why are you bothered by my visiting Samuel's grave?"

"*Bothered* is too strong a word," he said slowly. "I'm just wondering if you're really ready to date."

Her breath caught. She let it out. "That's a strange question to ask all of a sudden." She searched his face but couldn't read his expression. "Have you forgotten that I warned you that I didn't feel I was ready when we first started seeing each other? We agreed we'd be friends, and we'd take things slowly. It doesn't feel like you're doing that."

"Maybe I haven't," he told her in a low voice, avoiding her eyes. "Turned out to be harder than I thought it would be."

Then he turned to look at her, his eyes intense. "Someone told me that you visit Samuel's grave a lot."

"Who would say such a thing? And what's 'a lot'?"

He looked up to check on Sarah Rose and saw her edging closer to the pond. "Excuse me—Sarah Rose! Step back from the pond! Now!"

Turning back to Anna, he rubbed the back of his neck. "Doesn't matter who said it. Is it true?"

Was Martha—a busybody if there ever was one—gossiping again? She'd caused Naomi some problems once.

"I know how I feel about you and I think you know it," he said. "But two people have to want the same thing. Take some time and let's get together and talk later this week when there aren't little ears around." He paused, looking for Sarah Rose again and nodding when he saw her still standing by the pond.

Stunned, Anna didn't know what to say. Who'd have thought that a casual picnic would turn into a tense discussion of where their relationship was heading—or not heading?

He got to his feet and then held out a hand to help her up. They walked to the water's edge and saw that Sarah Rose was studying her reflection in the still pond. She smiled when she saw their reflections on either side of her, and then her smile faded. Her gaze went from one to the other, and she frowned.

"What's wrong?"

"Nothing," Anna said quickly, and she gave Gideon a warning glance. She wasn't having the child upset. "It's just time to go home now."

Sarah Rose turned and scanned their faces. She slipped her hand into one of her father's and one of Anna's and started walking toward the buggy.

Feeling helpless, Anna exchanged glances with Gideon over her head. He shook his head, his expression pained. As if she'd say anything!

Usually, no one got a word in edgewise because of Sarah Rose's chatter. Today, she stayed silent, occasionally giving them a worried look. *How quickly she picks up on tension*, Anna thought.

Gideon pulled into Anna's drive and stopped. Before she could get out, Anna sensed movement behind her and felt Sarah Rose's arms slip around her neck.

"I'm sorry I was bad!"

Anna turned around and saw the tears on the little girl's face. "You weren't bad! I just had to get home. Besides, it looks like it's going to rain soon." She hated not telling the truth, but it seemed justified here. "I'll see you in a day or two, all right?"

Seeing Sarah Rose about to wipe her nose on her sleeve, Anna quickly found a tissue and handed it to her. "Now, no more silly talk."

"I'll walk you to the door," Gideon said.

Anna shook her head. "No, there's no need. You both need to get home. It's good we left when we did."

"I love you."

The words stopped her. Anna turned and smiled at Sarah Rose. "And I love you."

Anna let herself into the house and closed the door behind her. After taking off her jacket and hanging it up, she put the teakettle on to boil. Feeling chilled, she grabbed the knitted shawl from the peg on the wall and wrapped it around her shoulders. The house felt even emptier than usual after the time she'd spent with Gideon and Sarah Rose. People were fond of saying alone didn't mean lonely but today . . . well, she felt lonely.

Things had been good before he'd brought up his question about whether she was ready to date. Where had that come from anyway? If she hadn't been interested in him, if she could never be able to commit to another man, she wouldn't have toyed with his affections. She cared about him and wouldn't do that to him. Obviously, since Samuel had been the one and only man in her life since they'd been schoolmates, it had been horrible for her . . . it had only felt like her heart had been ripped out of her chest. But that inexperience with men . . . she didn't know how to toy with a man's affections, to see him and be insincere about one day being married to him.

She poured hot water into her mug when a thought suddenly struck her: maybe Gideon was the one who was having cold feet and didn't want to see her anymore. . . . Jamie was always complaining that the men she knew blamed her when they broke up with her. What if that was what Gideon was preparing to do?

Restless, she wandered into the living room to her favorite overstuffed chair and sat there, her legs tucked under her, cradling her mug of tea in her cold hands.

Not quite warmed up by the tea, she set the empty mug on the table beside the chair, pulled one of Naomi's quilts over her lap, and reached for her knitting in the basket by the chair. Knitted baby hats with floppy bunny ears were going fast at the shop since Easter wasn't far off.

Her knitting needles clicked, and the pink bunny ears grew. But as the minutes passed, the events of the day came back to haunt her, and she sat in the growing dark, her knitting lying in her lap.

16

Mary Katherine was sitting on the bench in front of the shop when Anna, Naomi, and their grandmother arrived one morning.

"Did you lose your key?" Anna asked as she walked up. Then she stopped and peered at her cousin. "Are you all right?"

"No," Mary Katherine said through gritted teeth. "But turn and wave at Jacob so he'll leave."

Anna did so, but then she turned and sat down on the bench. "Why do you want him to leave if you're not all right?"

"Something wrong?" Naomi asked as she approached.

"Turn and wave at Jacob!" Mary Katherine hissed.

Naomi did as requested, but then demanded, "What is going on?"

"I just can't walk right now, but if Jacob knows, he'll insist I go home."

"But if you're not feeling well—"

She closed her eyes and seemed to withdraw from them. "I'm not sick. It's just that the baby is kicking so hard!"

"That's good," said Leah, patting her shoulder. "It means he's healthy and strong."

"And going to kick his way out of here," Mary Katherine said, opening her eyes. "There, he's stopped. I'm fine now."

She frowned and batted her arms at her cousins as each of them took one of her arms to help her up from the bench. "Stop that! I'm pregnant, not an invalid!"

Before they could get her inside, a buggy pulled up in front of the shop.

"Good morning, ladies!"

Mary Katherine turned. "I saw you leave!"

"I thought it was kind of suspicious that everyone was waving to me and you weren't going inside the shop. What's going on?"

She rolled her eyes. "Nothing. Don't you need to get going? You have a lot of work on the farm."

"I need you to tell me the truth."

"The baby's just really active, that's all."

Jacob looked at Leah. "Is that all?"

"That's what she says. We have to take her word for it."

He got out and walked around the buggy to stand before her. "You tossed and turned all night, and you were abnormally quiet this morning on the way here."

"I'm just uncomfortable," she insisted. "That's how pregnant women get sometimes."

"We'll see," he said, scooping her up into his arms.

"Jacob!"

"I'm taking her to the doctor," Jacob told Leah. "I'll bring her back after, if the doc says she's okay."

Mary Katherine argued with him all the way to the buggy, but Jacob turned a deaf ear to her. As they drove away, she stuck her head out and called to them that she'd be back.

"Talk about romantic," Naomi said, and she sighed.

"Maybe."

Naomi blinked at her. "I think he was showing he cared about her."

Anna shrugged. Seemed to her that he wasn't listening to Mary Katherine. She had a right to decide how she felt. Then she told herself that she shouldn't be critical of Jacob. He was just being caring. There was no comparison with Gideon deciding things.

"Anything wrong?" Leah asked, sitting on the bench and patting the place beside her. "You've been quiet the last few days."

"Everything's fine." She looked around her. "Spring's finally here."

Leah nodded. "Gideon will be busy planting soon."

Anna nodded.

"He didn't come for a knitting lesson this past week."

"No, he couldn't make it. He dropped off Sarah Rose. But you know that." She turned to her grandmother and sighed. "You and your questions. You're relentless."

"I've heard your cousins call you that when you wanted to know something." Leah smiled. "Where do you think you got it?"

Anna laughed and shook her head. "Not from my mother. She's one of the quietest women I know."

"True." Leah's smile faded, and she patted Anna's hand. "What's happened, *kind*? Are things not working out with Gideon?"

"I don't know. Something happened last time." She twisted one of the ribbons of her *kapp* around her finger. "He started saying he wasn't sure that I was ready to be dating him because he'd heard I often went to the cemetery to see Samuel."

Leah's eyes widened.

"I hadn't heard that. And I think someone would have told me. They'd have been worried about you and think I should know."

"Exactly." She hesitated. "I got to wondering if maybe he's changed his mind and he's looking for a reason to back away."

She put her hand to her mouth when her lips trembled. "I'm not going to feel sorry for myself. I think only of him, but if he's wanting to back away, then, well, I have to wonder if he's not the man God set aside for me." She shook her head. "I'm confused."

"Well, don't get ahead of yourself," Leah cautioned. "No relationship goes perfectly smoothly."

"Mine with Samuel did." Anna lifted her chin. "We never fought."

Leah grinned. "That's because he adored you and let you have your way."

Anna compressed her lips, and then she laughed and nodded. "Mostly." She sighed. "And maybe I'm just like so many other widows who remember our late husbands in a better light than we did when they were alive.

"Samuel was everything to me. He was a friend first and a protector of me, stepping in to make another boy stop teasing me in school, and then one day we looked at each other and had that first kiss."

She blushed. "And I knew then that I wanted to be with him for the rest of my days."

She drew in a deep breath. "You know, I was so happy with Samuel. I'm not willing to settle for less. God sent someone along for you. He'll do it for me."

Leah smiled and squeezed Anna's hand. "Good for you."

A woman walked up and stopped in front of them. "Oh, I must be early. I thought you were open at eight."

"We are. Naomi's inside, and we'll be right in, Mrs. Selby."

"No hurry," she said. "Oh, look, she's in the window." She walked inside the shop.

"Window?" Anna said, momentarily confused. Then, when she glanced over her shoulder, she saw Naomi wave, then go back to redoing the display window.

"It's time to get to work."

⸎

As mistakes went, Gideon figured he'd made one of the biggest of his life.

Not only did he miss Anna, but his daughter had been registering her disapproval of him all week.

He stirred the soup in the pot on the stove and shut off the gas flame beneath it. "Supper's ready. You'll have to finish your homework after."

The night before, he'd tried making her finish, but all that had accomplished was to make him wait a half hour for his meal.

Her lower lip stuck out as she scribbled on her paper. "I'm almost finished."

"Five minutes," he compromised. "If you're not done then, we'll eat and you can do your homework and go to bed."

She looked up, her eyes stormy. "No bedtime story?"

"Not if there's no time."

The lower lip pushed out even more.

"Watch out, you'll trip over it," he murmured.

"What?"

He bit back his grin. "Nothing."

She lifted her head and sniffed. "What are we having?"

Here it was. The big question. So far this week he hadn't pleased her once. "We're having Three Bear Soup and grilled cheese sandwiches."

She opened her mouth to object and then, to his surprise, shut it. Her pencil zoomed across the paper, and one minute later she was done and closing her notebook. She got up and started setting the table. When she put three bowls on the table, his heart sank. Would it be Anna she hoped would appear for supper?

Or the imaginary kitty she'd invented when he hadn't let her bring Anna's kitten home?

"Who's the bowl for?" he asked, hoping she wasn't going to bring Anna up again.

"It's not for her. It's for Kitty."

"Sarah Rose, put the bowl back. You don't have a kitty, and if you did, it wouldn't be allowed to eat at the table."

She stared at him for a long moment and then, with a long-suffering sigh, picked the bowl up and flounced over to the cupboard to put it back.

Gideon carried the pot of soup to the table, then piled the sandwiches onto a plate and set it next to the soup. They took their seats and bent their heads in prayer, then he served her soup and half a sandwich.

"Why do they call it Three Bear Soup?" he asked as he tasted a spoonful.

"Because it's what the three bears had on the stove when Goldilocks went to their house," she said, taking a big bite of her sandwich. "And it wasn't too hot; it wasn't too cold; it was just right. Just like the beds." She slurped some from her spoon.

Before he could admonish her on her table manners, she smiled at him. "It's good, all warm in my tummy."

He decided to hold off on the table manners lecture. Maybe his making her one of her favorite meals was thawing her out a little.

"Are you going to see Anna tomorrow after church?"

"I am. Do you want another half sandwich?"

"Yes." Then, "Thank you," she added. "Where are we going?"

"You're going to visit with your grandmother, remember? She told me she has something planned for the two of you to do."

"I'd rather go with you and Anna."

"Sorry, not this time."

"But why?"

She was *so* persistent, he couldn't help thinking for probably the thousandth time since she'd started talking. Where had she gotten such a trait? He wasn't like that. Mary hadn't been.

"Sometimes adults need to spend time with each other."

She frowned and started to say something, but he got up quickly, went to the refrigerator, and pulled a carton of ice cream from the freezer. A war immediately raged in his daughter—sulkiness warred with an interest in the ice cream Gideon had brought to the table.

"Do you want some?" he asked her casually as he filled a dish with scoops of butter pecan.

"Yes!" She got up and took their plates to the sink.

By the time she came back to the table, he'd set the dish at her place.

"Kitty just said she wanted some."

Grateful for the change in subject, Gideon got a saucer from the cupboard, placed a small scoop on it, and set it next to Sarah Rose's. "Just this once," he said.

"Sarah Rose told me you made her Three Bear Soup last night," Jenny Bontrager said as Gideon went into the kitchen after church. "I'm glad she likes it so much."

"I appreciated you giving me the recipe," he told her, bending to hug his daughter. "It's easy to make."

She smiled. "I wasn't the best cook when I got married." She gave her daughter Annie a sharp glance. "No comments from the peanut gallery."

"Peanut gallery?" Sarah Rose looked up at Gideon. "Why is she calling you that?"

Annie laughed. "*Mamm* talks a little funny sometimes. She was *Englisch* before she became Amish."

"I do not!" But Jenny was smiling as she worked with the other women to set out the after-church light meal.

"But what's a peanut gallery?" Sarah Rose, persistent as ever, wanted to know.

Gideon couldn't help thinking he wished it was as easy to get Anna to forgive him as it had been Sarah Rose last night. If only Three Bear Soup, grilled cheese sandwiches, and butter pecan ice cream . . .

Instead, she regarded him with some wariness as they got into his buggy after church and set out for a ride. He glanced at her a couple of times as they pulled away from the Bontrager house, and he felt her look at him.

"I brought a picnic lunch," he told her. "Or we can go to a restaurant if you'd rather."

"No point wasting food."

He nodded. "Let's go to that little park with the pond."

When she stiffened, he remembered that was the park where they'd had the picnic. Maybe it wasn't wise to take her back there . . .

"Wherever you want is fine," she said before he could suggest someplace else.

Gideon wondered if it was a good sign that she was being agreeable. But she didn't smile and didn't say anything. He didn't think that boded well for their discussion.

They spread a quilt on the grass. He put sandwiches he knew were her favorites and a pile of potato chips on paper plates. But she didn't eat.

His mouth suddenly dry, Gideon twisted off the cap on a bottle of water and drank. Okay, this wasn't going to be easy. But it had to be done.

"Anna, I'm sorry for what I said last week," he said simply. Taking off his hat, he ran a hand through his hair. "I've been feeling restless lately. It didn't seem that things were moving as fast as I was hoping. So I figured you were holding back because you weren't ready."

"Gideon, we talked about taking things slowly right at the start."

"I know."

"And even when everything was moving smoothly and we were madly . . ." she hesitated, then lifted her chin and looked at him directly, "even if we were madly in love, we couldn't get married until the fall, after the harvest."

"I know."

"You hurt me," she blurted out. "You decided something about me that wasn't true based on what someone said about me. That wasn't fair. You told me. You didn't ask."

"You're right."

"One person's not supposed to be the sole decider in a relationship."

He hadn't ever heard the word *decider* used before, but what he remembered of her in school was that she loved to read. Besides, he knew what she meant. He'd decided—he'd assumed—something that day when he'd *told* and not *asked* if she went to the cemetery to visit Samuel's grave often.

That assuming . . . suddenly he thought he might know how to get her to forgive him.

"I made an assumption," he told her, emphasizing the first the three letters in the word. "So we know what I made of myself."

He saw the corners of her mouth lift just a little. But then she pressed her lips together, and he knew she wasn't going to let him off the hook so easily.

"You always were good at charming your way out of things."

"Just our teacher. Not Mary. She didn't let me get away with anything. And I can tell you won't, either."

She lowered her eyes, then looked out at the pond. "You talked about feeling restless. About being impatient. Maybe it's because you should date someone else."

"*What?*"

"Maybe you should date someone else."

"Why would I want to do that?" Feeling panic rise up inside him, Gideon searched her face, trying desperately to understand what was going on.

"I've been thinking about what you said," she told him. "Maybe you're feeling restless because things aren't going as well as you'd hoped, and you're worried you won't have someone to marry in the fall."

"Now don't go putting words in my mouth!" His voice was sharper than he wanted it to be, but he couldn't help it.

She smiled slightly. "How does it feel?"

He scowled. "That's not funny."

"Can you understand how it felt to have someone just decide?"

"I didn't think," he admitted.

"I wouldn't do that to you," she said quietly. "I wouldn't let you think I cared about you and still be pining for Samuel." She sighed. "You know there's never a point where you say to yourself that you're over someone you love and you're ready to move on. But I did open my heart to you, Gideon, and it feels like you just handed it back."

She got to her feet and walked down to the water's edge, standing there with her arms wrapped around herself.

Her words hung in the air between them, damning him. He sensed that what he said next would make all the difference between them, and it terrified him. She'd said he was good at getting out of trouble, and he had been when he was younger and got into trouble at school.

But he wasn't as charming, as glib as she thought—at least not as she seemed to think. Maybe he'd settled down a bit because he'd married Mary and they'd made a home on the farm and started a family. Losing Mary had shaken him to the core, sobering him, making him appreciate the life they'd created together. Making him know that he wanted the joy and yes, even marriage again.

But Anna hadn't seen that side of him. They'd bonded in the beginning over shared pain of losing a spouse and her helping him figure out how to deal with Sarah Rose's difficulty with losing her mother.

Then he'd wanted to get past that and be a couple starting their own story. Their late spouses would always be a part of them, but it was time to write a new chapter.

He wondered whether he'd been a little jealous of Samuel, wanting Anna to think only of him once they started dating. So he'd jumped to the conclusion that she'd been visiting Samuel's grave often. He was surprised that she hadn't said he had a double standard—he visited Mary's, but maybe she realized that lately it was more for Sarah Rose's sake so that she could leave cards and flowers for her mother.

Gideon got to his feet and walked down to join her. "I'm sorry," he said quietly. "It wasn't fair of me to question whether you're ready to be dating. You're right—you wouldn't do that to me or to Sarah Rose."

He held out his hand, hoping she'd take it. To his relief, she did, although he sensed her reluctance.

"And I don't want to hear any more about maybe I should date someone else," he said. "You're the one for me. I'm going to prove it to you."

When he saw her eyes widen with surprise, he knew he was going to win her trust again.

And there could be no more worthy pursuit.

∽❧

"I can climb up myself," Sarah Rose told him as he lifted her into the buggy. "I'm a big girl."

"You are," he agreed. "But let your *daedi* enjoy helping you. After all, your hands are full carrying that basket and your tote. By the way, what do you have in it?" It was too small for her knitting—that was why she had the tote bag slung over her shoulder.

"Kitty is going with us to the store," Sarah Rose told him. "I put a ball of yarn in the basket for her so she could play with it while we knit."

He didn't know what to say. No matter how he'd talked to her she was firm in her belief that she had a new kitten. She talked to it, played with it, even said she was taking it to bed with her at night. Since it was imaginary, he could hardly tell her she couldn't tuck it in with her under her quilt . . .

And he couldn't tell her the kitten couldn't go into the shop, either.

Anna just smiled when he came into the back room where she was taking a break before the lesson.

"I think that's sweet," she told him, pouring him a mug of coffee before she turned back to stir a pan of hot chocolate.

"What's sweet?" asked Thelma. "Other than that adorable little girl of yours, Gideon."

She nodded when Anna held up the coffee pot, silently asking Thelma if she wanted a cup.

He rolled his eyes. "Well, thank you, but she's a bit mischievous this past week. She's decided she has a kitten."

"Oh, well, that's nice. It's good for a child to have a pet. Teaches them responsibility."

Anna chuckled. "It's an imaginary one. Gideon doesn't want her to have a kitten yet."

"Oh, I see," Thelma said. "Well, one of my kids had an imaginary pet, too. But as I remember it, it was a dragon, and my son said it ran away about six months after it moved into his room."

She poured a generous amount of cream into her coffee and turned. "Well, hello, Sarah Rose."

"Hello," the girl said politely. "Anna, can I have some hot chocolate?"

"May I?" her father prompted automatically.

"May I?"

"Of course. I've already started it for you."

Thelma sneezed. She plucked up a paper napkin from the coffee tray and dabbed at her nose.

"God bless you," Anna, Gideon, and Sarah Rose told her.

"Achoo! Achoo!" Thelma said loudly.

"Goodness, are you all right?" Anna asked her.

Thelma nodded. "Why, yes," she said, nodding. "Hmm. I don't usually sneeze like this except when there's a cat around. I'm allergic, you know."

Anna and Gideon exchanged a look. "No, I didn't know," Anna told her.

Sarah Rose moved the basket she was carrying in one hand to behind her back.

"Well, I'm going to go sit down out in the shop," Thelma said. "Lettie's here and I'm dying to find out how her vacation was."

Anna set the cup of hot chocolate on the table for Sarah Rose. "Be careful. It's hot."

Nodding, Sarah Rose took a seat and blew on the hot drink, smiling when her breath made the little marshmallows Anna had added bob and swirl around on the surface.

A few minutes later, after the three of them had finished their hot drinks, Sarah Rose stood. "I'm going to leave Kitty here, so Thelma won't sneeze."

Anna and Gideon looked at each other, and he nodded. "Good idea."

They waited until she walked out of the room and then turned to each other and laughed.

"*Kinner*," said Gideon.

"*Kinner*," she agreed.

He reached for her hand and held it, smiling at her until Leah came into the room to tell them that all of the class had arrived.

17

$\mathcal{A}$nna!"

She glanced up from her knitting to see where the voice was coming from.

"Anna!"

Getting up, Anna walked toward the front display window where she found Naomi kneeling inside.

"An—oh, there you are!"

"Why are you yelling?"

Naomi grinned. "Didn't know where you were."

"So instead of going to look for me . . ."

"Hey, I'm tired. I saved myself some steps by not going to look for you. It's been a long week helping Nick with some paperwork for his business. Do you have the knit caps for the display window?"

"I'll get them. I just finished another one last night." She went for the box and returned with them. "You decide which ones to use. I can't. I don't know if I like the ones with the bunny ears or the cupcake hats better."

"Let's do some of both." Naomi handed her a doll they used to display the hats in the window. "Has Mary Katherine come in yet?"

Anna shook her head. "She had a doctor appointment this morning, remember? She should be here soon."

"Can you help me?"

"Sure."

They worked together to place Mary Katherine's woven vests—perfect for *Englisch* women to wear for warmth over blouses and turtlenecks. Naomi had made several special quilts that were lighter weight and a couple of tote bags with a quilt square on the front. Anna's baby hats that looked like little cupcakes were always popular, but she added more of the little Easter-themed hats after the few she'd knitted last year had sold quickly. The little hats with bunny ears were quick and easy to knit, and she enjoyed thinking about the babies and toddlers who'd wear them.

Naomi sat back on her heels in the bay window. "Mary Katherine should have been back by now."

"I know." Anna frowned, then she turned to pick up the fabric wall hangings Jamie had made that were like little seasonal pictures composed of fabric scraps.

"Here are the new dolls I promised you for the window," Leah announced. She handed over a box filled with them and glanced at the contents of the window. "Nice work. Should get the attention of people walking past."

The bell over the door rang as a customer walked in. Leah hurried over to help her.

"How's Gideon?"

"Fine. Busy with spring planting. I haven't seen much of him lately."

Naomi touched her arm. "Is everything okay?"

"Fine. I'm just taking things slowly. It's a big step."

"You don't have to tell me that."

Anna went still. "Should I be asking you if everything is all right?"

"With Nick and me? Yes, things are great." She smiled. "He's sweet and thoughtful and very gentle with me. Nothing like John."

It was a narrow miss, Anna thought as she watched her cousin arrange her grandmother's dolls in the window. Naomi had almost convinced herself that she had to stay with her former fiancé even though he was showing signs that he'd be an abusive *mann*.

"How did you do it?"

Naomi's eyebrows went up. "Do what? Break things off with John or marry Nick?"

"Both."

"I wasn't willing to be in an abusive marriage," Naomi said. "I deserve more than that."

"But it can't have been easy to trust after being with someone like John."

"It wasn't. You know that. It took a long time."

"Are you having trouble trusting, Anna?"

Anna's mouth nearly dropped open. She shouldn't have been surprised at her cousin's perception. The three of them had always been closer to each other than the many cousins in the family.

Looking up, Anna met Naomi's concerned gaze. "Yes." She sighed. "It's hard when it was Samuel and me for so long." She hesitated. "I think Gideon's concerned that I'm not ready for a relationship yet. That I'm not over Samuel."

She folded her arms across her chest. "I hate when people talk like you can ever be over someone who was such an important part of your life! How can you be? They'll always be a part of it. You just learn that you have to go on. You have to find a way to live without them."

She stopped and gazed at the people passing the window, on their way to shop or find a good restaurant for some Amish food.

"And if you loved someone and felt that love from them, how could you not want that again? If nothing else, Samuel told me he wanted me to marry again."

"Do you think Gideon is feeling insecure? Maybe he doesn't think he can live up to what Samuel was to you."

"I don't know. I hadn't thought of that. I certainly am not as good a person as Mary was."

"Maybe not."

"Hey!" Indignant, Anna looked away from the tourists outside to Naomi.

"Well, she was a very sweet person."

"What am I? Sour?"

Naomi laughed and poked Anna with her elbow.

"I've changed."

"Yes, you have. I haven't been interrogated for ages."

"Well, I figure I have to be careful asking certain questions now that you're married."

Naomi laughed and blushed.

Anna laughed and pointed a finger at her. "I wouldn't ask that!"

"The old you might have."

Laughing, Anna nodded. "You're right! I would have! Nothing was off limits, especially when we were having a Girls' Night Out with Mary Katherine and Jamie!"

"What's so funny?" Mary Katherine asked.

"You're back! We didn't see you come in!"

"The two of you were having too much fun laughing your heads off when we walked past."

Surprised, Anna looked up. "We were just talking about Naomi and Nick's love life."

"Anna!" Naomi stared at her, scandalized. "Don't listen to her, Mary Katherine! We weren't doing any such thing!"

"Well, it's a relief to see Anna looking more cheerful. She's been moping a little this past week."

"You didn't share anything about us, did you?" Jacob asked Mary Katherine.

Now Anna felt her face flame. "Uh—we didn't see you standing there, Jacob."

"Obviously not," he said with a grin.

"And I wouldn't share anything personal about us with these two," Mary Katherine assured her husband.

"Anna was just being outrageous," Naomi muttered.

She started to say something, but her attention was suddenly drawn to Mary Katherine's face, then Jacob's.

"What is it? What did the doctor say?"

⟳

The day had been long, and it wasn't over yet.

When Gideon looked up and saw Anna at the end of the field, though, the fatigue and hunger faded away.

She picked her way carefully through the clods of dirt, carrying a thermos and a paper bag. "Hi."

"Hi."

"I brought you some coffee and a sandwich to tide you over until supper."

"How did I get so lucky?"

She smiled. "Don't know. Where's Sarah Rose?" she asked as she poured him a cup of coffee from the thermos and handed it to him.

"With my mother. She's been helping watch her after school while I get the planting done."

Anna took the plastic cup from him when he finished and gave him the sandwich. She watched him peel the waxed paper from it carefully so he didn't touch it with his dirty hands. The sandwich was gone in a couple of healthy bites.

"This is great. It'll hold me over for a while. Can you stay for supper? Sarah Rose will be back then," he added as an incentive.

"Not tonight. I just wanted to stop by and share some good news. Mary Katherine and Jacob are having twins."

"*Zwillingbopplin*? That's great news!"

She nodded. "She's cutting back on her schedule a bit so we might not see as much of each other for the last few months."

"We already weren't seeing each other enough," he said softly, moving closer.

Anna backed away and started to trip, but he reached out and grabbed her arm and stopped her from falling.

He brushed at the sleeve of her dress. "Sorry, I got you dirty."

"It's okay. I'd have gotten worse if I'd fallen. I have to go. I'll see you later in the week."

"Later in the week." He sighed.

She bit back her smile at his expression. "You know, you look just like your daughter right now. Just like she did when you told her she couldn't have a kitten."

"Hey!" he called after her as she walked away, giggling.

A buggy rolled to a stop in the drive. Gideon stood there, wondering who was visiting, and lifted his hand in greeting when he saw Matthew Bontrager and Chris Matlock.

"How is your planting going?" Matthew asked when he got close enough.

"*Gut*. Yours?"

"The same. I have a brother-in-law living right next door to help."

Chris grinned at Matthew. "Is that the only reason to be glad I live next door?"

"Give me a minute. Let me think," Matthew said, folding his arms across his chest and staring up at the sky.

Then, catching the look on Chris's face, he clapped him on the back and chuckled. "Maybe watching the way you and Hannah managed to fall in love and get married without killing each other."

Chris laughed. "That sister of yours is no submissive woman, that's for sure."

"None of them are," Gideon told him. "Well, Mary was, somewhat. I'm finding Anna isn't.

"Wait," he said. "I didn't mean it to sound like that. I hadn't expected her to be like Mary. After all, we all knew each other from school. But between Anna and Sarah Rose, I don't think it's going to be a quiet house."

Matthew and Chris looked at each other, and then they burst into laughter. "Is there such a thing?"

Gideon thought about it. Matthew and Jenny had started their marriage with his three *kinner* and then added one of their own. Chris and Hannah—after almost losing their first child when Hannah developed complications—now looked forward to their second child in the fall.

"So how are you doing with the planting?" Matthew asked him, scanning the fields. "You still need some help?"

Gideon nodded. "You hear of anyone?"

"Ben Zook is looking for some extra work," Jacob told him. "He said he's getting married after harvest, and he's saving to get his own place."

"I'd like to talk to him."

"Mud sale's day after tomorrow. Why don't I tell him to meet you there?"

Gideon nodded. "Sounds good. *Danki.*"

"*Wilkumm.*"

"See you there."

Well, he might not have plans with Anna in the coming days, but he'd soon be able to talk to Ben about helping him with planting.

Gideon sighed. Such was his life right now. Well, the sooner he got the planting done, the sooner the crop would grow and thrive and be harvested. And at the end of the harvest, maybe he'd be getting married to Anna.

⟡

Anna touched her lips with her fingertips as she walked back to her buggy.

She'd swear they tingled.

Gideon's kisses . . . yes, Samuel had kissed her before they married, and yes, of course she had been attracted to Samuel. But they'd been so young, just a boy and a girl, really. Their kisses were youthful and exuberant.

These kisses of Gideon's . . . they were a man's, and now that she had been married, she knew what they promised.

She'd only kissed one man . . . been with one man in her life. It was such a big step to kiss another. Be with another. She was a widow, and she wanted to remarry. Every woman wanted that. At least here, in her community.

She was more than a little in love with Gideon already, despite saying that she wanted to take things slowly. Who wouldn't be? He was a handsome, hardworking man who understood her and supported what she did, who had taken what she'd said when she was upset with him about deciding things and not done it again. He'd listened to her. And there was no discounting how wonderful a father he was and would be again if God decided to give them the gift of children.

Thoughtful, she walked back to her buggy and drove home. She spent the evening as she usually did after work—she ate her supper in the kitchen, washed up the few dishes, and wandered into the living room.

As was her custom, she worked for a little while on knitting a baby cap, then tired of it. She picked up a book to read, couldn't get interested in it, and finally gave up and climbed the stairs to her room.

After she changed into a nightgown, she climbed into bed and tried to sleep, but soon found that despite being physically tired, sleep wouldn't come.

She reached for her Bible and thumbed through it. Reading it always calmed her. The pages seemed to fall open to the book of Matthew. It wasn't surprising. She turned to it often because there she found the answers to questions she didn't even know she had.

Tonight was no different.

⁓꒰꒷

Gideon kept Sarah Rose's hand firmly in his as they headed toward the sale. The event was crowded already with bargain hunters of all ages. Household goods, farming and yard equipment, furniture . . . there was a little of everything displayed for sale.

Delicious scents of frying doughnuts, bacon and egg sandwiches, kettle corn, and local sausages and cheeses wafted from the tables.

"Why do they call it a mud sale?" Sarah Rose wanted to know as she eyed the man using a big wooden paddle to stir a big cast iron kettle of popcorn. "They don't sell mud."

Before Gideon could answer, she'd run ahead of him and was standing at the edge of a mud puddle.

"Maybe because the ground's thawed and there's a lot of mud this time of year?" he asked. "And do *not* jump in that puddle."

To his utter surprise, she didn't. And she didn't pout about it, either. Instead, she smiled at someone standing behind him. He turned and found Anna.

"I didn't know you'd be here!" he told her, surprised.

"I didn't, either. My grandmother gave us a few hours off. There's a loom Mary Katherine wants to take a look at."

"How are you?" he asked her, careful not to ask something too personal.

His daughter, however, looked absorbed in Mary Katherine's pregnant abdomen. He reached for his wallet and thrust a dollar into her hands.

"Go get some kettle corn for us. Wait," he told her, handing her two more dollar bills. "Get some for Anna and Mary Katherine, too."

She brightened and ran to do his bidding.

"Good save," Anna told him, her eyes sparkling with mirth.

"It would have been all right if she wanted to ask a question," Mary Katherine chided him. "She's just curious about the baby." She paused. "Babies."

"I'm happy for you and Jacob," Gideon said, and it must have been the right thing to say, for she glowed.

Glowed. He glanced over to where Sarah Rose waited by the kettle.

"*Kinner* are a gift from God. Imagine, getting two at once." She shook her head in amazement.

"I don't know why you were so surprised. There are several sets of them on your side of the family," Anna reminded her.

"True. Still, sometimes things seem like a miracle when they're happening to you."

Anna smiled. It was so nice to see how happy her cousin was at being married and being pregnant.

Sarah Rose returned with three bags of kettle corn and handed them out with great care and a sense of importance. Gideon smiled when he saw that she didn't save the bag that seemed to have a little more in it than the others.

Mary Katherine glanced toward the items set up around the firehouse. "I need to go take a look at the loom before the auction starts."

"I'll come with you," Anna said.

"No need, I—"

"I promised Jacob I'd keep an eye on you." Anna slipped her arm through one of Mary Katherine's, then turned to Gideon. "I'll see you before we leave?"

Mary Katherine waited until they were a distance away before she turned to Anna. "I don't need a babysitter. You could have stayed to talk to Gideon."

"I came to be with you, not to turn this into a date with him."

"What were you and Naomi talking about so intensely that you almost didn't see me walk past the display window?"

"Nothing important."

"I think it was important, or you wouldn't have missed seeing me."

Anna smiled as she glanced at Mary Katherine. "It's pretty hard to miss you these days."

She just laughed when her cousin elbowed her. They found the section outside the firehouse where the loom was displayed. Anna watched as Mary Katherine looked it over and asked the owner questions about it.

Bidding was spirited on the Amish quilts, the hand-carved furniture, and farm equipment. Anna enjoyed watching but wondered if Mary Katherine was going to be able to endure the hard folding chairs they were seated on before she had to leave.

A man took the empty seat next to Mary Katherine. Anna looked over and saw that Jacob had shown up, pleasing his wife to no end.

"How did the loom look?"

"I love it. I'm going to bid on it."

He glanced at Anna and said hello, then the two of them held a quiet discussion on how much the loom was worth.

Bidding started a few minutes later. Mary Katherine bid, had her bid raised again and again. Anna scanned the audience to see who was interested in the loom and saw it was a woman who owned a craft shop. But Anna knew the woman didn't weave.

"She must just want it to decorate her shop," Anna whispered to Mary Katherine. "You said she buys some of the things in the shop from overseas."

"I want that loom," Mary Katherine said, her expression wistful. "I could work at home while the twins are little if I had it and just go into the shop a few days a week." She sighed and then her breath caught. "I have to go find a restroom."

After a quick whispered conversation with Jacob, she left them.

Jacob moved into her seat. "She really wants that loom. I know what she told me she wants to spend for it, but I'm determined to get it for her."

Anna dug into her purse and pulled out some money. "Here, you can have this if you need it."

He started to argue with her, but then the bid Mary Katherine had made was raised.

Jacob signaled he raised the bid, and the auctioneer focused on the woman bidder, cajoling her, and she nodded.

"Go for it," Anna hissed to Jacob. "You know Mary Katherine pinches pennies until they scream. If she comes back, she'll try to stop you from going higher."

She glanced around at the other woman, then turned back to Jacob. "Besides, I think that's as high as Mrs. Wilson is going to go."

Anna watched as Jacob swallowed and then raised his hand.

The auctioneer's voice rose in excitement. "Ma'am?" he said, looking at Mrs. Wilson.

The crowd turned to see her reaction. Indecision crossed her face, and then she shook her head.

The auctioneer slammed his gavel down on the makeshift podium. "Sold!"

Victorious, Jacob pumped the air with his fist. Then he caught sight of Mary Katherine standing beside him, her hands on her hips.

"You didn't!" she said, looking scandalized. "That was way too much! I told you not to go higher than—"

He jumped up and took her hand. "Come on. Let's go get your present."

"Present?"

"*Ya*," he said, grinning.

"This better be for the next five birthdays, Christmases, and anniversaries," she huffed.

But Anna saw her radiant smile before Jacob swept her off to get the loom.

"We'll be right back!" Mary Katherine called.

"Meet you out front where the driver dropped us off."

Anna turned and searched the crowd for Gideon as she walked. A group of people parted in front of her, and as they did, she heard familiar voices.

With all the noise surrounding her, all she could hear was snippets of conversation, but Gideon and the other men were discussing someone working on her farm.

Her farm.

Anna stopped in her tracks so quickly someone behind her ran into her, apologized, and then redirected his steps around her.

18

Anna heard her name called, but she ignored it and kept walking to the place where the driver would be picking up her and Mary Katherine.

A hand touched her elbow, and she stopped, not surprised to see Gideon at her side. "I was calling you. Are you leaving? You said you'd come see me before you left."

"I have to get back to the shop."

He frowned. "Okay. Sarah Rose is sitting with my mother. Let me tell them I'll be right back."

"There's no need to—" she stopped. He'd already hurried away. It would be rude to leave without him now.

And she was in no mood to get into a discussion now about what she'd overheard. She had told her grandmother they'd be back around lunchtime, and no one ever knew when the shop could get busy.

So she stood there, arms folded across her chest, and silently fumed at the delay and the conversation the men had been having. How presumptuous of Gideon! Another example of him being a decider.

"Anna! Good to see you!"

"Bishop. Are you enjoying the mud sale?"

"Yes, indeed!" He held up the sandwich in his hand. "The firemen make a great kielbasa sandwich."

Then he peered at her over the rims of his silver glasses and frowned. "Are you *allrecht*?"

"Fine. Thank you," she added and tried to unclench her teeth.

"Was that Gideon I saw a minute ago?" he asked, squinting against the bright sunlight in the direction Gideon had gone.

"Yes. Did you want to talk to him?" She tried to keep the hope from her voice. It would be a perfect way to quietly slip away and not have to talk to Gideon.

"No. Just thought I'd say hello to both of you. Speaking of saying hello, I thought I'd stop by and say hello to Leah and everyone tomorrow at the shop while I'm in town."

Anna felt herself relax a little. "She'd like that. You're so different from the last bishop."

"I'll take that as a compliment. As long as you understand I'm not advocating pride."

She smiled and then, when she saw Gideon approach, tried not to let it slip.

"Interesting," he murmured as he turned to look at her.

"What?"

"That's not the reaction I expected of a woman to her future *mann*."

She felt her eyebrows go up. "Who said—"

"I know. Nothing's been announced," he said sagely, stroking his beard. "Gideon, have you bought anything?"

"Only snacks so far," he said. "You know *kinner*. They can eat an hour before and still want to eat here."

The bishop held up his sandwich and chuckled. "Well, I'd better be getting back to my dear *fraa*."

He began to walk away and then turned back. "See you tomorrow."

Anna could almost feel Gideon come to attention. He turned to her.

"You're seeing the bishop tomorrow?"

"He's just stopping in at the shop to say hello to my grandmother."

"Oh."

Mary Katherine walked up, licking an ice-cream cone. "Hi, Gideon." She turned to Anna. "I'm ready to go when you are. Jacob is putting the loom in our buggy."

"Tell Sarah Rose I said good-bye," Anna told Gideon.

"When will I see you again?"

"Later. I have to go now." Anna slipped her arm into Mary Katherine's and started walking toward their ride.

"What was all that about?" Mary Katherine asked when they were far enough away that Gideon couldn't hear.

"Don't know what you're talking about. We have to get back."

Mary Katherine shivered and Anna stopped, concerned. "Are you cold?"

"Sure felt it back there."

Anna rolled her eyes and began walking again. "Very funny." She sighed. "I'm just upset with Gideon about something."

"I guessed that. He looked a little confused. Does he know what you're upset about?"

"No. I didn't want to talk about it here. Too many people. And we have to get back to work."

"Don't wait too long," Mary Katherine advised. She finished the cone, wiped her mouth with a paper napkin, and threw it in one of the trash receptacles. "It causes all kinds of problems when a couple doesn't work things out as quickly as possible."

A couple? Anna wasn't so sure she and Gideon would be a couple after they talked . . .

True to his word, the bishop stopped by for a visit the next afternoon.

Leah took him for a little tour around the shop, and Anna noticed that he nodded with approval as he looked at the displays of authentic Amish quilts and the ones that were designed and sewn to brighten the homes of *Englischers*.

Mary Katherine was in that morning—she worked at the shop Mondays, Wednesdays, and Fridays and went home before closing. He stopped and watched her weave for a few minutes, asked a question, and made a comment that made her smile before he moved on.

Jamie walked past with bolts of fabric that needed restocking on shelves, and the bishop complimented the fabric wall hanging she'd done that hung on a nearby wall.

"I hope you'll continue to feel welcome to attend church with us," he said, and after Jamie nodded and he walked on she looked over at Anna, who raised her eyebrows and did a thumbs-up sign.

Anna remembered how he'd been perceptive enough to notice that she was upset the day before at the mud sale. Briefly, she toyed with the idea of going to him to talk about Gideon. His questions had shown that he was concerned.

"Do you have time for coffee?" she heard Leah ask him.

"I'd love some."

But before she could show him to the back room, a customer came in asking for her.

Anna stepped forward. "Let me show you where we take our breaks. I'm sure Grandmother will only be a few minutes."

She poured a cup of coffee and set it before him with a pitcher of cream and the sugar bowl. Then, after a moment's hesitation, she poured herself a cup and sat down.

"May I ask you a question?"

"Of course." He leaned back in his chair and smiled.

She took a deep breath. "I was thinking about what you said yesterday. I was upset—*am* upset about something. As you said, Gideon and I have been seeing each other. But there's been some . . . problems."

"Problems?"

"I'm wondering if he expects me to be like Mary."

"Tell me how that is."

"Quiet. Submissive."

"That's certainly not you."

"Exactly." Then she frowned. "You don't think I should be, do you?"

"Oh my goodness, no. Why would you think that?"

She traced a pattern on the tablecloth and shrugged. "Well, I have seen some men—especially the last bishop—have the opinion that men should decide things." There was that word again. "I didn't think Gideon was like that. But he seems to be that way lately."

Quickly, she told him about how Gideon had listened to someone saying she was visiting Samuel's grave too often, so maybe she wasn't ready to be dating him. And how she'd overheard him at the mud sale talking about getting someone to work on her farm.

He leaned back in his seat, steepling his fingers as she talked. "Sounds like you need to talk to him, clear the air."

"I never had to do that with —" she stopped.

"Oh, are you expecting Gideon to be like Samuel?" he asked seriously.

She saw the twinkle of mischief in his eyes. "No, I—" she began, but then she stopped. "Maybe. I just think we should be partners if we get married."

He leaned forward and patted her hand. "I think you could be great partners. I've seen the way the two of you have already worked together to resolve some problems Sarah Rose was having. That tells me a lot."

Her eyes widened. "I hadn't thought about it like that."

"I'll say a prayer for you. If God has guided the two of you together, nothing will set you apart."

"But He put Samuel and me together and look what happened."

He stroked his beard. "I know you've struggled with His will about that. Perhaps we should talk about it sometime."

Leah walked in. "Sorry that took so long."

"Anna here kept me company," he told her.

She got to her feet. "Please excuse me, Bishop. I'll let the two of you talk."

As she walked back into the shop, she considered what he'd said. While his words had been short and simple, there was a lot of truth behind them. She needed to speak up, and she needed to do it now. It was obvious to the bishop that she wasn't like Mary, and if that's what Gideon wanted, it would be better to get that out in the open now.

No matter how much she was coming to care for Gideon, she had seen what happened to women she knew who were pressured by their husbands—or who pressured themselves— into roles they weren't comfortable with.

Anna didn't usually watch the clock when she was working but she caught herself doing it a number of times that afternoon. She didn't know what the end result might be, but she had to speak up now.

⸘

Gideon had stopped for a quick break and cool drink on the porch. Facing the road, he saw Anna before she saw him.

He watched her get out of the van and look out at the fields, searching for him. When she didn't see him, she turned, and he waved at her from the porch.

She started for the house, and he watched the way she seemed to march up the walk and then the steps.

Uh-oh, he thought. *Trouble is brewing.* He remembered the way she'd seemed distant and cool as she was leaving, but she'd said she had to get back to work so he'd left it alone. If there was a problem, he figured they'd talk about it soon enough. Or she'd get over it. Mary always had.

He rose as Anna climbed the steps, unsmiling, and took the seat next to his that he indicated.

"Can I get you some iced tea?" he asked, holding up the glass in his hand.

She barely glanced at it. "I'm not Mary," she said without preamble.

Startled, he sat with a thump. "I know you're not. What brought this on?"

She pinned him with her gaze. "You keep making decisions without me."

Puzzled, he ran back through the events of the past few days. "You accused me of being a 'decider' once, and I didn't do that again."

"I overheard you talking with Matthew and Chris at the mud sale. You were arranging for a friend of Matthew's to do some work on my farm. Gideon, we're seeing each other. We're not married."

"So that's it," he murmured. "I was talking with them about getting some help with my planting. The man who'll be helping me is looking for some extra work—"

"So you were talking about getting him to help me without discussing it with me first?"

"I was only talking with them. I wouldn't arrange anything before I discussed it with you."

He watched her get to her feet and pace the porch. "I'm quite capable of arranging these things myself, Gideon."

Feeling a little affronted, he stood as well. "I know that. I didn't arrange anything."

"That you'd even talk about it with someone else." She shook her head. "I just can't believe it."

"I was trying to make things easier for both of us. I'm short on help since the Stoltzfus brothers have their own farm now. I'm getting some help for me and happened to hear I might be able to help you."

He frowned. "Don't you want me thinking of how I can help you with all you do?"

"Have I said I need help?"

"Well, no."

She sighed. "It's too soon. Do you understand it's too soon?"

"No, what's too soon?" Confused, he pulled off his hat and dragged a hand through his hair.

"We're . . . butting heads over your getting so involved in my life when we're supposed to be dating, taking things slowly! Gideon, I've been managing on my own for more than two years now!"

"So you don't need me," he said slowly.

"Not the way you're doing things. I've had to learn to be independent, Gideon. Don't you understand that?"

He reached for her hand, but she put them behind her back. "But you don't need to be that way anymore, Anna."

"But I do. I can't give that up again. If you had any idea how hard it was to lose Samuel and feel so adrift, feel I couldn't make decisions afterward on my own after making them with him."

"I can't give up control again. No, *control* isn't the right word."

She looked out at the fields surrounding the house. "I need to feel I'm a partner in a marriage. I don't think you were a partner with Mary. I think you had a very traditional marriage with her with you being the one in charge. That's fine if that's what you both wanted, but that's not what I'm looking for the next time I marry."

Gideon felt his heart sink. "Are you saying you want to stop seeing each other?"

She was silent for so long he felt his nerves stretch to the screaming point. "I don't know. Maybe we need to back off a little," she said finally, so quietly he almost missed what she said.

There was a commotion in the drive. Sarah Rose was jumping out of his father's buggy. When she spotted Anna, she flew toward the porch. His father grabbed at her, but she proved too fast for him. He chuckled and waved a hand at Gideon before he climbed into the buggy and left.

Sarah Rose hopped up the steps and threw her arms around Anna's knees. "Anna! Are you here for supper?"

She glanced at him, sending him a silent signal as she stroked Sarah Rose's braids that were coming undone. "Not tonight. Another time."

He couldn't argue with her. A van was already pulling into the drive. "Her ride is here, Sarah Rose. You need to say good-bye."

Anna bent and hugged Sarah Rose, and then she hurried down the steps and crossed the lawn to get into the van. Gideon stood there on his porch and watched as it backed up, then headed down the road.

"*Daedi*? Can I go play next door?"

"Did you do your homework at your grandmother's?"

"She helped me with my math."

"Make sure it's okay with Sadie's *mamm*. And be back in an hour. Ask her to tell you when it's time. And no snacks."

Gideon watched her run next door and waited until his neighbor stepped out onto her porch and waved to show the visit was okay.

He'd been ready to call it a day before Anna had visited, but now he scanned the sky and calculated how much daylight he had left. It might be good to work off the uneasiness he was feeling at what had just happened between him and Anna.

Big Jim, his lead plow horse, shook his head when he approached. "Let's get a little more work in, and I'll make sure you get a treat when we go to the barn."

The horse shook his head again and snorted but moved forward. Gideon climbed up into his seat behind them and began the slow, steady trek up a row, down a row. Most days he enjoyed the work, but today all he could think about was the sparkle of tears he'd seen in Anna's eyes as she left him.

They reached the end of the row and traveled down another, then another. Each time they came to the end, the horses moved in a slow turn in tandem, a movement and rhythm born of years working together on the farm.

"Let's head home, Big Jim," he called on the last turn.

Big Jim must have been so happy to hear the call that Gideon saw him bump into Dale and the second horse stumbled. Gideon called out to them, waiting for them to settle into rhythm again.

Then a wheel hit a rut, the world tilted sickeningly, and he flew through the air, slamming into the hard, unplowed ground. The plowshare swerved up into his view, and he threw up his arms to protect his face. Pain exploded in his head, and then the world went black.

The lines on the shop order form were blurring. Anna decided to take a few minutes' break and rest her eyes.

She hadn't slept well after she talked to Gideon. It had just been too upsetting, and nothing had really been resolved before Sarah Rose had come home. After she'd gone home, she'd tried to relax but eventually went to bed, where she'd tossed and turned, tossed and turned.

Following her usual pattern, she'd finally gotten up, fixed a cup of chamomile tea, and knitted for a while. Finally, she returned to lie in her bed, wide awake, but forcing herself to rest. Working in the shop meant being on her feet many hours of the day so her body was tired even if her mind raced.

Now she was having trouble getting through her day.

Naomi stuck her head in the back room. "Phone call. It's Sarah Rose, and she sounds upset."

Anna picked up the phone. "Sarah Rose? Slow down, I can't understand you." She listened, feeling colder by the second. "I'll go to the hospital right now."

She hung up and stood there for a moment, trying to think what to do. Then she realized Naomi was trying to get her attention.

"What's wrong, Anna?" She turned and called for their grandmother.

Leah rushed in. "What is it?"

"Sarah Rose said Gideon's been hurt. He's in the hospital." Anna pressed her fingers to her temples. "I need to go there."

"I'll get you a driver. Get your things. I'll go with you."

Anna didn't argue with her grandmother. Fear had her in its grip, and she wasn't going to pretend she couldn't use some support.

It seemed like hours before a driver got there, but it was only minutes. Anna and Leah rode to the hospital holding hands and praying.

Only when they got to the hospital did Anna think about how quickly she'd dropped everything to come to see him . . . what if he didn't want to see her?

Gideon's parents were waiting at the hospital. They embraced her like a daughter. Obviously, Gideon had either not told them that they were having problems, or they were simply too upset with what was happening.

"Gideon's neighbor called us. She saw his horses in the field and Gideon lying on the ground," Amos said heavily. "They called 9-1-1 and brought him here. He lost a lot of blood. Broke an arm and his left leg. He's been in surgery for several hours already."

"And will be for hours more." Tears filled Esther's eyes. "We've been praying since we heard."

"Us as well," Leah said, and Anna felt her squeeze her hand.

They sat and waited, drinking cups of coffee Esther would fetch them. They formed their own little world insulated from the swirling, noisy one of the hospital, sitting in a circle in a corner of the room to hold hands and pray.

Every so often, a nurse would come to tell them how Gideon was doing in surgery. He was "holding his own," they were told. Such a strange expression. But it was good news, the nurses assured them.

Anna knew that things could change in the blink of an eye, but it seemed impossible to connect Gideon with such a devastating accident. Both Mary and Samuel had fought the battle to live for months before dying. Gideon was such an energetic, vital man. He'd been doing the same work he'd done for years, carefully plowing his land, and something had gone wrong and the equipment had thrown him and then when the horses panicked, the metal from the plow had—

"Anna?"

She stared up, trying to focus. "Yes?"

Amos put his hand on her shoulder and smiled at her. "Gideon got through the surgery. They're taking him to the recovery room now."

"Thank You, God," Anna whispered through trembling lips. She turned to her grandmother, and the tears began.

Leah rocked her like a babe and patted her back. "Sssh," she soothed. "He's going to be all right. Don't cry so. You'll make yourself sick." She dug in her purse for a tissue and pressed it into Anna's hand.

Anna watched as Amos and Esther talked with the doctor. They listened intently, and then they walked over to join Anna and her grandmother.

"It's going to be at least another hour or two before family can see him," Esther said. "The doctor said one of us can see him for five minutes each hour as long as he's stable."

She leaned forward and touched Anna's hand. "We want you to go first."

19

Anna tried to argue with Gideon's parents, but they insisted she be the one to see him first.

"I—I can't do that," she told them quietly. "It wouldn't be fair to either of you. The last time we saw each other we argued."

Esther turned to Amos. "When was the last time we argued?"

"This morning," he said with a slight smile.

"Like I always tell him, it's all right if he doesn't agree with me. I can't force him to be right."

They were trying to make her feel better. She loved them for it, for the way that they looked past their own worry and pain. But it didn't change what had happened between her and Gideon.

Anna stood and paced. "You don't understand. We talked about not seeing each other again."

"I know how Gideon feels about you," his mother told her. "All couples go through rough patches. Let's get through this, and you'll see. Everything will be fine."

Her grandmother patted her shoulder. "Esther is right."

They sat there, waiting, and when Leah smothered a yawn, Anna glanced at the clock on the wall and realized how late it was getting.

"You need to go home," she told her grandmother.

"I'm fine. I'll stay with you until you get to see Gideon."

"It might be hours."

"We'll see."

Not long after, a nurse came to get Anna.

"We don't expect him to wake up for hours," she told Anna. "Don't be alarmed by the swelling in his face. It'll go down in the next day or two."

"But he doesn't have a concussion?"

The nurse shook her head. "The biggest worry right now is infection. He had some nasty cuts they cleaned out, and he's taking antibiotics intravenously."

Even with the warning it was a big shock to see Gideon lying so still in the bed. Casts encased his left arm and leg. His face looked pale and swollen against the pillow. A line of stitches ran along one side of his forehead; bruises bloomed on one cheekbone.

Anna's knees went weak, and she sank down into the chair beside the bed, barely registering the nurse reminding her that she could visit for five minutes.

He was such a strong person, so full of life . . . what a shock to see him like this. Surely, at any minute his eyes would open, and she'd be accusing him of trying to decide everything and dominate.

As she sat there and listened to the machines recording his vital signs, all she could think about was that she wanted to turn back time. She knew she loved him, but she'd thought she couldn't continue to go on the way she had feeling that she couldn't be herself in a relationship with him. But now . . . now she wondered if God was testing her to see if she really meant it.

It was as if He said, *Oh really? Maybe you'd like to see what it's like to be without Gideon?*

No, God didn't work that way. Her anxiety and her imagination were running away with her.

She didn't want to wake him, but she needed to tell him that she was sorry—not for what she'd said. An accident didn't wipe away her frustration, her concern about how they were getting along exactly. She was sorry for the pain he was feeling, the worry he'd undoubtedly feel the minute he opened his eyes.

Some said people could hear when they were unconscious. Several times when Samuel seemed out of it, he'd told her later what she'd said to him.

Leaning over, she whispered his name. When he didn't stir, she raised her voice a little. Still nothing. She felt a little guilty. After all, if he woke, he'd likely feel a lot of pain from the broken bones and the surgery.

"It's Anna. I'm here." She lifted his hand that lay on the bed, held it with hers. "Sarah Rose got your neighbor to call me."

He didn't move, didn't say anything, but she hadn't really expected him to. They had been seeing each other for months, moving slowly as she'd asked. Now, she wondered if God was taking him. There'd be no more taking it slow or telling him—like the last time she'd seen him—that she just didn't know if she could handle someone being so dominant in the relationship.

She felt helpless, something that had been too much a part of her life near the end with Samuel. Then, she'd prayed to keep him, prayed so hard, but he'd still slipped away.

Now she bent her head and prayed as she'd been doing since she'd heard that Gideon had been seriously hurt.

She opened her eyes and took a deep breath. "You've got to get better. Your daughter was scared to death when I talked to her. She needs you. Your parents need you."

Her lips trembled, and she touched them with her fingers. "Okay, and maybe I need you, even as aggravating as you can be."

She heard footsteps approach the door. The time she'd been given was up. She hadn't been ready to say it before, and maybe she still wasn't. Once she'd given her heart, and it had hurt so badly to be left behind. She couldn't bear it if it happened again.

But if she never said it and he left this world tonight, could she live with that? Tears burned behind her eyelids as she leaned forward, willing him to wake and hear her. "I love you."

"You should go home and get some rest," the nurse advised. "He's probably not going to wake up until late tomorrow morning."

"I don't think his parents will leave until they've seen him, so I'm going to stay until then."

The nurse checked an IV drip and then walked with her out of the room. "When are you getting married?"

Anna didn't know what to say. "I don't know."

"Oh wait, don't I remember that the Amish get married in the fall, after harvest?"

"That's right."

Anna thanked the nurse and rushed from the room. She wanted to just keep going and leave the hospital, but it wouldn't be fair to Gideon's parents. They had given up that chance to see how he was doing first. She owed them.

So she tried to steady herself and walked into the waiting room to tell them how their son looked.

❧

Gideon woke slowly, floating and trying to figure out where he was. The last thing he remembered he'd been lying on the ground, staring at the sky, feeling his plow horses had fallen onto him.

A face swam into view.

"Well, hello there. Decided to join us, eh?"

"I'll tell the doctor," someone he couldn't see said.

"You're in the hospital," the beaming face over him announced. "How are you feeling?"

"Like I've been run over."

"From what I understand, that's pretty much it. Except it was by having a piece of farming equipment rolling on you, not a truck."

"Sarah Rose!" he croaked, wondering why his voice sounded rusty, as if he hadn't used it in a long time. "I have to make sure she's all right—"

He thought he sat up, but he was flat on his back and couldn't move. The woman wasn't holding him down. Under the pain, he felt something hard pressing on an arm, a leg. What was going on?

"That your daughter? Don't you worry. She's just fine. You should be able to see her in a few days when you transfer to a different unit."

Gideon tried to look down. "How bad?"

"Broken arm, broken leg, lots of cuts and bruises," she rattled off, ticking the injuries off on her fingers. "Lost a lot of blood. Took two transfusions. You wouldn't believe how many friends and family came to donate."

He groaned.

"Don't worry. We're going to get you well," she assured him.

"I need to see Sarah Rose today," he said, fighting the dragging need to go under again. "Today."

"I can't—"

"She lost her mother two years ago," Gideon told her. "She'll be so scared."

He lost the battle and slipped under.

The next time he woke, he could hear whispering. He opened his eyes and he saw her—saw them. The two most important people in his life.

"He's awake," Sarah Rose said, her voice rising in excitement.

Anna looked over at him, her expression doubtful, and then he watched it change to joy.

He lifted his free hand, and Sarah Rose slid from Anna's lap to run to his side and clasp it in hers.

"Be careful. Don't bump him." Anna came to stand beside the bed, resting her hands on Sarah Rose's shoulders. "I'm glad you woke up. They'll only let us stay for a few minutes. You'll have to thank Vickie—that's the nurse who was on duty earlier. She insisted you get to see Sarah Rose."

He listened to his girl chatter, letting it wash over him as he and Anna stared at each other. "Thank you for bringing her."

"Your parents picked me up on the way here. She's staying at their house."

"*Mamm* will be worn out in a couple of days," he said with a rueful laugh that turned into a wince of pain.

"Don't worry. I'll watch Sarah Rose for a while to give her a break."

A nurse entered the room and smiled at the child. "Would you like to give your daddy a hug before we make him take a nap?"

She laughed. "Daddy never takes a nap."

"He has to this time. Doctor says. That's how he'll get well. Here, I'll show you how you can hug him without hurting him."

It still hurt a little to be hugged, even though the nurse held his daughter carefully and showed her where to slip her little arms around his neck, but Gideon embraced the pain. Feeling pain meant he was alive. Feeling her hug meant love. No one needed to tell him things could have gone very differently . . .

"We'll say good-bye then," Anna said, backing away from the bed. "Your parents will want to come in and see you."

It was easy to see the signs that his mother had been crying. But Gideon saw the moisture in his father's eyes as well, the way he turned and wiped his nose on a bandanna he took from his pocket.

"We finished the field you were working on," his father said gruffly.

Something was coming back to him. "Big Jim. I need you to have Doc Wells take a look at him. Seemed like something was wrong with him just before things went haywire."

His father patted his shoulder. "Don't go getting upset," he told him. "It's not good for you right now."

"The planting—"

"God will provide, *sohn*. Rest."

His mother leaned over him and kissed him on the forehead. "We'll see you tomorrow."

He reached for her hand and squeezed it. "Thank you for everything."

"Especially for bringing Sarah Rose and Anna," she said, nodding and smiling.

"She's upset with me. Anna, not Sarah Rose."

His mother squeezed his hand back. "Things change. If she was upset enough to break things off with you, she wouldn't have come to the hospital."

"Well, she did that because you asked her to." Gideon shifted, trying to get comfortable.

"Today we did. Not the first night. Now, we have to leave, or they won't be letting us come visit again."

Shocked, Gideon stared after them. Anna had come to the hospital when she heard about his accident?

❦

The time for indecision was over.

Anna sat in the drive of Gideon's house and told herself she needed to get out and go talk to him. He'd been home for several days, and there was no more putting it off. Several weeks had gone by since they'd had that last talk before his accident.

She'd gone over what they'd said so many times. When she'd gone to talk to him that day, she'd felt frustrated at the way she felt he just charged ahead in decisions that affected them both. She knew that she still guarded her heart, afraid of the pain giving it and having it bruised might cause. But she hadn't felt he'd understood.

"I need to feel I'm a partner in a marriage," she'd told him.

He'd reacted with surprise when she said that she didn't feel that he and Mary had been partners. Theirs had looked to be very traditional with him being the one in charge and Mary being a submissive wife.

That was fine if that's what both people in the relationship wanted, but that hadn't been what she and Samuel had and that wasn't what she wanted the next time she married. Being widowed and working at Stitches in Time had forced her to become independent.

Well, *forced* wasn't exactly the word she was looking for. No, it hadn't been a step that she'd willingly taken—only when Samuel had died had she taken those first steps to independence. It hadn't always been easy or what she'd have done if there'd been a choice, but so much good had come of it. Now she was proud of the woman she'd become—especially when she'd stopped being angry with God and started trusting Him with her life again.

Gideon had asked her if she wanted to stop seeing him, and she hadn't known what to say. Finally, she'd stammered that maybe they needed to back off a little, and then she'd rushed out of there.

It hadn't taken long for her to wonder if he'd been upset, distracted, and that had been why he'd had the accident. After all, it had only been a day, hadn't it? She'd been so upset it was hard to remember.

But men didn't let things upset them the way women did, did they?

She shook her head as if to clear it and got out of the buggy, reaching in to lift the box she'd brought. No one was in the front of the house so she was able to climb the stairs and leave the box on the side of the porch before she went to the door and knocked on it.

Sarah Rose answered it, and she beamed, obviously glad to see her. "I was just going to help *Daedi* go out on the porch," she announced. "He needs some fresh air. He's been cooped up in the house all day."

Anna saw that someone had built a small wooden ramp onto the front doorstep so that it was easier for wheelchair access. She wanted to help Sarah Rose maneuver the chair, but it was obvious that the child wanted to do it herself so she stepped back and waited to see what happened next.

"I think what I said was someone had been cooped up for a while and needed to get outside for a while."

"Maybe everyone would enjoy some fresh air," Anna said, holding open the door and watching his progress down the wooden ramp.

"I can help *Daedi*," Sarah Rose said, pushing the chair from behind.

"Careful, sweetheart, you're going a little fast," her father told her.

Anna noted his face paled and moved quickly to his side, prepared to stop the child if necessary.

"Here, *Daedi*, this is a nice sunny spot." Sarah Rose stopped in the corner of the porch, and Anna helped her set the brake. "My grandmother says he's looking awful white from being inside so much. He can get a tan here."

He still looked pale, and there were dark circles under his eyes. His left arm and leg still wore casts, but oh, he looked wonderful to her.

"I'm thinking you're looking a little green around the gills myself," she told Gideon quietly as Sarah Rose hopped from one foot to the other. It was obvious that the two of them had come outside so that she could burn off some energy.

"Sarah Rose, I think there's something in that box over there for you," she told her, gesturing at where it sat in the corner of the porch.

The little girl raced over to it, pulled back the flaps, and out popped the head of the kitten she'd fallen in love with at Anna's house.

Anna wasn't sure who was more surprised—Sarah Rose or the kitten. Sarah Rose screamed and clapped her hands. The kitten jumped straight up and when it landed, it ran to Anna and tried scaling her skirts.

Laughing, she disentangled the pet and stroked it until it calmed before handing it to Sarah Rose. "Sit down with her and help her calm down," she urged.

"Are you talking to my daughter or the kitten?" Gideon asked, leaning back in his chair and watching.

"Can I keep her? Please, *Daedi*, can I keep her?"

"What was this about me deciding things?" he asked Anna, his brow raised in irony.

"See how it feels?" she asked him with a touch of mischief. "I know, I shouldn't have. But she needs a new home."

"What's wrong with the one she has now?"

"Sarah Rose, your *daedi* and I need to talk for a few minutes. I put a carton of milk and a bowl in the box. Do you think you could take her inside and give her some?"

The little girl looked from one to the other. Then she must have decided it would be more fun to feed the kitten. She nodded and scampered off with the kitten slung over her arm, the bowl and milk in her hands. The screen door slammed behind her.

Anna walked over to a rocking chair, sat, and fanned herself with her hand. "Getting warmer."

He nodded, watching her.

"How are you feeling?"

"As good as a man can when he can't take care of himself, let alone his farm."

She looked out at the fields and nodded.

"Everyone turned out to finish the planting," he told her, his gaze going with hers, seeming to look at the fields. But there was a faraway expression in his eyes, as if he were looking beyond the fields. "But you know. You were here to help feed the men on more than one occasion."

He turned to her suddenly. "Grace doing all right? And the baby?"

"Eli, too." Grace had gone into labor, and Eli had to leave to take her to his parents' house where they'd planned a home birth.

"I passed them on the way coming home from the hospital that day," he told her.

Anna found herself blinking hard against the hot tears that crowded the backs of her eyelids. "It could have been so different. I—" she stopped. She couldn't say the words—*I could have lost you.*

He moved forward awkwardly in his chair. "But it didn't. Obviously that wasn't in God's plan . . . although I'm not certain what God's plan is yet."

"Me, either." She twisted her hands in her lap.

He reached out with his free hand. "There's one thing I know, though. I've had a lot of time to think, being laid up. I don't want to lose you. I want us to work things out. I need you to tell me if you'll give me another chance."

Anna bit her lip. "Will you give me another one, too?"

"You? Why do you think you need to ask that?"

"Because I've had a lot of time to think, too, and I realized that I might have overreacted. I looked for a reason to think we weren't suited, that you'd overwhelm me, instead of trying to work out a way of us working together instead of against each other. A way so I wouldn't just think I had to walk away."

She took his free hand and lifted it, pressing one of hers against it. "This is what I should have done. Pushed back more."

The screen door creaked. "Anna? Did you bring kitty any food?"

"I did. I'll bring it in soon."

"'Kay." The door slammed again.

"So why does the kitten need a new home?" Gideon asked her, staring at her intently.

She turned back to him. "I'm thinking of moving. Of selling my farm."

"Really?"

Nodding, she took a deep breath. "Samuel and I worked hard to start a life there, and it's time to let someone else do it. I want to sell it to Eli and Grace. They'll continue what Samuel and I started—in their own way, of course. Raise children there and fill the house with them and their laughter and their noise."

She realized that he'd used his good foot to pull the chair closer to her. "And where will you live, Anna?"

"Here, if you'll ask me to marry you again," she said, feeling the butterflies in her stomach and trying to breathe. "With my heart in hand, I'm ready to give you all of it and not hold back."

He took her hand in his, caressing the palm with his thumb. "I'll take it and cherish it, Anna. And give you mine as well." Leaning forward, he kissed her until she was breathless.

Lost in the kiss, they didn't hear the sound of the screen door opening. When they broke apart, they were startled to see Sarah Rose standing there, the kitten clutched to her chest, grinning at them.

"Are you gonna come live with *Daedi* and the kitten and me here?"

Gideon laughed. "I don't think you get to say no," he told Anna. "Or at least, you may have trouble getting the kitten back."

"Yes, I'm going to come live here, when your *daedi* and I get married after the harvest," she said, stroking her hand over the girl's head.

Sarah Rose grinned. "*Gut.*"

She hugged Anna's neck, and the kitten squealed at being smooshed too closely between them.

Then she stood back. "Now can I feed the kitten?"

Anna and Gideon exchanged a bemused look.

"Get the box and we'll open it for you," he told his daughter. "Priorities," he told Anna with a shake of his head.

Anna pulled the can, a spoon, and a dish from the box. She quickly opened the can and put a few spoonfuls in the bowl. "There you go," she said, handing it to Sarah Rose.

She watched the girl set the bowl on the porch floor and hunch down to watch the kitten eat.

"Do you know what made me think we belonged together?" she asked Gideon.

"Aside from the fact that we love each other?"

Anna smiled. "Aside from that. Because love isn't always enough. It was something the bishop said. He told me that he'd watched how we behaved with Sarah Rose when he saw us at church and such. Gideon, he said we were already behaving like parents and working things out as a family."

Gideon's eyes were warm and full of love—and more. "And there'll be more," he promised and she felt herself blush.

"If God wills," she whispered.

"If God wills," he agreed.

But somehow, deep in her heart, she knew he was right.

RECIPES

Creamed Celery

4 cups finely chopped celery
½ tsp. salt
½ c. sugar
2 tablespoons vinegar
1 tablespoon flour
½ c. milk
2 tablespoons mayonnaise

Cover celery with water in saucepan, add salt, sugar, and vinegar, and cook until tender. Drain. Combine flour and milk and bring to a boil. Stir in mayonnaise. Add cooked celery and mix until blended. Serve hot.

Snickerdoodles

½ cup butter, softened
1 cup sugar
¼ teaspoon baking soda
¼ teaspoon cream of tartar
1 large egg
½ teaspoon vanilla
1 ½ cups all-purpose flour
4 tablespoons granulated sugar
1 ½ teaspoons cinnamon

Preheat oven to 375 degrees. Using mixer, beat butter for 30 seconds, then add sugar, baking soda, and cream of tartar, and beat until combined. Add egg and vanilla, then slowly add flour until all is used. Cover bowl with plastic wrap and chill for an hour. In small bowl combine the 4 tablespoons sugar and cinnamon. Shape dough into one-inch balls, roll in cinnamon sugar mixture, and place on ungreased cookie sheet. Bake for about 10-12 minutes until golden brown. Cool on wire rack.

White Hot Chocolate

1 cup white chocolate chips
1 cup heavy cream
4 cups half-and-half
1 teaspoon vanilla extract
Peppermint sticks or candy canes, optional

Place chips in a saucepan over medium heat, add cream and stir until chips are melted. Add half-and-half and extract. Serve warm with peppermint sticks or candy canes as stirrers.

Three Bear Soup
(great for sick kids)

3 tablespoons olive oil
1 onion, diced
1 pound stew meat or lean hamburger
2 large carrots, diced
3 stalks celery, diced
1 16-ounce package frozen mixed vegetables
1 28-ounce can whole peeled tomatoes, juice included
1 tsp salt
½ tsp pepper
1 tsp dried parsley
2 quarts beef or vegetable broth

Sauté onion, meat, carrots, and celery until meat is no longer pink. Add remaining ingredients, bring to a boil, then reduce heat and simmer for at least an hour (two hours are even better). Serve at a temperature that is not too hot, not too cool, but just right and see sick kids perk up.

Soup is even better the next day.

Alphabet macaroni or seashell macaroni may be added.

Glossary

allrecht—all right

boppli—baby

bruder—brother

daedi—daddy

danki—thank you

dat—father

dawdi haus—addition to a house where elderly parents can live and be cared for, similar to an *Englisch* mother-in-law apartment.

Der Hochmut kummt vor dem Fall. "Pride goeth before the fall."

Englisch, Englischer—Non-Amish person

fraa—wife

guder mariye—good morning

gut—good

hungerich—hungry

kaffe—coffee

kapp—prayer covering or cap worn by girls and women

kich—kitchen

kind, kinner—child, children

kumm—come

liebschen—dearest or dear one

maedel—young woman (maid)

mamm—mother

mann—husband

nee—no

Ordnung—The rules of the Amish, both written and unwritten. Certain behavior has been expected within the Amish community for many, many years. These rules vary from community to community, but the most common are not to have electricity in the home, not to own or drive an automobile, and to dress a certain way.

Pennsylvania Deitsch—Pennsylvania German

rumschpringe—time period when teenagers are allowed to experience the *Englisch* world while deciding if they should join the church. It is not the wild period so many *Englisch* imagine, according to Amish sources.

schul—school

schur—sure

schweschder—sister

sohn—son

wilkumm—welcome

wunderbaar—wonderful

ya—yes

zwillingbopplin—twins

Discussion Questions

Caution: Please don't read before completing the book because the questions contain spoilers!

1. Anna and Gideon have been widowed at a young age. Why do you think God would put two people together only to take one away?

2. Have you lost someone you loved? How did you deal with the loss?

3. Some people would think that Anna and Gideon have a lot in common. What do you think they have in common? What were their challenges to their relationship?

4. How did Anna help Sarah Rose deal with the loss of her mother?

5. What do you think parents can learn from the Amish?

6. Work is an important element of life in both the Amish community and the *Englisch* community. Anna, her cousins, and their grandmother find a way to be creative in their work life. Sometimes being able to deal with people is being creative. How do you use creativity in your own work life?

7. Knitting is not just Anna's work—it is an activity that keeps her centered. What activity do you use to stay centered?

8. Anna is afraid to give her heart to Gideon. If you knew Anna, how would you help her learn to trust God and love again?

9. Do you feel it makes any difference if couples are engaged a short time or a long time?

10. Gideon is a strong male who likes to help, but Anna finds it hard to accept that help. What would you say to Gideon? To Anna?

11. Gideon's accident makes him feel vulnerable and unable to run his life. Have you ever experienced something similar? How did you cope? What did you learn?

12. The community comes together to help Gideon after his accident. How do the people in your community rally to help someone?

Abingdon Press is delighted to announce a return to the Quilts of Lancaster County series in fall 2013 with *Annie's Christmas Wish*, a story about one of Jenny and Matthew Bontrager's daughters.

Come travel with us to visit with old friends and new ones in the Amish and *Englisch* community of Paradise, Pennsylvania, in the first chapter of *Annie's Christmas Wish*.

1

$\mathcal{A}$nnie lay on the quilt-covered bed tucked up in her cozy little attic bedroom. She held up the snow globe and shook it, watching the little snowflakes inside swirl and swirl and then float gently down to cover the skyscrapers of New York City.

It was her favorite Christmas present ever, brought back from the big city by her *mamm* when she went to see her editor years ago. After she'd received the globe with its tiny glimpse of the city, Annie had borrowed books from the library and studied the photos and read everything she could. New York City seemed like such an exciting place, filled with such towering, fancy buildings, its streets lined with so many types of people from so many places. Stories were everywhere, stories of hope and joy and death and loss and—well, her imagination was soaring just thinking about them.

She might be twenty-one now, a woman and not a child. But she was no less interested—some might say obsessed— with the city than when she first received the globe. Her one big wish had become to visit New York City, and now it was finally coming true.

Life here in her Plain community of Paradise, Pennsylvania, wasn't boring. Not exactly. She loved everything about it. But she'd always been a seeker, endlessly curious about even the tiniest detail of life. She'd been like that even before her *mamm* had moved here and married her *daed*. Before she had been Jenny Bontrager, her mother had been Jenny King, a television news reporter who specialized in traveling around the world and showing people what war did to innocent children.

Annie thought the work sounded amazing. All the travel, so exciting. Meeting all kinds of people. Telling the story of someone who needed attention to their story to help them. Annie had never lacked for a meal. She'd always had a comfortable bed.

And even though she had lost her mother at a young age, she'd always had so many people around her to love her and make her feel safe and happy. The children her mother had seen overseas in war-torn countries had often lost parents, their homes . . . even been injured or killed themselves. And sometimes there was little food.

She looked up when there was a knock on the door frame.

"Hi. May I come in?"

"Of course." Annie moved so her mother could sit on the bed with her.

When she saw her mother's gaze go to the snow globe she held, she handed it to her. Jenny shook it and watched the snowflakes settle on the skyscrapers inside, just as Annie had done.

"I remember when I gave this to you."

"You came back from a trip there and told us you were going to have a baby."

"Seems like just yesterday."

"Seems like he's been around forever to drive me crazy." She grinned. "Don't worry. I don't mean it. He's a good little brother."

"You mean when he's not being a little terror?"

Annie laughed and nodded. "Right. He's not afraid of any-thing. Must have some of the adventurer spirit you have inside him."

Her mother glanced down at her traditional Amish dress and laughed self-deprecatingly. "I'm not much of an adven-turer now."

"You have a spirit of adventure in your heart," Annie told her.

She studied her mother, looking so slim and pretty in a dress of deep green, her dark brown hair tucked neatly under her snowy white kapp still showed no gray. Jenny never missed the fancy clothes of the *Englisch* . . . never missed anything from that world, from what she said. Annie wondered how she would feel visiting the city she'd made her home base for so many years.

"Getting excited?"

"It's going to be so amazing!" She looked at her mother. "I'm still surprised *Daed* said he wanted to go."

She sat up and hugged her mother. "But I'm glad he did. He's so, so proud of you. We all are."

"I appreciate it," Jenny told her. "But we're not going to the event for them to make a fuss over me. You know that's not our way."

"I know." Annie pretended to roll her eyes. "It's because the organization is helping children. And because your friend, David, is being honored, too. "

"Exactly." Jenny paused and grinned. "Of course, it doesn't mean we can't have some fun while we're there."

Annie reached under her pillow and pulled out a handful of brochures. "I sent off for these. Look, the Statue of Liberty, Rockefeller Center, Times Square . . ."

"And the *New York Times*?" Jenny looked over the informa-tion packet for the newspaper. "Hardly a tourist attraction."

"Please?" Annie bounced on the bed like a kid. "I want to go so bad. Badly," she corrected herself.

Jenny chuckled. "I guess it *would* be attractive to someone who wants to be a writer."

She glanced over at Annie's small desk. "I remember when you started keeping a word journal. How you loved finding new words to tell us about."

"So this is where you went." Annie's father appeared in the doorway.

He filled the doorway, this tall and handsome father of hers. She and her brothers and sister had gotten their blond hair and blue eyes from him.

"Matthew, look! Annie's gotten all sorts of brochures of places to visit for us to look at before we go to New York City."

"*The New York Times?*" he asked, sounding doubtful. "I'm not sure your brothers and sister are going to be thrilled with going on a tour of a newspaper."

Annie looked imploringly toward her mother.

"Maybe we can think of someplace you and the rest of the family would like to go, and Annie and I will go on the newspaper tour, maybe the television studio where I used to work," Jenny suggested.

"It's no surprise the two of you would want to go there." He picked up the brochure of the Niagara Falls. "This looks amazing. Amos and Esther went there last year and said the boat ride was exciting. Bet Joshua would love this."

They heard a crash downstairs.

"The Bontrager children are never quiet," Jenny said, sighing. But she wore a smile. "I'd better go see what they're up to."

She patted Matthew's cheek as she passed him. "Supper in ten."

"Smells wonderful."

Laughing, she shook her head. "I'm making baked pork chops."

"One of my favorites."

She glanced back. "And something easy I can't mess up. Well, at least when I set the timer."

Matthew waited until she left the room and then he looked at Annie. They laughed.

"I heard you!" Jenny called back.

He struggled to suppress his grin. "It's still fun to tease her about her cooking."

"You have to stop," she told him sternly.

"You do it, too. It's just too easy to tease her when she makes comments first. But she's become a good cook. Not that I'd have been any less happy to be married to her if she hadn't." Tilting his head, he studied her. "So I guess you're going to miss Aaron while you're gone."

She frowned at him. "Don't tease."

"He's a nice young man."

With a shrug, Annie gathered up the brochures and tucked them under her pillow.

"Annie? Is there a problem?"

"No, of course not."

"We used to be able to talk about everything."

She looked up and felt a stab of guilt. He looked genuinely disappointed.

"He's afraid I'm going to stay there," she blurted out.

Matthew pulled over the chair from the desk and sat down. "You're not, are you?"

She frowned. "Of course not."

But oh, to stay longer than the four or five days they planned to visit. There was so much to see, so much to write about . . .

"*Gut*," he said, looking relieved.

She stood. "I should go down and help *Mamm* with supper."

He nodded. "I'm right behind you. She might need me to get the apple pie I smell baking out of the oven."

"Men!" she said, laughing as she walked from the room. "All you think of is your stomachs."

"Hey, a man works hard, he needs to eat."

When she got downstairs, she saw her mother didn't need her help—Mary was visiting and staying for supper. She stood at the counter slicing bread while Johnny set the table. Joshua was no doubt out in the barn finishing his chores. There was nothing he liked better than to feed and water the horses.

She'd known her siblings would be doing their evening chores. But it had been a good excuse for getting out of a discussion of Aaron with her father. She hadn't liked what Aaron said about her going to New York City. And there was no need to be getting into it with her father in any case. Such things weren't discussed with parents until you actually knew you were getting engaged and right now, she and Aaron were just friends.

It was fun going to singings and church activities and things with him, but she wasn't ready to get married yet. Fortunately, her parents wouldn't dream of pressuring her to do so. Many of her friends were waiting a little longer than their parents had before they married. After all, marriage was forever in her community.

At least, until death did you part.

She'd been so young when her mother died Jenny had been the only mother she'd ever known. Although Jenny moved with only a trace of a limp from the car bombing she'd suffered overseas, she'd experienced problems recovering from it that had affected her speech. Annie had bonded with her when her father had offered to drive Jenny to speech therapy on the days Annie went for help with her own childhood speech problem.

But maybe Annie was closer to Jenny, too, because Jenny had lost her mother when she was young and knew how it felt.

Their shared interest in writing came as her mother helped her with schoolwork and found Annie loved to put her active imagination on paper. Now her tiny room was full of boxes of journals and bound collections of poems and short stories.

Annie watched the way her family worked together in the kitchen getting the family meal on the table—especially loving the way her parents got along. Her father had come down the stairs and insisted on checking on the pie. Her mother shooed him away from the oven, insisting it needed five more minutes. She smiled at the way they pretended to argue, all the while teasing each other and loved seeing them occasionally sharing a kiss when they thought their *kinner* weren't watching.

They were different than the parents of most of her friends. Jenny's father had been born Amish, but decided not to join the church, so she was familiar with the Amish ways and had visited her grandmother here for years. Although Jenny and Annie's father had fallen in love as teenagers, Jenny had left one summer to go to college, and her father had married Annie's mother some time later.

But then the terrible bombing overseas years later had an amazing result: Jenny's grandmother had invited her to recuperate at her house, and Jenny had been reunited with Annie's father. After she joined the church, the two of them had gotten married. So they were different from the parents of her friends in that respect. Annie always wondered if they seemed more in love than other married couples because of all they'd been through. Then again, Amish couples didn't usually indulge in public displays of affection.

"Go tell Phoebe supper's ready," Jenny told her.

It was a simple thing to do—just a few steps across the room and a knock on the door of the *dawdi haus*.

Phoebe opened the door with a smile. "No need to knock, child. Mmm, something smells so good."

"Matthew thinks the pie should come out," Jenny said as Phoebe stepped into the kitchen. "I think it needs five more minutes. You decide."

Phoebe opened the oven door and nodded. "Jenny's right, Matthew. You know you're just impatient to be eating it."

He sighed and pulled out her chair. "You're right."

She patted his cheek before she sat. "Be patient. Even after it's done you'll need to let it cool a little."

Joshua came in from the barn, letting in a cold blast of wind. He took off his jacket, hung it on a peg, and went to wash his hands.

The wind picked up and rattled the kitchen window. "Hope it doesn't snow early this year," Phoebe said. "It'd make travel to the big city hard."

"It wouldn't dare snow and interrupt Annie's trip," Jenny said as the family took their seats at the big wooden kitchen table.

"Annie's trip? I thought it was Jenny's trip," Matthew remarked.

"I think she's even more excited than I am."

She grinned. "You're right."

They were just about to thank God for the meal when they heard a knock on the door.

"We know who it is," Joshua said, rolling his eyes.

"Be nice," Jenny told him with a stern look. But Annie saw the smile playing around her mother's lips.

"I'll get it," Annie said, but there was no need. No one else was getting to their feet.

She opened the door and found Aaron standing there, wearing a big smile.

"Good evening," he said, smiling as he stepped inside and took off his hat. "Sorry I'm late."

The Stitches in Time Series

Stitches in Time is a very special shop run by three cousins and their grandmother. Each young woman is devoted to her Amish faith and lifestyle, each talented in a traditional Amish craft and in new ways of doing business—and yet each is unsure of her path in life and love. It will take a loving and insightful grandmother to gently guide them to see that they can weave together their traditions and their desire to create and forge loving marriages and families of their own.

And now for a sneak peek into the first chapter of *Her Restless Heart*, Mary Katherine's story, the book that started the Stitches in Time series.

1

A year ago, Mary Katherine wouldn't have imagined she'd be here. Back then, she'd been helping her parents on the family farm and hating every minute of it.

Now, she stood at the front window of Stitches in Time, her grandmother's shop, watching the *Englischers* moving about on the sidewalks outside the shop in Paradise. Even on vacation, they rushed about with purpose. She imagined them checking off the places they'd visited: Drive by an Amish farmhouse. Check. Buy a quilt and maybe some knitting supplies to try making a sweater when I get back home. Check.

She liked the last item. The shop had been busy all morning, but now, as people started getting hungry, they were patronizing the restaurants that advertised authentic Amish food and ticking off another item on their vacation checklist. Shoofly pie. Amish pretzels. Chow-chow. Check.

"Don't you worry, they'll be back," Leah, her grandmother, called out.

Smiling, Mary Katherine turned. "I know."

She wandered back to the center of the shop, set up like the comfortable parlor of an Amish farmhouse. Chairs were arranged in a circle around a quilting frame. Bolts of fabric of every color and print imaginable were stacked on shelves on several walls, spools of matching threads on another.

And yarn. There were skeins and skeins of the stuff. Mary Katherine loved running her hands over the fluffy fibers, feeling the textures of cotton and wool and silk—even some of the new yarns made from things like soybeans and corn that didn't feel the same when you knitted them or wove them into patterns—but some people made such a fuss over it because it was using something natural.

Mary Katherine thought it was a little strange to be using vegetables you ate to make clothes, but once she got her hands on the yarns, she was impressed. Tourists were, too. They used terms like *green* and *ecological* and didn't mind spending a lot of money to buy them. And was it so much different to use vegetables when people had been taking oily, smelly wool from not very attractive sheep and turning it into garments for people—silk from silkworms—that sort of thing?

"You have that look on your face again," her grandmother said.

Mary Katherine smiled. "What look?"

"That serious, thoughtful look of yours. Tell me what you're thinking of."

"Working on my loom this afternoon."

"I figured you had itchy fingers." Her grandmother smiled.

She sighed. "I'm so glad you rescued me from working at the farm. And *Dat* not understanding about my weaving."

Grossmudder nodded and sighed. "Some people need time to adjust."

Taking one of the chairs that was arranged in a circle around the quilt her grandmother and Naomi worked on, she propped her chin in her hand, her elbow on the arm of the chair. "It'd be a lot easier if I knitted or quilted."

Leah looked at her, obviously suppressing a smile. "You have never liked easy, Mary Katherine."

Laughing, she nodded. "You're right."

Looking at Naomi and Anna, her cousins aged twenty and twenty-three, was like looking into a mirror, thought Mary Katherine. The three of them could have been sisters, not cousins. They had a similar appearance—oval faces, their hair center-parted and tucked back under snowy white *kapps*, and slim figures. Naomi and Anna had even chosen dresses of a similar color, one that reminded Mary Katherine of morning glories. In her rush out the door, Mary Katherine had grabbed the first available dress and now felt drab and dowdy in the brown dress she'd chosen.

Yes, they looked much alike, the three of them.

Until Mary Katherine stood. She'd continued growing after it seemed like everyone else stopped. Now, at 5'8", she felt like a skinny beanpole next to her cousins. She felt awkward next to the young men she'd gone to school with. Although she knew it was wrong, there had been times when she'd secretly wished that God had made her petite and pretty like her cousins. And why had He chosen to give her red hair and freckles? Didn't she have enough she didn't like about her looks without that?

Like their looks, their personalities seemed similar on the surface. The three of them appeared calm and serene—especially Naomi. Anna tried to be, but it didn't last long. She was too mischievous.

And herself? Serenity seemed hard these day. In the past several years, Mary Katherine had been a little moody but lately it seemed her moods were going up and down like a road through rolling hills.

"Feeling restless?" Naomi asked, looking at her with concern. Nimbly, she made a knot, snipped the thread with scissors, then slid her needle in a pincushion.

Anna looked up from her knitting needles. "Mary Katherine was born restless."

"I think I'll take a quick walk."

"No," Leah said quickly, holding up a hand. "Let's eat first, then you can take a walk. Otherwise you'll come back and customers will be here for the afternoon rush and you'll start helping and go hungry."

Mary Katherine was already mentally out the door, but she nodded her agreement. "You're right, of course."

Leah was a tall, spare woman who didn't appear old enough to be anyone's grandmother. Her face was smooth and unlined, and there wasn't a trace of gray in her hair worn like her granddaughters.

"I made your favorite," Leah told Mary Katherine.

"Fried chicken? You made fried chicken? When did you have time to do that?"

Nodding, Leah tucked away her sewing supplies and stood. "Before we came to work this morning. It didn't take long." She turned to Naomi. "And I made your favorite."

Naomi had been picking up stray strands of yarn from the wood floor. She looked up, her eyes bright. "Macaroni and cheese?"

"Oatmeal and raisin cookies?" Anna wanted to know. When her grandmother nodded, she set down her knitting needles and stood. "Just how early did you get up? Are you having trouble sleeping?"

"No earlier than usual," Leah replied cheerfully. "I made the macaroni and cheese and the cookies last night. But I don't need as much sleep as some other people I know."

"Can you blame me for sleeping in a little later?" Mary Katherine asked. "After all of those years of helping with farm chores? Besides, I was working on a design last night."

"Tell us all about it while we eat," Naomi said, glancing at the clock. "We won't have long before customers start coming in again."

"I worry about Grandmother," Anna whispered to Mary Katherine as they walked to the back room. "She does too much."

"She's always been like this."

"Yes, but she's getting older."

"Ssh, don't be saying that around her!"

Leah turned. "Did somebody say something?"

"Anna said she's hungry," Mary Katherine said quickly. "And happy you made her favorite cookies. But everything you make is Anna's favorite."

Anna poked Mary Katherine in the ribs, but everyone laughed because it was true. What was amazing was that no matter how much Anna ate, she never gained weight.

Nodding, Leah continued toward the back room. "We'll have it on the table in no time."

Anna grabbed Mary Katherine's arm, stopping her. "Shame on you," she hissed. "You know it's wrong to lie." Then she shook her head. "What am I saying? You've done so much worse!"

"Me? I have not! I can't imagine what you're talking about."

Turning so that her grandmother wouldn't see, Anna lifted her fingers to her lips and mimed smoking a cigarette.

Mary Katherine blushed. "You've been spying on me."

"Food's ready!" Leah called.

"Don't you dare tell her!" Mary Katherine whispered.

Anna's eyes danced. "What will you give me if I don't?"

She stared at her cousin. "I don't have anything—"

"Your afternoon off," Anna said suddenly. "That's what I'll take in trade."

Before she could respond, Anna hurried into the back room. Exasperated, Mary Katherine could do nothing but follow her.

The minute they finished eating, Mary Katherine jumped up and hurried over to wash her dishes. "I'll be right back," she promised, tying her bonnet on the run as she left the store.

Winter's chill was in the air. She shivered a little but didn't want to go back for her shawl. She shrugged. Once she got moving, she'd be warm enough.

She felt the curious stares as if she were touched.

But that was okay. Mary Katherine was doing a lot of staring of her own. She had a great deal of curiosity about the *Englisch* and didn't mind admitting it.

She just hoped that her grandmother didn't know how much she'd thought about becoming one of them, of not being baptized into the Amish church.

As one of the tourists walked past, a pretty woman about her own age, Mary Katherine wondered what it felt like being covered in so little clothing. She suspected she'd feel half-naked in that dress. Although some of the tourists looked surprised when she and her cousins wore bright colors, the fact was that the *Ordnung* certainly didn't mandate black dresses.

Color had always been part of Mary Katherine's world. She'd loved all the shades of blue because they reminded her of the big blue bowl of the sky. Her father had complained that she didn't get her chores done in a timely manner because she was always walking around . . . noticing. She noticed everything around her and absorbed the colors and textures, and spent hours using them in her designs that didn't look like the quilts and crafts other Amish women created.

She paused at the display window of Stitches in Time. A wedding ring quilt that Naomi had sewn was draped over a quilt rack. Anna had knitted several darling little cupcake hats for babies to protect their heads and ears from the cold. And there was her own woven throw made of many different fibers and textures and colors of burnt orange, gold, brown, and green. All echoed the theme of fall, of the weddings that would come with the cooling weather after summer harvests.

And all were silent testament to Leah's belief in the creativity of her granddaughters, thought Mary Katherine with a smile. The shop featured the traditional crafts tourists might expect but also the new directions the cousins came up with.

It was the best of both worlds, thought Mary Katherine as she ventured out into the throng of tourists lining the sidewalks.

∽❧∾

Jacob saw Mary Katherine exit her grandmother's shop. His timing was perfect because Anna had told him once what time they took a break to eat at the shop during the day.

He watched her stop to gaze at the display window and smiled—the smile that had attracted her to him. Oh, she was pretty with those big brown eyes and soft skin with a blush of rose over her cheekbones. But her smile.

She hadn't always smiled like that. He started noticing it just a few months ago, after the shop had opened. It was like she came to life. He'd passed by the shop one day a couple of weeks ago and stopped to glance inside, and he'd seen her working at her loom, a look of absorption on her face, a quiet smile on her lips.

Something had moved in his chest then, a feeling he hadn't had before. He'd resolved to figure this out.

He hadn't been in a rush to marry. It had been enough to take over the family farm, to make sure that he didn't undo all the hard work that his *daed* had done to make it thrive. He didn't feel pride that he'd continued its success. After all, Plain people felt *hochmut* was wrong. In school, they had often practiced writing the proverb, "*Der Hochmut kummt vor dem Fall.*" Pride goeth before the fall.

But the farm, its continuity, its legacy for the family he wanted one day . . . that was important to him. To have that family, he knew he'd have to find a *fraa*. It was important to find the right one. After all, Plain people married for life. So, he'd looked around, but he had taken his time. He likened the process to a crop—you prepared the ground, planted the right seed, nurtured it, asked God's blessing, and then harvested at the right moment.

Such things took time.

Sometimes they even took perseverance. She'd turned him down when he approached her and asked her out.

He decided not to let that discourage him.

She turned from the window and began walking down the sidewalk toward him. *Look at her,* he thought, *walking with that bounce to her step. Look at the way she glances around, so animated, taking in everything with such curiosity.*

He waited for some sign of recognition, but she hadn't seen him yet. When they'd attended school, their teacher had often gently chided her for staring out the classroom window or doodling designs on a scrap of paper for the weaving she loved.

Mary Katherine moved through the sea of *Englisch* tourists on the sidewalk that parted for her like the waters for Moses when she walked. He watched how they glanced at her the way she did them.

It was a mutual curiosity at its best.

He walked toward her, and when she stopped and blinked, he grinned.

"Jacob! What are you doing here?"

"You make it sound like I never come to town."

"I don't remember ever seeing you do it."

"I needed some supplies, and things are slower now with the harvest in. Have you eaten?" He'd casually asked Anna when they took their noontime break, but he figured it was a good conversational device.

"Yes. We ate a little early at the shop."

He thought about that. Maybe he should have planned better. "I see. Well, how about having supper with me tonight?"

"Did you come all the way into town to ask me out?"

Jacob drew himself up. "Yes."

"But I've told you before—"

"That you're not interested in going out."

"Yes."

"But I haven't heard of you going out with anyone else."

She stared at him, oblivious of the people who streamed around them on the sidewalk. "Who did you ask?"

Her direct stare was unnerving. His collar felt tight, but he knew if he pulled it away from his neck, he'd just appear guilty. "I'd have heard."

"I'm not interested in dating, Jacob."

When she started past him, he put out his hand to stop her. She looked down at his hand on her arm and then met his gaze. "Is it you're not interested in dating or you're not interested in dating me?"

Her lips quirked. "I'm not interested in dating. It's not you."

"I see."

She began walking again.

"Do you mind if I walk with you?"

"*Schur.*" She glanced at him. "Can you keep up?"

He found himself grinning. She was different from other young women he knew, more spirited and independent.

"Where are we going?"

She shrugged. "Nowhere in particular. I just needed to get out and get some fresh air."

Stopping at a shop window, she studied its display of tourist souvenirs. "Did you ever think about not staying here? In Paradise?"

"Not stay here? Where would you go?"

She turned to look at him and shrugged. "I don't know. It's a big world out there."

Jacob felt a chill race up his spine. "You can't mean it," he said slowly. "You belong here."

"Do I?" she asked. Pensive, she stared at the people passing. "Sometimes I'm not sure where I belong."

He took her shoulders and turned her to face the shop window. "This is where you belong," he told her.

She looked at the image of herself reflected in the glass as he directed. He liked the way they looked together in the reflection. She was a fine Amish woman, with a quiet beauty he'd admired for some time. He'd known her in school and, of course, they'd attended Sunday services and singings and such through the years. He hadn't been in a rush to get married, and he'd noticed she hadn't been, either. Both of them had been working hard, he at his farm, she in the shop she and her grandmother and cousins had opened.

He began noticing her shortly after the shop opened. There was a different air about her. She seemed more confident, happier than she'd been before.

He reminded himself that she'd said she didn't date.

So why, he asked himself, *am I trying again?* Taking a deep breath, he turned to her. "Mary Katherine—"

"Jacob!" a man called.

He turned and saw a man striding toward him, someone who had returned to the Plain community after years away.

Though the man hailed him, his attention was clearly on Mary Katherine. He held out his hand. "Daniel Kurtz," he said. "We met last Sunday."

Out of the corner of his eye, Jacob saw Mary Katherine turn to the man and eye him with interest.

"You're Rachel's cousin from Florida."

"I am." He eyed the shop. "So, this is your shop?"

"My grandmother's. My cousins and I help her."

Daniel nodded. "Very enterprising." He glanced around. "Is this the size of crowd you get this time of year?"

Mary Katherine nodded. "After-Christmas sales bring them out. But business slows down while people eat this time of day."

"I came into town to pick up a few things and I'm hungry. Have you two eaten?"

"I asked Mary Katherine but—"

"We'll join you," she said quickly.

Jacob stared at her. But the two of them were already walking away. With an unexplained feeling of dread washing over him, he followed them.

Want to learn more about author
Barbara Cameron and check out other great
fiction by Abingdon Press?

Sign up for our fiction newsletter at
www.AbingdonPress.com
to read interviews with your favorite authors,
find tips for starting a reading group, and stay
posted on what's new on the horizon. It's a
place to connect with other fiction readers or
post a comment about this book.

Be sure to visit Barbara Cameron online!

www.BarbaraCameron.com
www.AmishHearts.com
www.AmishLiving.com
and on Facebook

Abingdon Press fiction
a novel approach to faith

Plan your escape.

For more information and for more
fiction titles, please visit
AbingdonPress.com/fiction.

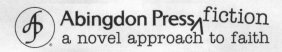

Abingdon Press fiction
a novel approach to faith

The Quilts of Lancaster County Series

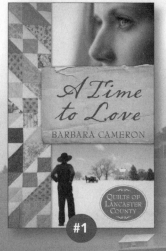

#1

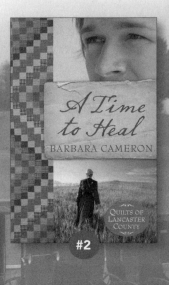

#2

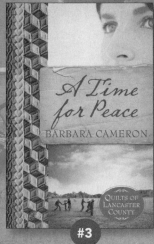

#3

"Each book in the *Quilts of Lancaster County* series is a tribute to the Amish faith." —*RT Book Reviews*

For more information and for more
fiction titles, please visit
AbingdonPress.com/fiction.

What They're Saying About...

The Glory of Green, by Judy Christie
"Once again, Christie draws her readers into the town, the life, the humor, and the drama in Green. *The Glory of Green* is a wonderful narrative of small-town America, pulling together in tragedy. A great read!"
—Ane Mulligan, editor of *Novel Journey*

Always the Baker, Never the Bride, by Sandra Bricker
"[It] had just the right touch of humor, and I loved the characters. Emma Rae is a character who will stay with me. Highly recommended!"
—Colleen Coble, author of *The Lightkeeper's Daughter* and the *Rock Harbor* series

Diagnosis Death, by Richard Mabry
"Realistic medical flavor graces a story rich with characters I loved and with enough twists and turns to keep the sleuth in me off-center. Keep 'em coming!"—**Dr. Harry Krauss, author of *Salty Like Blood* and *The Six-Liter Club***

Sweet Baklava, by Debby Mayne
"A sweet romance, a feel-good ending, and a surprise cache of yummy Greek recipes at the book's end? I'm sold!"—**Trish Perry, author of *Unforgettable* and *Tea for Two***

The Dead Saint, by Marilyn Brown Oden
"An intriguing story of international espionage with just the right amount of inspirational seasoning."—*Fresh Fiction*

Shrouded in Silence, by Robert L. Wise
"It's a story fraught with death, danger, and deception—of never knowing whom to trust, and with a twist of an ending I didn't see coming. Great read!"—**Sharon Sala, author of *The Searcher's Trilogy: Blood Stains, Blood Ties,* and *Blood Trails*.**

Delivered with Love, by Sherry Kyle
"Sherry Kyle has created an engaging story of forgiveness, sweet romance, and faith reawakened—and I looked forward to every page. A fun and charming debut!"—**Julie Carobini, author of *A Shore Thing* and *Fade to Blue*.**

Abingdon Press fiction
a novel approach to faith

AbingdonPress.com | 800.251.3320

BKM112220003 PACP01034642-01